BI...
ON...

Lia Anderssen

SILVER MOON BOOKS LTD LEEDS
PO Box CR25, Leeds LS7 3TN

New authors welcome

Silver Moon Books of Leeds and Silver Moon Books of London are in no way connected.

The following Silver Moon titles can be ordered from bookshops for £4.99 or by post from us at £5.60

ISBN 1-897809-01-8 BARBARY SLAVEMASTER (Allan Aldiss)
It was in 1809 (by the Christian calendar) that the Pasha of Marsa instructed Rory Fitzgerald, a renegade Irishman serving in the Turkish Janissaries, to buy, train and march into the interior a group of white slavegirls as gifts to induce the cruel tribesmen to abandon their liason with Napoleon.
Also by Allan Aldiss (to be read in any order):
ISBN 1-897809-03-4 BARBARY SLAVEGIRL
ISBN 1-897809-08-5 BARBARY PASHA
ISBN 1-897809-14-X BARBARY ENSLAVEMENT

By REX SAVIOUR (See extracts on end pages)
ISBN 1-897809-02-6 ERICA, PROPERTY OF REX
ISBN1-897809-99-9 BALIKPAN I:ERICA ARRIVES (£9.99)

ISBN 1-897809-04-2 BIKERS GIRL (Lia Anderssen)
The near future - a beautiful young runaway loses her clothes and remains naked through many highly painful episodes in which she revels unashamedly until the Biker of her dreams sweeps her off her feet.   Also by Anderssen:-
ISBN 1-897809-07-7 THE TRAINING OF SAMANTHA
ISBN 1-897809-11-5 THE HUNTED ARISTOCRAT

ISBN 1-898809-05-0 BOUND FOR GOOD (Gord, Saviour, Darrener)
Comprising:- *Bound for Good,* surely the ultimate bondage novel
Robin, Property of Ogoun, a girl runs from her sadistic husband
Teacher's Pets, Mr Robinson has trouble with nubile school leavers

ISBN 1-897809-10-7 CIRCUS OF SLAVES :An erotic fantasy (Janey Jones)

ISBN 1-897809-16-6 RORIG'S DAWN (Ray Arneson)
Not to be missed - Book I of *SLAVES OF KHAEA* - our answer to the Gor series!!

There are also three Silver Mink Books - our erotic fiction for women, on similar themes, widely read by men!
ISBN 1-897809-09-3 - WHEN THE MASTER SPEAKS (Josephine Scott)
ISBN 1-897809-13-1 - AMELIA (Josephine Oliver)
ISBN 1-897809-15-8 - THE DARKER SIDE (Larry Stern)

SILVER MOON READER SERVICES
PO BOX CR25, LEEDS LS7 3TN

BIKER'S GIRL
ON THE RUN

by
Lia Anderssen

**This is fiction -
In real life practice safe sex - with a willing partner!**

Copyright Mike Walsh
First published 1994

See opposite for other books by Lia Anderssen

Chapter One

The day was already warm, the early morning sunlight penetrating the canopy of trees and shedding a dappled light on the grass below. The wood made a perfect setting of peaceful bliss. The only sound was that of the river as it swept gently by, small wavelets lapping at the river banks. A group of rabbits sat by its edge, nibbling at the grass, and in the sky above the occasional bird call was audible. The scene was idyllic, and apparently untouched by humans.

But this rural spot, despite initial appearances, was not deserted. Indeed there was unmistakable evidence of the presence of man. In a small clearing close to the river's edge, something gleamed brightly in the sun, looking strangely out of place in this green and pleasant setting. It was a motorcycle. A large, powerful machine with thick, rounded tyres and wide upswept exhausts, a leather jacket draped carelessly from the handlebars. Its presence, there among the flowers and trees was enough to make any casual observer stop and stare, and to wonder what it was doing there.

The bike was, however, not the only thing that gave a somewhat incongruous air to the scene. Beside it lay a figure in the grass. A figure that would have captivated anyone who encountered it.

It was a girl, slim and beautiful, with an air of youthful innocence about her that made her seem very vulnerable as she blinked her eyes, clearly awakening from a deep sleep. She was totally naked, her full, firm breasts tipped with large brown nipples that pointed up to the treetops. Her waist was slim, her belly flat, her legs long and slender. But there was something else about her. Something that would have turned the head of any red blooded male who stumbled across her. Her pubic mound was completely shaved of hair, so that lying as she was, with her legs were spread slightly apart, the full pink lips of her sex were totally exposed.

The girl stretched languorously in the soft grass, then sat up and gazed about her.

"Thorkil?"

As she called the name there was a rustling in the grass nearby and a young man emerged. He was tall, well over six foot, his hair hanging in golden tresses that reached to his shoulders. He was clad in a leather

5

biking suit, the zipper open almost to the waist. He crossed to where she sat, and stood gazing down at her.

"Did you sleep well?"

"Mmm. I just went straight out."

"After the way you were behaving last night I should think you were tired out."

She blushed. "You did enjoy me, didn't you?"

"Very much," he smiled. "Now come on, we really should be getting back on the road."

"Where are we going?"

"Back to my base."

"Your base?"

"Yes. Depot twenty-nine."

"Depot twenty-nine? What's that?"

"That's where I live. And that's where we'll be going after I've checked in with some friends."

"What friends?"

"Very good friends. I'm sure you'll like them."

"And that's where we're going now?"

"Yes,"

The girl rose to her feet, glancing nervously about her. It was as if she had only now become aware of her nudity, and was suddenly feeling very exposed.

"Isn't there something I could wear?" she asked.

He shook his head. "Not unless you know how to weave leaves together."

She lowered her eyes. "You mean I'm to stay naked?"

He grinned. "I prefer you like that."

"But surely if I'm to meet your friends..."

He moved close to her, running his hand gently over her breast.

"I expect they will like you naked too."

"But Thorkil..."

He placed a hand over her mouth. "There's nothing more to say," he murmured.

For a second she looked as if she might protest. Then she sighed and shrugged her shoulders. If that was the way he wanted it, then it was not for her to object. The decision was a sensible one. After all, it was to him that she owed her freedom. He it was who had tried his best to buy her imprest, but had been cheated out of it. And, more to the point, it was he who had rescued her from the Black Cat, and from the clutches of the dreadful Helda, who had sold her body to anyone able to pay for it. All

6

this meant that she belonged to Thorkil now, and would do whatever he wished.

The girl's name was Lia. She had been captured by the Bikers more than four months earlier, whilst on the run after nearly murdering the warden of the hostel where she had lived. A group of Bikers had found her wandering along the highway naked, trying to buy a ride in a truck with her body. The Bikers had claimed her, selling her imprest at auction to Helda, the cruel owner of the Black Cat. There she had been kept as a plaything for men and women alike, permanently naked. Shaved and available to be chained, beaten or taken by anyone who could afford the price.

Then, just the night before, she had been rescued by her knight in shining armour, Thorkil.

Thorkil, like Helda, was a Biker. The Bikers had ruled the highways since law and order had all but broken down years before, leaving the cities as nightmarish areas where crime was rife and to venture out at night without protection had become extremely dangerous. The Bikers' great service depots were scattered all over the country, each a tribal area in its own right. In these places, young men and women were pressed into service to repair and maintain the great trucks that roved the highways. Outside the cities the Bikers were in charge, the genuine law enforcement officers simply paying lip service to their jobs, content with the backhanders they received from the men and women in black leather.

And now, in Thorkil's hands, Lia was a Biker's girl.

Thorkil reached out for Lia's hand, pulling her toward him. She stepped forward willingly, turning her face up to his as he closed his lips over hers. She felt his tongue force its way between her lips and she opened her mouth to accept it, licking at it with her own tongue as she pressed her naked body against him, rubbing her crotch against his strong thigh.

They kissed for a full minute, then he broke away.

"Suck me," he ordered, his voice full of quiet authority.

Lia was used to obeying, and she did not hesitate. At once she dropped to her knees before him, looking for all the world like one kneeling in front of an idol in worship. She reached eagerly for his zip, and tugged it down until the suit fell open.

Underneath he was naked, his body muscular and tanned. She gazed at him for a moment in admiration, taking in the broad chest, with its scattering of golden curls, and his lean torso.

His cock was long and fat and it hung down from his groin, still dormant. Lia took it in her fingers. It felt warm and soft, and she squeezed it gently, cupping his heavy balls with her other hand.

Raising her head, she took him into her mouth and began to suck him. His manhood tasted salty, and the smell of him sent a thrill through her as she contemplated what was about to happen.

Almost at once she felt his penis begin to swell, filling her open mouth. She stroked his balls, happy to be kneeling subserviently before her Biker and doing his will. He took hold of her head and pressed it to his groin, and she responded at once, sucking harder at his organ, taking it further inside her, flicking her tongue back and forth over the tip as it stiffened to its full size.

Once he was hard she began in earnest, bobbing her head up and down as she sucked hungrily, his cock sliding in and out of her mouth, her saliva dribbling down its thick shaft. In response he gave a low moan and pressed her harder against him. Lia glanced up at him momentarily. His eyes were closed and his head was thrown back, his expression intent. The sight of his obvious arousal spurred her on, and she felt a wetness begin to seep through her sex as she pleasured him.

Suddenly he withdrew from her mouth, his weapon wet and glistening. She looked up questioningly.

"Over the bike seat. Face down."

Lia sprang eagerly to her feet and scurried across to where Thorkil's bike stood. She approached it from behind, lowering her body forward over it. The plastic seat felt warm in the sunshine and her nipples tingled as they brushed against its surface.

She flattened herself onto it, her lovely rounded backside thrust backwards and upwards, ready for penetration. For a fleeting moment she felt a pang of shame, and wondered what he must think of her lasciviousness. There had been no hesitation whatsoever in her actions, and there was no doubting her desire. She wanted desperately to feel him inside her, and would obey his every whim.

But there was no time now for prudishness. With a gasp she felt his hands slide up her inner thighs towards the very centre of her pleasure.

His fingers prised apart the cheeks of her bottom, laying her open for his inspection. She groaned as she felt his fingers trace the crevice of her behind, stroking the tight star of her anus before working lower to the hot pink slit that gaped so invitingly.

He slid two fingers inside her, making her body start as the pleasure overwhelmed her. He began to frig her, his fingers making a slight squelching sound as they moved in and out of her hole. Lia remained where she was, her cheek pressed against the bike seat, biting her lower lip to prevent herself from crying aloud with pure lust.

8

At last she could bear it no more.

"Fuck me Thorkil," she cried.

He smiled. "Ask me nicely."

"P-please fuck me Thorkil."

"Again."

"Oh! Oh please fuck me. Please put your cock into me Thorkil. Fuck me!"

The last word was almost lost in a strangled cry as she suddenly felt the thick bulb of his glans pressing against her slit. She pushed her backside back at him eagerly, and with a cry felt him slide his cock into her, deeper and deeper until it filled her completely.

Then he was fucking her. Driving his thick weapon hard into her, his stomach slapping against her backside as he took his pleasure in her. Lia was beside herself with passion. He was giving her precisely what she craved. The night before he had been gentle and loving, but now he was simply taking what was rightly his, ramming his cock into her with an almost animal urgency, and she realised with a shock that that was the way she preferred it. To be utterly his and prey to his every whim.

The force of his thrusts became harder, pounding her body, and she began to fear that the cycle might fall over. She clung to the tank as tight as she was able, her breath coming in loud grunts as she was hurled forward with every stroke.

Then he gave a shout, and she felt his sperm pumping into her. Almost at once her own orgasm was triggered and she too was crying aloud as her lustful desires overcame her. Sensing her passion, he continued to plunge his great cock into her as it spurted again and again deep within her. She wanted to laugh and cry at the same time, such was the pleasure of her own climax and her stomach slapped wetly against the plastic of the bike seat as he rode her down the slope from her peak, slowing gently now as the pleasure began to gently ebb.

At last he was still, and she lay panting beneath him, exhausted. His fingers traced her spine as he gazed down at her, his cock still embedded within her.

"My passionate little Biker's girl," he murmured.

Chapter 2

At the Black Cat, Helda was watching as the third of the three gatekeepers who had allowed Lia to escape slumped to the ground, his teeth and jaw broken, his eyes blackened, his nose a bloody pulp. She kicked him twice in the ribs, each blow resounding to the crack of broken bone. She turned and left the servants to drag the three groaning men back to their cells.

She strode back to her office and slumped into the chair behind her desk. Then she leaned forward and pressed a bell. Almost immediately her assistant Stefan was with her.

"Is the transmitter working?" she asked anxiously.

"Oh yes - did you get someone in Thorkil's camp to attach it to his machine?"

"Of course. You didn't think I'd risk him getting away with her, did you?" she snapped. "Oh no! I still have plans for that young lady! So where are they?"

"About twenty-five miles down the highway. They seem to have pulled off into some woods."

"Good. They're bound to join up with the rest of his cronies. Set an ambush for when they arrive there. We'll leave them to their fun for now. After all there's plenty of time."

A thin, evil smile began to play about her lips.

Lia clung hard to Thorkil as they roared down the road. He rode the machine hard, leaning low into bends, then grabbing a handful of throttle as they straightened up so that she had to hug herself close to him to avoid being flung off the back. The machine was a large one, and the thrill of the speed accompanied by the vibration of the engine induced an almost sexual pleasure in the naked girl as they sped along. Her arousal was increased by the other drivers on the road, who would point in fascination at her lovely young body as they were passed, grinning and making rude gestures at the sight of her. Lia in return would grin back, sometimes thrusting her lovely behind back at them, making their eyes wide with desire.

They rode on for what seemed many miles before the bike suddenly slowed. Then they were swinging left, off into the wooded countryside with which Lia was becoming so familiar since falling into the hands of the Bikers.

They followed a track that wound through the trees for about a mile. The whole area seemed deserted, and Lia wondered where he could possibly be taking her. Then, suddenly, the track widened into a clearing, in the centre of which was seated a group of black-clad figures.

Thorkil braked to a halt and cut the engine, the sudden silence taking Lia by surprise. It took her ears a second to accustom themselves to the quiet of the wood.

They had come to a halt by a group of bikes parked under a tree. Thorkil kicked down the stand and climbed off. Lia sat where she was, nervous and embarrassed now as she looked across at the group in the centre of the clearing.

"Who are they?" she asked timidly.

"Just friends. Friends who assisted me in getting you out. They're all looking forward to meeting you."

"But I'm naked."

He looked at her rather sternly. "Listen," he said. "You are a beautiful and sensuous girl, and I rescued you because I wanted you, and I believe you wanted me. Am I right?"

"You know you are."

"Then you must realise the role of a Biker's girl. It is to serve her man in whatever way he pleases. If I choose that my friends see you naked, then that is what will happen."

She hung her head. "Yes Thorkil," she mumbled.

He wrapped his arms about her and kissed her. "Good," he said.

She looked into his eyes. "Must I always obey you?"

"Yes. Unless and until you gain your leathers. Then you become a Biker yourself. But that will take some time."

"How long?"

He placed a finger on her lips. "Enough questions for now. Come and meet my friends."

She followed him across the clearing, her face glowing red with embarrassment as they approached the group. Somehow, her position at the Black Cat, as a plaything, had made her enforced nudity easier to bear. Here she was being asked to meet Thorkil's friends in an otherwise normal social situation, and her lack of clothes made her feel very conspicuous indeed.

There were six Bikers, all seated on logs about a small fire. They looked up and waved to Thorkil as they came closer, and Lia realised with surprise that two of them were girls. They were clad in the same way as the men, indicating that they had 'gained their leathers' as Thorkil had described. The presence of the females only served to increase her discomfort. The contrast between their bodies, clad in the black one-piece leather suit that many Bikers wore, and her own, totally exposed, her breasts and sex bare for all to see, seemed to make her the more conspicuous.

They came to a halt in front of the group.

"This is Lia," said Thorkil.

All eyes were on her, and she wanted to turn away. Clearly Thorkil sensed this.

"Stand straight," he ordered. "Legs apart. Hands behind your head."

Reluctantly Lia took up the familiar submissive stance before the six pairs of eyes, her legs spread so that her shaven sex was open to their gaze.

One of the men whistled. "Whew! Very nice, Thorkil," he said. "I can see why you wanted to rescue her."

Thorkil sat down on the log, grinning. "Yeah. Quite something isn't she?"

"Stunning," said one of the girls.

"Really sexy," said the other

Thorkil waited until they had all had a look, then sensing Lia's embarrassment, changed the subject.

" Now what about something to eat?" he said.

As he spoke, Lia realised that she too was extremely hungry. Resting in the embers of the fire was a cooking pot, and there was a wonderful smell coming from it. One of the men lifted the lid to reveal a steaming stew inside. He grabbed a ladle and scooped two large portions into bowls. He passed one across to Thorkil, then offered the other to Lia. She glanced down quizzically to Thorkil, who gave a little nod. Unclasping her hands from behind her head, Lia took the bowl and, still standing, began spooning the food into her mouth. The stew was hot and tasty, and she consumed every morsel, drinking the last of the gravy from the bowl before placing it at her feet and putting her hands behind her head once more.

The Bikers began to talk amongst themselves and Lia stood, passively listening to their conversation. Thorkil described in detail how the escape had gone, and the six Bikers attended with interest, firing questions at him all the time. One of the men, though, seemed unable to take his eyes off Lia. He was short and balding slightly, a pink patch of skull showing through at the back of his dark, lank hair. She could tell from his belly that he was a beer drinker, and he confirmed this by frequently swigging from a can that lay on the grass beside him.

Lia gathered from the chat that this man's name was Rico.

Once Thorkil's story had been told, they turned to Lia, and began to question her about her life at the Black Cat. Rico in particular was curious and Lia found herself blushing deeply as she was made to describe the beatings and gang bangs she had experienced. Throughout most of this Thorkil was silent, and she wondered what he must be thinking of her.

At last they seemed to have heard enough. Then, to Lia's surprise Rico rose to his feet and took her arm.

"You're quite a girl," he said.

She dropped her eyes. "Thank you."

He took her chin in his hand, turning her face toward his.

"Now what about coming and having a little fun with me?"

She stared at him. How could he ask such a thing? And in front of Thorkil as well!

"What do you mean?" she asked.

"What do you think I mean? Here you are, starkers, that shaven pussy of yours displayed for all to see. It makes me horny as hell. Now come on."

"No!" She pulled away from him. "Thorkil..."

Thorkil looked up at her. "Rico is a good friend," he said. "Without his help I'd never have traced you to the Black Cat. He's earned your gratitude."

"But you can't make me go with him," said Lia in dismay.

"Is that how a Biker's girl talks to her man?"

The words came from one of the two girl Bikers. She was called Lara, and was tall and slim, with magnificent breasts and long flowing blonde hair. She rose now and joined Rico beside Lia.

"I reckon you're going soft, Thorkil."

"She's new," replied Thorkil. "She'll soon learn her place."

"Even so," replied Lara. "Talking back to you like that should at least earn her a smacked bottom."

"All right," said Thorkil. "But just six mind."

Lia stared at him. A smacked bottom? After all she'd been through he was going to have her bottom smacked like some recalcitrant schoolgirl? She opened her mouth to protest, then caught his eye and saw a dark look cross his face. She closed her lips and hung her head. Of course it was she that was at fault, not Thorkil. He had explained her position only a few minutes before, and already she had forgotten. She was a Biker's girl now, and as such must respect her position. To defy Thorkil in front of his companions was to underlie his stature in the group, and that was something she knew he could never allow. She relaxed and stood passively awaiting her orders.

Lara took her hands and turned her round, so that she was facing away from the fire. Then she puled her gently forward, bending her over until her palms rested on the log on which they had been sitting. She shoved Lia's legs wide apart, presenting her rear beautifully to those watching. Once in position Lia kept her body as still as she could, her eyes fixed on the ground.

"You gonna whack her Thorkil?" asked Lara.

"No, you go ahead," he replied. His voice sounded nonchalant, and Lia turned her head to look at him. He gave her a slight smile and winked, and she knew he was no longer angry with her.

Smack!

Lara's hand came down flat on the left cheek of Lia's backside. The blow stung, but she held her position.

Smack!

This time her right cheek was assaulted, the blow cracking down onto her tender flesh. But now the pain triggered another feeling. As so often in the past, the humiliation and pain of her punishment had ignited a perverse spark of arousal in the girl, and she felt the muscles of her cunt convulse slightly as she anticipated the next blow.

Smack!

The third blow caught the underside of her pretty behind, rocking her body so that her dangling breasts shook tantalisingly. Her bottom was smarting dreadfully, and she could imagine how it must look, the handmark reddening as the others watched.

Smack!

The fourth blow fell precisely where the first had, redoubling the pain in the hapless girl's behind. Lia's backside had been beaten many times since she had fallen into the hands of the Bikers, and a smacking from a girl was far from the worst punishment she had received. But Lara was striking with deadly accuracy and the pain was very real indeed. And so was the arousal, the juices within her beginning to flow now as her ordeal went on.

Smack!

It was all Lia could do to prevent herself crying out as Lara's hand caught her once more. She closed her eyes as she awaited the last blow.

Smack!

Lara's hand descended for the sixth time onto Lia's backside. Then it was over, and the girl was helping her to straighten up. Lia's behind stung terribly, and she knew it must be bright red. But the heat in her bottom was as nothing to that in her belly, and the shortness of her breath was more a panting desire than anything else. Lia was now extremely aroused, and she knew that the evidence was visible to all on the glistening lips of her sex as she turned to face them.

"Wow!" Rico grinned. "That's turned her on. Look at her!"

Lia's face glowed almost as red as her behind as she felt her nether lips twitch once more. She turned to Thorkil, who rose to his feet and, taking her in his arms, kissed her on the lips. She responded eagerly to his kiss, pressing herself against him, her entire body alive with lust, but he broke away.

"Rico," he said shortly, and nodded to her.

She gave Thorkil a final lingering look, then turned to face Rico. He reached out his hand and she placed hers into it.

Suddenly she felt her other hand grasped and turned to see Lara on her other side.

"I'm coming too," she said. "I want a bit of this action."

And with that the two of them led the naked girl off towards the trees.

Chapter 3

Lia glanced back over her shoulder toward Thorkil as she was led away by Rico and Lara. He gave her a small wave, then turned back and continued talking to the others. Lia's mind was in a whirl. On the one hand she was surprised that he was able to just stand and calmly watch as she was taken away like this. He must know what the two Bikers' intentions were, but he was seemingly unworried. At the same time, she was slightly shocked by her own feelings. She knew that she should be protesting, fighting to escape from this pair. But inside, all she could feel was the most extraordinary thrill. Lia was very turned on indeed.

They made their way toward the spot where the bikes were parked, and for a moment she thought they were going to drive her away. But they passed the gleaming machines and made instead for the trees.

They entered the wood by a narrow path, the barefoot Lia treading gingerly as she was led along. They didn't go far, just to a small clearing about fifty yards from the one they had left. In the centre was a large fallen tree trunk about three feet in diameter, and it was to this that the Bikers took their naked young companion.

"Sit down on there," ordered Rico, indicating the trunk.

The two released her hands and Lia approached the trunk nervously, turning to face them and lowering her sore backside onto the hard wooden surface. Rico and Lara stood side by side watching her, and she gazed quizzically back at them waiting to discover what they wanted.

"Open your legs," said Rico.

Slowly, reluctantly Lia did as she was told, spreading her legs wide so that her bare sex was once again exposed to the two watchers. When they were as far apart as she could get them she once more looked across at the Bikers.

"Play with yourself."

"What?"

"You heard me. Play with yourself. Get those delectable nipples of yours erect first."

"But I..."

"No buts. You've been wandering about flaunting yourself enough. Now let's see some action."

Lia looked from one to the other. She felt extremely embarrassed by Rico's demand. Yet, at the same time there was a warm sensation spreading within her as she felt their eyes on her body. She hesitated for a moment longer, then slowly moved her hands up to her breasts.

She took them, one in each hand, and began gently to caress them. Her fingers rubbed the soft flesh and almost at once her nipples began to respond, the brown flesh puckering to hardness so that they stood out invitingly from her firm globes.

Lia's fingers worked on, caressing and kneading her plump mammaries, then holding them up and out as if offering them to the leather clad pair who stood and watched her. In no time at all, the sensation of her own caresses began to have the effect they had wanted on her, and her face was a picture of rapt concentration as she continued her self arousal.

"Now your cunt."

Once again she looked, wide-eyed at Rico.

"Your cunt. Let's see that clit of yours shine with come," he said. "Frig yourself, you randy little slut."

Lia didn't need to be asked a second time. Whilst her left hand continued to play with her breasts, her right reached eagerly for her open slit.

She slid her fingers down over her pubic mound, giving a little start when they came in contact with her clitoris. She eased it out from between her sex lips, flicking gently at it as it came erect. When she knew it was hard and visible, she raised her eyes to Rico's and let her fingers run down lower over the wet surface of her slit. Gently she prised apart her nether lips, exposing the pinkness inside. Once more she paused, her eyes fixed on Rico's. Then her hand moved again, her long, elegant digits delving into her aching love hole.

Lia knew she had her audience spellbound, and it had been her intention to tease the watching pair with her lascivious actions for as long as possible. But once she had penetrated herself, the familiar lustful feelings returned and she felt her control begin to slip away.

She began to frig herself, her fingers working in and out of her cunt, making a slight squelching sound as they did so. Her body responded enthusiastically to the sensation and she found herself opening her legs still wider as her passion overcame her. She planted her feet firmly on the ground and raised her bottom up off the tree, thrusting her sex forward as her fingers slid in and out. Her breath was coming in short gasps as she masturbated, her whole self concentrated on the delicious sensation that her fingers were bringing her.

"Stop."

For a moment Lia did not obey, being too intent on her own pleasure. Whack!

Rico had removed the belt that went round the waist of his suit, and he used it now to deliver a stinging blow across the naked girl's thighs.

The blow caught Lia by surprise, and she stopped pleasuring herself at once, looking up startled at her companions, her face redder than ever. She wondered at the sight she must make, stretched there totally nude, her breasts swollen, the nipples hard as nuts, her legs spread wide apart so that they could watch the convulsions of her dripping sex lips as they tried to close about an imaginary cock.

"Jeez," said Lara. "Thorkil told us you were hot, but you've surpassed yourself. That little slit of yours looks like it would positively eat a cock if it could. And speaking of eating things..."

As she spoke, Lara moved forward, toward Lia, pushing her backwards gently so that she lay across the trunk, her back arched backwards, her breasts forced forward and upwards. Lia made no protest, allowing the female Biker to manipulate her body into the position she wanted. Then she felt Lara's lips close over her nipples and she gave a cry of pleasure.

Lara took hold of Lia's left breast, squeezing it hard as she sucked noisily on the nipple. Lia squirmed with pleasure, a pleasure that was doubled when she felt Rico's mouth close over the other one.

"Oh!" Rico's hand reached for Lia's shaven pussy, eliciting yet another cry from his naked captive as he slid his fingers into her warm, wet love hole. Lia pressed her crotch against his hand, her whole body arched upwards as the two Bikers took possession of her young body. Once again her control was lost as she writhed beneath their hands and mouths, totally abandoned to her own pleasure, her juices flowing down her thighs in a silvery trickle.

"Wow," gasped Lara as she lifted her mouth from Lia's swollen nipple. "This bitch is something else. I just gotta have her lick me."

With that she rose to her feet, reaching for the zipper at her throat, pulling it all the way down and round her crotch almost to the top of her backside whilst Lia looked on, her heart thumping with anticipation.

Lara peeled off her suit. Underneath she was totally naked and Lia felt the hotness within her increase as she surveyed Lara's lovely body. Her breasts were magnificent, the biggest Lia had ever seen, yet barely drooping at all. The dark brown nipples were large and prominent and projected slightly upwards. Beneath them her body curved in to a trim waist, then widened again, her hips in perfect proportion to her breasts. Lia fixed her eyes on Lara's crotch. Her pubic mound was a mass of thick blonde curls below which her sex lips showed thick and prominent. Lara stretched herself in the sun, arching her body proudly, clearly enjoying the attention it was receiving from her two companions. Then she moved closer to Lia again, but this time approaching her from above her head, standing so that her legs straddled Lia's face as she stood gazing down at her.

All Lia could see was Lara's pink slit hovering just above her face. Then, even as she watched, Lara began lowering herself onto her face.

"Right," she said. "Now it's your turn. Lick me, you randy little bitch. Get that tongue of yours working!"

Lia had little choice, but even if she had been given one the result would have been the same. Lara's sex descended onto her and for a second her senses were filled with the sight and smell of a woman's arousal. Tentatively she protruded her tongue, running it gingerly over the soft lips of Lara's slit. As she did so the Biker gave a groan and pressed herself down harder on Lia's face.

Lia sought out the girl's clitoris, lapping at it and flicking it back and forth with darting movements of her tongue. She felt the little bud swell and took it gently between her teeth, sucking it in between her lips. Lara gave a little cry at this and Lia felt her hips begin to move back and forth. The prostrate girl reached her arms up and around Lara's thighs, her hands grasping the woman's buttocks. This allowed her to control her movements better and to co-ordinate herself with the pumping of Lara's hips.

Suddenly Lia felt the fingers that had been inside her wet crotch slide out of her. Then something else was probing her sex. For a second she abandoned Lara's pussy and gazed down between her breasts. Rico had unzipped his suit to the crotch and, beneath his heavy beer gut, Lia could see his cock jutting proudly erect. It was this that he was pressing against her as he sought to penetrate her. She gave a little moan of pleasure which was stifled as Lara pressed down onto her face once more.

Lia spread her legs as wide apart as she was able, raising her backside from the wood once more as she willed Rico to penetrate her. Then she gave a gasp as she felt him shove his hips forward and he was inside her, his cock filling her as he rammed it home.

Rico began working his hips back and forth as he took his pleasure in her. Above her Lara moaned and wriggled as Lia's tongue went to work, probing her vagina now, the sleek little muscle worming deep into the Biker's throbbing slit.

For herself, Lia's arousal was intense. Never before had she serviced a man and a woman simultaneously in the open air like this. She reached a hand up to feel for Lara's breast, only to find Rico's already there, squeezing and mauling at his fellow Biker whilst all the time shafting Lia hard.

Together the three of them made an extremely erotic sight. The lovely young girl stretched backwards across the tree trunk, her hair hanging down behind her, her face buried in the other woman's crotch as she slurped noisily at it. Lara meantime was pumping her hips back and forth, pressing down on her lover's face whilst locked in a passionate embrace with Rico. Their lips were pressed together in a bruising kiss, their tongues intertwined as he stroked her magnificent breasts. And all the time he was thrusting his cock into Lia, fucking her for all he was worth.

Lara's moans were turning to cries now, and the juice flowed copiously from her, dribbling down Lia's cheeks as she tried to lap it all up. Rico's cock was pumping harder and harder, and Lia knew she could not hold back much longer.

Rico came first, his cock throbbing as he unleashed his load into Lia's love hole. He gave a groan of pleasure, which was echoed almost at once by Lara, her cunt muscles twitching uncontrollably as her orgasm overcame her. All this was too much for Lia and she too let herself go, the pleasure flowing through her in waves as she screamed her pleasure into Lara's open sex.

For a second it was as if the three of them were frozen. Locked together cock to cunt, mouth to cunt and mouth to mouth, their bodies joined in a crescendo of pleasure that seemed to flow from one to another like some strange electric energy. Then, with a collective gasp they let go, Lara and Rico collapsing into each others' arms as Lia flopped backwards, her tired muscles slowly relaxing as she lay back, gasping for breath.

She remained where she was, watching as Rico pulled up his zipper and Lara climbed back into her leathers. She knew she must look a sight, her face glistening with Lara's come whilst Rico's sperm was streaked down her thighs. But she didn't care. She was proud of herself. All that mattered to her now was that she was a Biker's girl, Thorkil's girl. And it was for him alone that she gave herself so freely to whoever it pleased him to offer her to.

Rico and Lara took her hands again, pulling her to her feet. She rubbed her backside, brushing off the scraps of wood and grass that stuck to it. The redness had faded now, but it still felt sore to the touch.

Nothing was said as they made their way back to the camp. Lia wandered dreamily along between them, anxious to be back with Thorkil, her body glowing with pleasure.

They had almost broken into the clearing when they heard the bikes. The roar of powerful engines was unmistakable and Rico and Lara stopped in their tracks.

"What the hell?" said Rico startled. "Where are they going?"

"Hang on," said Lara. "Those aren't our bikes."

They began to run, dragging Lia along between them. As they broke cover into the clearing they saw the source of the sound. It was a group of about fifteen Bikers, They were speeding across the clearing, away from where the three were standing, bearing down on the small group by the fire.

"Oh shit," said Lara. "It's Helda."

Chapter 4

Lia stood frozen to the spot as she watched the Bikers tear across the clearing, their machines roaring deafeningly as they rode helter skelter toward the group gathered around the fire. All wore the familiar black leathers of Bikers, but the insignia on their backs was different from that sported by Thorkil and his companions. She recognised it instantly as the logo used by Helda, and, at that very moment, she realised with a start that the figure leading the attack was indeed Helda herself.

"Quick," shouted Rico. "Let's get them." He set out at a run in the direction of his companions.

But Lara held back momentarily. She could see that they were hopelessly outnumbered. It was also clear to her why Helda was attacking. She turned to face Lia.

"Listen," she said. "There's too many of them to fight successfully. It's you they're after, so you've got to get the hell out of here."

"But where?" asked Lia, despairingly."

"It doesn't matter where. Can you ride a bike?"

Lia nodded. They had taught her to ride during her time at the Black Cat. Some of the clients found it a turn-on to be picked up by a naked Biker. Helda invented a scenario by which the man was walking along the road, hitching, and Lia would ride up and offer him a lift. Then she would speed around the estate with the man perched behind her, his hands roaming over her body whilst she drove. The final act would always involve her parking the machine in some remote corner and then submitting to his desires. This little piece of play-acting had become extremely popular with the Black Cat's customers, and soon Lia was riding with some skill. Now, ironically, it appeared that the biking tuition would prove to be her salvation.

Lara dragged her across to where the bikes were parked. The attacking Bikers were still concentrating on the group round the fire, and had so far failed to notice the two women. She pulled one of the bikes off its stand.

"Get on," she ordered.

Lia swung a leg over the machine and took hold of the handlebars. As she did so Lara kicked the starter and the engine roared into life. Then she slapped Lia's bare behind.

"Right, on your way," she shouted. Lia opened her mouth to ask where, but Lara was already running towards the scrimmage in the centre of the clearing.

Lia engaged first gear and let go of the clutch. Too fast. The machine reared up onto its back wheel, and for a moment she feared she would lose it. She closed the throttle, letting the front wheel drop again. Then she twisted it open and was moving, skidding the bike around and heading for the track along which they had come.

She glanced over her shoulder, and her heart sank. One of the Bikers had spotted her and was already heading after her at high speed. Despite her skill at handling the machine, she had no doubt that his would be the greater.

Lia slowed her machine and glanced back again, anxious to see how close the other rider was. As she did so, she noticed the figure of Lara, between her and the other Biker, running across to intercept the man. For a second it looked as if Lara would be mown down by the speeding cycle, but at the last minute she sprang aside and thrust something into the man's front wheel. At once the wheel locked up, sending the bike sideways and flinging the rider off into the dust. Lia offered a little prayer of thanks and crouched low over the handlebars of her machine as she sped away down the track.

Lia had to think fast. She knew that the advantage she had gained was only a temporary one, and that she would easily be outridden by Helda and her men once they realised where she was going. Her only hope was to get off the beaten track and drive deeper into the wood. She checked the road ahead. To her left there was a small clearing and she slowed the machine as she approached it. Sure enough there was a game track, winding off into the depths of the wood. Lia braked the machine almost to a stop and turned in slowly, anxious that there be no mark in the road to betray where she had left it. Then she was on the path and plunging down through the trees.

Negotiating the track took all the skill she could muster. The trees hung low and there were obstacles round every bend. On more than one occasion she came within a hair's breadth of striking something, or sliding into the undergrowth. But she stayed on, her teeth gritted in grim determination as she penetrated ever deeper into the wood.

The vegetation was no more than a green blur, so fast was Lia travelling. The path twisted this way and that, and she fought hard to stay in control of the machine as she sped along. She had no idea how far she had travelled. Five miles? Ten? All she knew was that she was getting away. Putting as much distance as she could between herself and Helda.

It was some time before Lia felt secure enough to slow her pace. She eased back the throttle at last though, and began to look about her. For the first time she wondered where she might be. There were no landmarks she could recognise. Perhaps she had come a little too far?

Suddenly there was an odd popping sound from the bike's engine. It faltered, then picked up again momentarily before faltering again. Then it was slowing, the throaty roar reduced to a sucking sound as the now dead engine exerted a braking effect on the bike. Lia pulled in the clutch and coasted on as far as she could, but the machine soon came to a halt.

Lia gave a little cry of dismay. She climbed off and gazed uncomprehendingly at the engine. On an impulse she fiddled with the fuel cap and at last succeeded in opening it. The tank was empty.

At that moment she felt very alone and isolated. Whilst she had had the bike, she at least knew she could eventually find her way out of the forest. Without it she was quite lost. She cursed the bad luck that had brought her right back where she had started. She was in exactly the same position as when she had been swept away by the river all those weeks ago. In the middle of a thick forest completely alone and, worst of all, totally naked.

She glanced about her. There were no distinguishing features to the place at all. Her only hope was to find some high ground, as she had on the previous occasion.

Lia set off down the path, abandoning the now useless motorcycle. She guessed there was little chance of accurately retracing her steps through the maze of pathways, but she knew that in order to find safety she must somehow find her way back to the road.

As she walked, she thought of Thorkil and his friends. She hoped desperately that they were all right. With any luck, Helda's Bikers would have abandoned the attack when they realised their quarry was no longer there and set off after her. She knew their chances of finding her here were virtually zero. They would expect her to have headed for the highway and would be searching miles away. The trouble was that Thorkil would have no idea of her whereabouts either. Her heart sank as she thought of her predicament, lost and miles away from the ones she loved.

She walked on for a full hour, searching for something she could recognise, but to her consternation the more she walked, the less familiar was the terrain. The trees here were strangely shaped, and the flowers were like nothing she had ever seen before. Clearly she had strayed far from the path she had followed on the way in.

All at once, she heard the sound of water and realised how thirsty she was after walking so far. She set off in pursuit of the sound and soon found a small stream. It was clear and inviting and she knelt down and drank gratefully from it, gulping down the cool water.

Once she had drunk her fill, it occurred to her how hungry she was. It seemed ages since she had eaten the Bikers' stew and her stomach growled with emptiness. She looked about her for something to eat.

An odd shaped tree caught her eye. It was quite tall, but not very broad, its trunk no more than fifteen inches across. Hanging from its upper branches she could see large yellow fruits, that looked as though they might be good to eat. The lower part of the tree was like none she had ever seen before. At even spaces around it were odd protrusions, like stunted branches, each one no more than ten inches long. They sprang out at an upward pointing angle, and from where she stood they resembled nothing more than erect penises. She moved closer to the foot of the tree, taking one of the branches in her hand. At this range the resemblance to a male organ was, if anything, heightened, the thick stem opening into a bulbous end. Even the hole in the tip was in place. She ran her hand over the surface of the thing. It was a little rough to the touch, with slight undulations running across it, giving it a ribbed appearance.

Lia tested the knob for strength and calculated that it would easily support her weight. She placed a foot on it and levered herself up, using another one higher up as a hand hold. She began to climb the tree, stepping from one projection to another and hauling herself ever further up the trunk and closer to the fruits. They hung a good twenty feet above the ground and she clung tightly to the tree as she rose higher and higher.

At last the fruits were within her grasp. She reached up and took one in her hand. Its surface had a furry texture, like a peach, and the flesh felt soft. She twisted it round and it snapped off easily. Then she let it drop, watching as it bounced in the soft grass below. She detached two more in the same manner, then began to descend again.

She eased herself down carefully, stepping gingerly from foothold to foothold, taking great care not to scratch her bare flesh. She was no more than five feet up when disaster almost overcame her. The projection on which she was standing suddenly gave way with a loud crack. For a second she was completely off balance. Then she made a grab for a large knob just by her hand and managed just to prevent herself from falling.

Gently she lowered herself to the ground, then leant back against the tree, grateful to be back on terra firma.

When she had regained her breath she searched for the piece that had snapped off. It lay in the long grass just a few feet away, and she stooped down to pick it up. The base was green and soft, indicating that it was living tissue rather than the remains of a broken branch. Once more she fingered it, fascinated by its phallic shape. It was just like the dildo that clients of the Black Cat would make her use, standing her on a table in the middle of the night club and making her pleasure herself for the entertainment of the guests.

For a moment a strangely erotic feeling passed through her as she remembered her former brazenness. She stroked the object again, and as she did so, her hand dropped almost unconsciously to her shaven sex her fingers running lightly over her clitoris. For a few seconds she was in an almost dream like state, the sensation of her fingers on her sex sending a thrill through her body. Then she suddenly realised what she was doing, and the blood rushed to her face. She dropped the thing as if it had suddenly become red hot and, snatching her fingers from her love hole, she turned her back on the tree and went over to where the fruits had dropped. She gathered them up, then sat herself down on the ground, deliberately facing away from the tree. She took a tentative bite at one of the fruits, sucking at the juice that leaked from it. It tasted very good indeed, something between a peach and a mango in fruitiness and texture. She began to devour it hungrily. Then the second and third. Soon all that was left were three brown stones.

The afternoon was warm, and Lia felt a drowsiness overcome her. She stretched languidly, enjoying the feel of the soft grass against her bare skin. She lay back, closing her eyes and breathing in the fresh air and the scent of the flowers. She had not intended to doze, but the excitement of the day and the long walk soon got the better of her and she fell into a dreamless sleep.

It was the shadow falling across her face that wakened her.

"Who on earth are you?" a man asked.

Chapter 5

It took Lia a few seconds to focus her eyes as she blinked up into the bright sunlight. At first she thought she must be dreaming, but slowly she became aware that the group of people standing staring down at her were real enough. There were eight of them. Five men and three women.

They were dressed in a way she had never seen before. The men wore jeans, which looked extremely worn, many of them torn and ragged. Some were bare chested, others wore unbuttoned shirts that flapped in the wind. On their feet were sandals, and their faces were unshaven. The women wore long, shapeless dresses that hung below their knees. These too were shabby and torn in places. All of them, both men and women, wore jewellery of various kinds draped round their necks and wrists, and many of them had tattoos on their arms and chests and even on their faces.

"I said - who are you?"

Lia turned to face the man who was speaking, and simultaneously she remembered her nudity. She clutched her hands to her breasts and sex in a vain attempt to hide herself from their gazes.

"Speak!"

The man who addressed her was taller than the rest, and was distinguished by the thick gold chain round his neck. On the end of it dangled a jewelled medallion. It reminded Lia rather incongruously of a mayoral chain of office.

"My name is Lia," she said quietly.

"And what are you doing here, in this sacred place?"

"Sacred?"

"Certainly. This is the Tree of Birth. It is at the very heart of the living forest. Your presence in that disgusting state will have angered the spirits here."

"Spirits? What spirits?"

"The all-knowing Spirits of the Woods."

Then, suddenly, Lia understood. She had stumbled into a community of New Agers.

After the breakdown of law and order, many previously established organisations had been changed beyond all recognition. Attendance at conventional churches had been falling for years, and many of the great cathedrals now stood empty and derelict, their windows smashed, their great interiors turned into cardboard cities for the homeless. At the same time many people had begun to turn to alternative religions. Some worshipped ancient gods, others earthly things. Various different cults sprang up, each professing to have discovered the true meaning of life, and for a long time they remained in the cities, trying desperately to recruit people to their causes.

Some attempted to declare parts of the cities safe, preaching peaceful coexistence, but inevitably being wiped out by the tough gangs that roamed the streets. Many others left the urban areas, setting up communes in remote places where they could carry out their rites in peace. For the most part they were ignored by the Bikers, and were allowed to live quietly and practice their religions as long as they stayed away from the highways and service areas which the Biker's considered their own province. Despite the relative poverty in which they lived, the members of these communes began to preach to anyone who would listen of the dawn of a new age. Inevitably they became known as the New Agers.

And now Lia had found them. Or they had found Lia. She glanced from face to face, still clutching her hands to her body, wondering what they wanted with her.

"I - I'm sorry I was in your wood," she said. "I didn't realise it was sacred."

"But where are your clothes? Don't you realise it is sacrilege to be naked here, except during the most hallowed of services? Why is your body uncovered in such a provocative way?"

"I ... I haven't any clothes."

"Look Kieran," said one of the women suddenly. "The fruit. She's been eating the fruit."

The woman pointed at the fruit stones on the ground beside where the confused girl lay. Kieran, the man with the gold chain, picked one of the stones up and studied it. Then he turned to Lia, his eyes wide.

"It's true," he said. "You have been eating the fruits of the tree. Don't you realise that no-one is permitted to eat the fruits?"

"I didn't know..."

"Wait!" shouted one of the men. "Here is further proof of the little strumpet's evil." He held up the piece of the tree that Lia had snapped off. "She has removed a member from the Tree."

A collective gasp went up from the New Agers as they stared openmouthed at the object in his hand.

"Give me that," said Kieran, snatching it from him. He took the piece almost reverently, turning it over in his hands. Then he stared at Lia.

"Wicked girl," he shouted. "Look at what you have done to the Tree. This is a profanity that must not go unpunished."

"But it was an accident," insisted Lia. "I didn't know the tree was sacred."

"Ignorance is not an excuse," said Kieran, his eyes wide. "You must make amends to the Tree for what you have done." He turned to the man beside him. "Victor," he said. "She shall be offered to the Tree, and punished there."

"Offered to the Tree?" Victor was dubious.

"Yes. It is the fitting place for her punishment, and it will show her the supreme power of the tree. Do it!"

Before she fully realised what was happening, Lia found her arms grasped on both sides and she was hauled to her feet, her hands trapped behind her so that her intimate parts were visible to all the New Agers. She stood, confused, whilst the New Agers began pulling ropes from the bags that they carried. As they did so, Kieran started muttering some incomprehensible chant.

At a command from Kieran, Lia was marched over to the tree, where she was halted just in front of it.

"Oh Spirit of the Tree," chanted Kieran loudly. "We offer you this strumpet for your pleasure, to make amends for her behaviour. Please accept our offering."

With that Lia found herself being lifted bodily, and her legs pulled wide apart. For a second she was unsure of what they were doing. Then she realised.

They were going to impale her on one of the knobs!

She looked down with consternation at the protrusion. It was long and thick, and positioned just at the level of her sex. She tried to struggle, but the hands that held her were too strong, pushing her downwards onto it. She gave a little gasp as she felt the rough tip brush her sex. Then there were fingers probing at her. Rough, insistent fingers that delved between her legs from behind and stretched the lips of her sex apart. Fingers that found her clitoris and teased it into a hard little bud. Fingers that, despite her outward reluctance, began to have an inevitable effect on her, causing a warm wetness to flow within her.

For a full minute they held her suspended, stimulating her until she was lubricated and ready. Then they forced her downwards, so that the phallic tip was pressed hard against the opening of her vagina. Lia gave a cry of surprise as it slid into her. At that moment, despite herself, she felt her juices flow even more strongly, coating the rough wood with a sleek film as it penetrated her in the most intimate manner.

Down and down they pushed her, forcing the great wooden knob further and further into her until it could go no further, and her pubic mound was pressed against the trunk of the tree, her nipples brushing the gnarled bark.

As soon as he was certain she was completely impaled, Kieran shouted an order and two stakes were driven into the ground on either side of the tree. Ropes were wound round her ankles and secured to these stakes, leaving her legs spread wide apart. Then they took her hands, wrapping them round the tree and tying her wrists before dragging them up as high as they could and securing them out of her sight.

Lia was helpless, her naked body pressed hard against the tree, her sex filled with the solid wooden cock. All she could move was her head, and she glanced back at Kieran, watching him as he uncoiled a long, thin whip. Her stomach turned over as she realised the target she made, her whole back exposed from neck to ankle, her backside thrust back provocatively by the phallic projection.

And yet, mixed with the fear was a delicious sense of anticipation, and she felt the muscles of her sex tighten round the wooden cock as she braced herself for the beating.

Swish! Crack!

The whip came down across her beautifully presented rear with a force that drove the breath from her. She closed her eyes and gritted her teeth.

Swish! Crack!

It descended again, this time across her lower legs, cutting into her flesh. She tried to struggle, but she was held fast, the movement simply causing her exposed clitoris to rub against the harsh wood, making it swell still further.

Swish! Crack!

This time the leather fell across her back, the hard thong on the end whipping round and catching her breast, leaving a long red stripe that travelled halfway round her body. Lia's skin was bathed in sweat now, and her body glistened in the afternoon sunlight.

Swish! Crack!
Swish! Crack!
Swish! Crack!

The whip continued to descend on her punished flesh. But there was a new sensation filling her now, one that made the pain bearable. Pleasurable even. Each blow of the whip rocked her body forward, forcing the wooden shaft to slide back and forth inside her. It was as if the knob and the whip were conspiring together to fuck her, and the sensation to one as lustful as Lia was delicious.

Swish! Crack!

Swish! Crack!

Lia struggled to control her feelings as the blows rained down. The pain from the whip was excruciating, but somehow it paled into insignificance compared to the pleasure that ran through her every time she felt the object inside her work its way in and out of her sex. Her nipples had swollen to hard nuts as they were forced against the rough wood, further heightening the tingling lust that was rising within her.

Swish! Crack!

Swish! Crack!

Kieran paused for a second, and Lia turned to watch him, still gasping with passion as she hung there. He was drawing his arm right back and she gritted her teeth.

Swish! Crack!

The blow striped across her behind with enormous ferocity, raising a spray of sweat as it bit into her already reddened flesh.

Kieran lowered the whip, but Lia's body continued to writhe. She wanted to stop, but her arousal was too great. Her nakedness, her incredibly erotic position and the beating had raised her emotions to fever pitch and she drove herself down on the phallus, somehow spurred on by the fact that she was being watched. It was like the scene in the diner weeks before, where she had deliberately brought herself off with the neck of a bottle in front of all the truck drivers. She wanted to be watched. To demonstrate her wantonness to all who wished to see.

Lia's backside was pumping back and forth with a terrible urgency now, as she fucked the rough, hard tree. A loud moaning sound escaped her lips and she rammed her hips down harder and harder on the wooden rod, revelling in the sensation of its roughness as it ran back and forth over the walls of her sex. Her clitoris was hard and protruding as she ground it down against the wood, and such was her arousal that a silvery trickle of wetness was running down the trunk of the tree.

"Aah! Aah! Aah!" she shouted.

Then she was coming, the moan turning to a shriek as her passion exploded inside her. She hung, her muscles tensed, her entire body totally rigid except for her behind, which thrust forward in regular jabbing movements as her come flooded her. She threw back her head and cried aloud as the pain and the passion brought her to the most exquisite peak she could imagine, the bondage only serving to increase the sensation as the world seemed to disappear in a blur of pleasure.

Then slowly, by degree, her body began to relax, the breaths coming longer and deeper now as the muscles lost their tension. The movements of her backside slowed too and her whole frame seemed to slowly sag, until she hung from the tree like a spent rag, staring shamefacedly round at her audience.

Chapter 6

Lia was brought to her senses by the sensation of someone undoing the knots that held her wrists. She opened her eyes to see that it was Victor. Once he had freed her hands, she clung onto the trunk whilst he removed the ropes from her ankles. Only then was she able to separate herself from the tree, easing the phallic object from within her, gasping slightly as it's rough surface slid from her sex.

When it finally emerged from her, the wooden knob was wet and shiny with her juices. Lia stared down at it shamefacedly, wondering what they must think of her.

Kieran crouched down, examining the surface of the wood, and the trail of wetness that ran down the trunk.

"I think the Spirit has been appeased," he said gravely as he stood up.

"Wait," said Victor suddenly, pointing to the tree. "What's that?"

"What?"

"There, on the end of the thing. It looks like sperm."

"Don't be stupid," said Kieran. "It can't be."

"I tell you it is," Victor insisted. "Just look."

Kieran knelt down and inspected the tree once more. Then he gave an exclamation.

"By the Spirits," he said. "It is sperm."

Lia stared down at the object. It was no great surprise to her that some spunk had leaked from her. After all she had already been fucked by both Thorkil and Rico today, and the wooden knob had penetrated her right to the farthest reaches of her sex. But of course the New Agers had no way of knowing that.

Kieran rose to his feet. "This is indeed a sign," he said importantly. "The Tree has shown us the pleasure that this woman brings to it. We must take her back and show the High One."

"You mean the tree actually released it's seed into her?" asked one of the women.

"Of course. I tell you it is a sign from the spirits."

Lia was flabbergasted by their credulity. How could they possibly believe that the spunk had come from the tree? She had heard before of the New Agers' willingness to believe in anything remotely supernatural, but this was ridiculous. And yet they all seemed to accept it as the truth, kneeling by the tree and inspecting the evidence, expressions of wonder pouring from their lips. For a moment she pondered whether she should give them the real explanation. Wisely, she decided against it, fearing that she would appear to be ridiculing Kieran. He obviously had a good deal of power over these people and she was afraid he might make them turn on her if he found out.

Even if she had intended to explain, Lia was given no opportunity. Almost before she knew what was happening, her hands were being grasped and her wrists tied together behind her back. Then her elbows were fastened together, rendering her arms completely helpless. The bonds had the effect of thrusting her chest forward so as to accentuate the round creamy globes of her bare breasts.

Once he was satisfied that Lia's arms were secure, Kieran gave an order and the odd party set off through the forest. A length of rope trailed down from Lia's wrists which was firmly held by one of the women, who hurried her along, pushing and prodding her if she stumbled. As she marched through the forest, Lia wondered what would befall her. Her freedom had been very short lived indeed, and now here she was, once more a naked captive, being led into the unknown.

They walked for about fifteen minutes, penetrating deeper and deeper into the woods. The New Agers seemed to know where they were going, but Lia had lost her bearings completely. It seemed impossible she would ever be able to find Thorkil or his Biker friends again.

All of a sudden they crested a rise and the land seemed to drop away in front of them. Lia found herself gazing down into a large clearing. There she saw what she assumed was the New Agers' village. It was more of an encampment really, the buildings low and crude, built of wood and mud with thatched roofs. There were about sixty huts altogether, all gathered around a central square where stood a much larger building that dominated the entire village. Beyond it, right on the edge, was a similarly impressive edifice, resembling a fortress, complete with towers and ramparts.

At the sight of the encampment Lia found herself holding back. It was much larger than she had expected and appeared to be bustling with people. The thought of being led naked amongst so many strangers filled her with dread. A pinch on her still sore behind made her move on though, and they began their descent to the village. Soon they were passing the first of the houses, threading their way up a narrow street.

As they made their way between the buildings, people came to their doors and stared at Lia. She blushed scarlet at the sight she must make, her breasts jutting conspicuously, her sex hairless and visible, her back and bottom striped with the marks of Kieran's whip.

No sooner had they passed by than the people fell in behind them, whilst others were gathering in the square ahead, talking excitedly and pointing at the lovely young girl who was being led into their midst. Lia looked straight ahead, trying not to catch their eyes. She wished more than anything that she had some clothes. The humiliation of being naked before all these people was more than she could bear, and her face glowed a brighter red than her behind as she approached the square.

When they reached the square, the crowd parted in front of them. Ahead Lia could see a platform about three feet from the ground, and it was to this that she was being led. There were steps up the side of the platform, and the woman who held her lead shoved her up these to the top, where there was a single post about four feet high. There was a metal ring set in the post and the rope was secured to this, leaving her standing with her back to it, staring out over the crowd.

"Legs apart," ordered the woman.

Reluctantly Lia obeyed, aware that her elevated position left her sex totally exposed to the eyes of the onlookers.

"Who is she?"

"Where did they find her?"

"Why is she naked?"

"Look at the brazen hussy, displaying herself like that."

"Someone's been whipping her arse. Just look."

Lia heard the remarks of the crowd, but tried to block them from her mind. She searched the faces below, hoping for a friendly or sympathetic face, but in vain. Some were grinning, others open-mouthed, still others licking their lips as they surveyed her naked body. She looked about for Kieran. He didn't appear to be among the onlookers. Then she spotted him entering the large building at the top of the square. The door was guarded by two women, who wore tiny bikini-like garments that seemed to be made of animal skin. Both carried spears. They reminded Lia of the women in a film she had once seen about dinosaurs and cave men.

Lia was left on display in the middle of the square for a full hour. All that time men and women were approaching the dais for a view of her, pointing at her and making crude and suggestive remarks.

At first she felt nothing but a deep shame, wishing desperately that she was somewhere else, or at least that her breasts and sex were covered. But as the time passed, something odd began to happened in her mind. Somehow, despite her fears, she began to find her situation strangely arousing. To be placed as she was, bound, naked and open before all these people gave her an odd feeling in her belly. She thought back once more to the scene all those weeks ago in the diner, where she had been forced to stand naked on a table before a room full of truck drivers. She thought too of the cold hardness of the bottle that they had given her, and how delicious it had felt when she slipped it inside her. And as these thoughts went through her mind she felt her nipples harden and her sex lips convulse. All at once she was aroused once more, her head filled with thoughts of the men who had fucked her in so many different ways. Try as she might, she was unable to suppress these thoughts, even though she was aware that the crowds could see her arousal as they pointed and commented. She closed her eyes tight, trying to control her emotions, praying that Kieran would return soon and release her.

At last she saw the door to the large building open once more and two women, dressed in the same skimpy outfits as the pair guarding the door, came out. They crossed the square towards the platform where she was displayed and climbed the steps. The first of them took up a position before her, the cruel spike of her spear placed at Lia's neck, so that the hapless captive dared not move an inch. At the same time the other woman set about releasing her from the post. Once the rope was undone the spear was removed from her throat and she felt another prodding her back, indicating that she was to descend to the square.

They forced her across the square, the cold metal of the two weapons pressed into her back as she headed towards the large building. On either side stood the crowd, watching silently as she passed. She had been afraid that they might reach out for her body, with her hands pinned as they were, but no attempt was made to touch her and she had the feeling that this was in no small way due to the presence of her two guards.

The doors to the building were pulled open by the sentries as she approached and she walked inside. She found herself in a vast chamber, not unlike a church or cathedral. There were crude wooden benches on either side, laid out in rows, all facing the front. Before them was a large stone, which formed a kind of altar, on which was lying the body of a dead rabbit. The blood of the animal was still not dry and it trickled slowly down a channel that led to a bowl at the bottom which was already half full of the red, viscous fluid. The sight made Lia shiver slightly.

They led Lia past the altar and on to the back of the chamber, where there was an archway. She was taken through this into a narrow corridor, at the end of which she was ordered to halt outside a door. One of the women knocked on the door and went through, whilst the other remained at Lia's side, her spear point once more at Lia's throat.

Once the door had closed the guard turned to look at her captive.

"Such a pretty little thing," she murmured.

She lifted the spear up, so that the cold metal brushed Lia's cheek.

Lia stayed perfectly still. The point was razor sharp, and the slightest involuntary movement could have caused her skin to be pierced.

The guard moved the weapon, sliding the edge down Lia's neck, the feel of it making the hapless girl shiver. She slid it down her front and over her swelling breasts, just scratching her nipples, the sensation making them harden almost at once. The guard smiled at this and continued to tease them in turn, the rough edge of the steel sending a tremor through Lia's body.

Then she began to move it lower, prodding gently at her midriff before scraping it ever so lightly down to press gently against her prominent mound. Lia held her breath, aware of what might follow and afraid she would not be able to hold her body still.

Slowly, inexorably, the blade slid down between her legs and found her clitoris, the cold edge of the metal making her gasp aloud. The sensation of the hard edge on her love bud was extraordinary and Lia felt the wetness flow from her and onto the blade. The guard went on with her gentle probing, amused at the way the lips of Lia's sex twitched as she teased her.

At last she took her spear away, leaving the tethered girl panting softly. She raised it up to Lia's eye level, and let her see the drop of moisture that trickled down the cold steel. Without a word she held it in front of Lia's mouth.

"Clean it off," she ordered quietly.

Lia stuck out her tongue and licked the salty liquid from the spear's tip.

No sooner had she lapped the last of her juice from the blade than the door opened and the other guard appeared again.

"The High One will see you now," she said.

"Who is..."

"Silence!" snapped the guard. "You will not speak in the High One's presence unless specifically invited to do so. Disobedience of this rule will result in punishment. Do you understand?"

Lia bowed her head. "Yes," she said.

"I am a high priestess. Yes Sereneness is the correct form of address when you speak to me."

"Yes, Sereneness."

"Now listen. Once inside you will kneel before the High One and await his orders. Do you understand?"

"Yes."

Whack! The second guard brought down the handle of her spear across Lia's behind with a force that made her cry out with pain.

"Yes, Sereneness," she mumbled.

The guard brushed Lia's hair from her eyes, gave her a final check-over, then stood aside and indicated that she was to enter.

Inside, the room was lit only by candlelight and Lia blinked in the gloom, unable at first to make anything out. Then her eyes perceived a movement and she saw the figure of Kieran standing at the far end of the room. As they came closer to Kieran she realised that there was a second man present. He was seated on what could only be described as a throne. It was a massive piece of furniture placed on a stage a full yard above the floor. It was covered in a wine-red velvet material, with gold tassels hanging down from it. Above it was a canopy of similar hue.

The man seated in the throne was about fifty years old, his hair grey and thinning on top. His face was shrouded in a bushy grey beard that hung down almost to his waist. He wore a long multi-coloured robe, and had open sandals on his feet. His face seemed to be painted with some kind of war paint, and on his head he wore a golden spiked crown.

This was the High One.

The guards prodded Lia forward until she was almost underneath the figure, then the blades were placed on her shoulders, forcing her to her knees. Lia knelt obediently before the High One, her eyes cast down, her heart beating fast.

"So this is the mysterious young lady," said the High One. His voice was thin and nasal, not at all the booming voice of authority that Lia had been expecting. "Tell me, girl," he went on. "What were you doing in the sacred place? And in that state as well."

"I - I was lost sir," Lia stammered.

Whack! Once again the end of the woman's spear came down on Lia's behind.

"You will refer to the High One as Highness," barked the girl.

"But how did you come to be there?" persisted the High One.

Lia hesitated. The last thing she wanted to do was to admit that she was on the run from the Bikers. She feared that if they found out they would hand her over to Helda, and she would be back where she started. She decided to play on their gullibility. After all, if they had believed that the spunk on the tree had been supernatural maybe they would believe her.

"I don't understand it, Highness," she said, her eyes cast down. "I suddenly found myself there."

"But why did you steal the fruit?

"I... The tree told me to eat it Highness."

"Told you?"

"Yes Highness. I heard a voice in my ears bidding me to eat it."

"But you broke a piece from the tree!"

Lia was thinking fast now. She knew what she was saying was ridiculous, but there was no turning back once she had begun the lies.

"It wasn't broken Highness," she said. "It was a gift. From the tree."

"A gift?"

"Yes Highness."

"For what purpose?"

Lia's face reddened. "For me to... to use Highness."

There was silence for a few moments, then the High One spoke again. "Show me the piece," he said.

Kieran, who had merely stood apart listening all this time, stepped forward bearing the piece that Lia had snapped from the tree. It was about ten inches long, with the same ribbed surface and bulbous end as the one on which they had impaled her that afternoon.

The High One examined the object carefully, turning it over in his hands. Eventually he looked down at the kneeling girl.

"If what you say is true, then this is indeed a miraculous occurrence," he said. He turned to Kieran. "It is possible that she was sent for the Solstice Ceremony."

Kieran bowed. "That was what I thought, Highness," he said.

"We shall test her at the New Moon Gathering," said the High One. "Meanwhile I will leave her in the custody of the priestesses." He addressed the two guards. "You are to impose a regime of the strictest discipline upon her, so that she will be ready for the Gathering."

"But you mustn't keep me here," blurted Lia. "I have to find Thorkil."

"Silence!" thundered the woman, who stood behind her. "For that outburst you will receive six strokes."

Lia opened her mouth to protest, but catching sight of the glare on her guard's face she closed it again.

"Take her away," said the High One quietly. "And prepare her for the Gathering."

Chapter 7

Lia awoke the next morning to the feel of the sun on her face. She opened her eyes and saw that it was shining through a small barred window above her. She tried to cover her face, but her hands wouldn't move. She raised her head and looked down at herself.

She was naked, and chained to a narrow bed. Her wrists were attached to a ring in the wall behind her, whilst her legs were stretched apart and fixed to similar rings at either side of the bed at the bottom. The cell in which she lay was entirely bare apart from the bed. Opposite her was a strong oak door, with a small triangular window in it, no more than four inches square.

She couldn't believe her bad luck. After only a few short hours of freedom she was a captive once again. But for what? What had the High One meant about the New Moon Gathering? And the Solstice Ceremony? To Lia the New Agers were a complete mystery.

She had learnt no more from the guards the night before. By the time they had marched her out of the temple, the light was beginning to fade in the sky and the crowd had almost completely dispersed. The women had led her down the narrow path between the buildings, their spears at her back. At the very edge of the encampment was the building that resembled a fort, guarded by still more of the scantily clad young amazons she now knew to be priestesses. Her escorts had taken her in through a large gate that opened onto a courtyard. She had watched whilst the gate was secured behind her with a heavy iron lock, then they had taken her through a door on the far side of the yard, where there was a row of cells. As far as she could tell, all were empty. They had led her into the farthest one, locking the door once she was inside.

Here she had remained alone, the only other contact being when they brought her a meal just as darkness was falling. Once she had eaten they had chained her to the bed and left her to fall into a troubled sleep, haunted by dreams of Helda stalking her through the woods.

She lay for more than half an hour, gazing at the ceiling and pondering her fate. So quiet was it, that she began to imagine she had been abandoned, and that the entire commune had moved away overnight, leaving her to starve in this bare cell. But at last she heard a noise outside and she looked up to see a pair of eyes staring at her through the small window. She squirmed uncomfortably under their gaze, wishing she could cover herself. She was only too aware of the delightful sight her plump breasts and gaping sex offered to the onlooker.

The eyes stayed unmoving for about half a minute. Then she heard a key turn in the lock and the door swung open.

Standing in the doorway was a man. He looked strangely different from the New Agers she had encountered earlier. He was dressed in a grey shirt and trousers, clean shaven with none of the body paint or jewellery that the others had worn. He grinned as he stared down at her.

"Now you're a sight for sore eyes, that's for sure," he said, letting his eyes drift over her bare flesh. "It looks like those nutters have come up trumps for once."

He reached out and ran a hand over her breasts, staring into her eyes as he did so. Lia turned away, but he grabbed her chin and made her face him.

"I'm Delgado," he said. "Mr Delgado to you. You and I have to get to know one another better. We'll be seeing a lot of each other over the next few weeks."

"But what's going to..."

He placed a finger on her lips, silencing her instantly.

"No speaking unless you're spoken to," he said. "I could have you flogged if the priestesses find out. But I won't tell them just this once. In the meantime..." He stopped speaking suddenly and stared at her face. "Wait a minute."

"What is it?" she asked, slightly alarmed.

He narrowed his eyes. "Don't I know you from somewhere?"

"I don't think so."

He stared at her for a moment longer, then shook his head.

"I dunno," he said. "I don't usually forget a face."

He began undoing her shackles, and soon she was standing beside the bed stretching gratefully. He led her from the cell and down the corridor to a bathroom. In the middle of the room was a large bath filled with warm water. She wondered where the water had come from, as there was no plumbing that she could see. Nevertheless she was grateful when he nodded to it, and climbed in eagerly. She washed herself all over under his unblinking eyes. It was good to get clean again, but she longed for a little privacy. Clearly she would get none here.

When she had dried herself off, he motioned to a wooden table in the corner of the room.

"Sit on that," he ordered.

Obediently Lia did as she was told, the wooden surface feeling cold and hard against her bare backside.

Delgado opened a cupboard and removed a shaving mug and brush.

41

He poured a little water into the mug, then carried it across to her.

"Starting to get a little spiky down there," he said. "We can't have that. Now open your legs wide."

Lia had no choice but to obey. It had been two days since her pubic hair had been shaved and there was indeed a layer of dark stubble across her pudendum. She hated the idea of being shaved down there. Somehow it made her even more naked and seemed to emphasise her availability. It was like she was making a statement about her promiscuity to all those who saw it.

He began brushing the lather onto her, working all over her pubic mound, then down between her legs, smearing it onto the lips of her sex. She was relieved to discover that the water was warm, and the sensation as he spread it was really quite pleasant. She lay back and closed her eyes, trying not to think of the sight her naked body was presenting to him.

She heard a scraping sound and looked up to see him stropping a razor on a length of leather. It was an old-fashioned cut-throat razor and its blade gleamed as he worked it back and forth.

He began to shave her, letting the cold blade slide over her skin, carrying with it the small dark wiry hairs that had sprung through since she had left the Black Cat. He worked carefully over her mound, then began to shave her lips. As his fingers touched her down there she felt her muscles convulse.

"Steady now," he said quietly. "I wouldn't want to cut you."

It was all Lia could do to stay still as his hands brushed against her most private and sensitive place. She could feel her clitoris swelling and, with her legs stretched so wide, she knew he must be able to see it.

Delgado wielded the razor expertly and was soon finished, much to Lia's relief. He rubbed her over with a damp flannel, then replaced the shaving gear in the cupboard. Then he came back and stood between her legs, gazing down at her.

"Yes," he said quietly. "Not a bad job at all." He slid his hand down over her sex, allowing his thumb to slide into her slit. She rewarded him with a groan as his thumb found her love bud.

He smiled and withdrew his hand.

"No time for that," he said. "They'll be expecting you."

He took her from the bathroom into another room. This was some kind of store room, with cupboards and drawers all around the walls.

"Star sign?" he asked.

"I beg your pardon?"

"Star sign. Sign of the Zodiac. What is it?"

"I don't know. I don't believe in that sort of thing."

"Don't let those nutters out there hear you saying that," he said. "Round here everybody believes. Even me. Now, when were you born?"

"I'm not sure. Nobody ever told me."

"Well, for the sake of these people you'll have to be something." He fished out a small gold chain. "Here you are," he said. "Capricorn. That'll do."

He hung the chain about Lia's neck. There was a pendant hanging from it in the shape of a goat, and he adjusted it so that it nestled between her breasts. The metal felt cold on her skin, and Lia shivered slightly, not liking the ridiculous trinket at all.

He fastened a second, very fine gold chain about her waist, and another round her ankle. Somehow the jewellery seemed cheap and made her feel rather tartish

At last he was satisfied with her appearance and, after running a brush through her hair a few times, led her from the room.

He produced a pair of handcuffs and fastened her wrists behind her back. Then he opened a door and took her out into the sunlight.

The courtyard was empty apart from two guards who stood by the main gate. Delgado marched her smartly across the yard toward a doorway. When they reached it he rapped loudly on the door, then opened it, pushing her inside and closing the door, without entering himself

Lia looked about her. She was in a small hallway with a single exit opposite the door through which she had been pushed. She hesitated for a second. Then, since there was nowhere else to go, she pushed the door open and stepped through.

Chapter 8

The room Lia entered was large, with a high ceiling supported by thick wooden pillars. The walls were covered with murals depicting strange scenes. Creatures that were half man and half beast were depicted in unfamiliar landscapes. Some of the pictures seemed to have no form to them at all, just meaningless swirls and splashes of colour. In addition to the murals were the statues, some in recesses high in the walls, others free standing about the room. Many of these were of odd, ugly beings that stood on two legs, great phalluses projecting from their groins. Others were of winged beasts with long curved talons, some of them bearing the body of some hapless woodland creature.

The only other furniture in the room was a series of divans that stood around the walls, draped with brightly coloured cloths that had the coarseness of a fabric woven by hand.

Lia stood in the centre of the room, glancing round uncertainly. There was another door to the room on the far side, but her instincts told her to remain where she was.

She had been waiting for nearly ten minutes before she heard the sound of someone approaching. Her body stiffened. Her months with the Bikers had taught her to take a submissive stance when in such situations and, although she was unable to place her hands behind her head because of the cuffs, she was still able to straighten her back and place her legs apart before the door opened.

The beautiful young women who entered the room were all dressed in the same manner as the ones who had escorted her on the previous day. Only the colour of their skimpy outfits varied, some being almost white whilst others were a much darker hue There was no sign of the cruel spears. Each woman seemed to know her place and they made their way to the divans, where they draped themselves, some giggling as they pointed at Lia.

The one in the lightest coloured outfit went to a divan in the centre, close to where Lia stood. She reclined gracefully on it, then beckoned Lia closer to her.

"The High One tells me that you were found at the Tree of Birth. Is this true?"

"Yes, Sereneness."

"And is it also true that you had sex with the tree?"

At this one of the other girls giggled again, but a withering look from

Lia's interrogator silenced her almost at once.

"Well, is it?"

"Yes, Sereneness."

"And the tree actually released male seed into you?"

"So they said, Sereneness."

"Where do you come from?"

"I don't know, Sereneness." The answer was, at least in part, truthful, since Lia had been brought up an orphan and knew no details of her past. In any case, the woman seemed to accept it without question. What strange people these were, thought Lia. With their odd icons and customs and their curious titles for one another.

"What do you know of the Spirits of the Forest?" asked the woman.

"Nothing, Sereneness."

"Yet you were in the Sacred Place?:"

"I - I don't know how I got there."

The interrogation went on for some time, with Lia professing ignorance at every possible opportunity. Eventually the woman seemed to accept that she would learn no more from her young captive, and she began to talk about the New Agers themselves.

"I am Karla," she said. "I am the senior priestess of our colony. We escaped from the darkness of the city after the High One had a vision telling him of the Spirits of the Forest and urging him to come out here and serve them. Once in the forest, the Spirits guided him to the Tree of Birth, which is the most sacred place on earth. So we built our village nearby, erected the temple and began to worship. In return the Spirits have been kind to us and we have not gone hungry. Now, it seems, we have been sent you. The High One believes it is for the Solstice Ceremony, but first you must pass the test of the New Moon Gathering. The High One told you this I believe?"

"Yes, Sereneness."

"The Gathering is not for three weeks. Until then you will remain here in the Fortress Retreat with the priestesses. It is important that you understand who we are."

"Yes, Sereneness."

"The people of this community are dedicated to the service of the Spirits. It is also necessary, however, for them to build and dig and sow in order to sustain life. The Spirits are generous, but must be assisted in their work by the labour of the people. In order to ensure that the true meaning of the Temple is not obscured, therefore, they appoint us priestesses to offer praise and prayer. We carry spears, mainly for ceremonial reasons, but our chief duty is to the praise of the spirits and the High One.

For this reason we live here, in the Fortress Retreat and only venture out to guard the Temple and to join in the services there. Do you understand?"

"Yes, Sereneness."

"No man from the commune is allowed inside this fortress, and we are forbidden all contact with males during out five year tenure. Yes, I know that Delgado is allowed inside the Fortress, but he is not one of us, and even he is not allowed here, in the Inner Sanctum. Delgado has his reasons for wanting to hide from the outside world, and we do not question them."

"Yes, Sereneness."

"Whilst you are in the Fortress, you will carry out duties that will keep you occupied. Once a day you will attend the worship in the Temple, as the people will wish to see you. At all times you are to be obedient to the Priestesses and to the High One. Is that understood?"

"Yes, Sereneness."

"Good. Now, I believe Shuna has something to report from yesterday."

Two of the women rose from their divans, and Lia felt a sinking feeling as she recognised the two priestesses that had escorted her the day before.

"Speak, Shuna," said Karla.

Shuna was the girl who had gone ahead into the High One's reception room first, Leaving Lia and her companion, Lisbet outside. She frowned at Lia as she began to speak.

"This person has already transgressed," she said, her eyes cast down.

"Then it is your duty to speak, Shuna. How has she transgressed?"

Shuna frowned again. Lia wondered why she seemed so reluctant to tell Karla of her misdemeanour. She had shown no affection towards Lia up to now.

"She ... she spoke out of turn to the High One," said Shuna at last.

"And did the High One order a punishment?"

"Yes."

"Go on."

"He ... he has ordered six strokes."

"I see." Karla turned to Lia. "Is this true?"

Lia hung her head. "Yes, Sereneness," she muttered.

"Then the sentence must be carried out. On both of you"

Lia looked up in surprise.

"You see -" Karla was smiling as she explained - "here at the commune we believe guilt must be shared. We are duty bound to report any misdemeanours we come across, but in doing so we may appear to be sitting in judgement. So the punishment is meted out to the accuser, as well as the accused. And since Shuna was given the duty of reporting the punishment, then she must receive the same."

Lia shook her head. These people had the strangest customs she had ever encountered. No wonder Shuna had been so reluctant to report her.

"Right," said Karla. "Let me see your backside young lady."

Lia hesitated for a moment.

"Your behind," said Karla sharply. "Show it to me."

Slowly Lia turned around.

"Bend forward."

She obeyed, displaying her bottom to the priestesses. It was still red from her punishment the day before, with cruel marks across both cheeks.

"Hmm," said Karla. "It seems that you've been pretty well punished there already. I think a thong across those lovely white thighs might be in order."

The words sent a chill through Lia, and with it an odd sense of excitement as she thought about what was intended.

"Stand up and turn around," said Karla. She looked round at the young priestesses. "Now who shall have the honour of carrying out the punishment? Someone new, I think."

She pointed to a youngster, who was seated right on the outside of the gathering.

"Stand up Charlotte," she said.

The girl rose to her feet. She looked about nineteen years old. She was slim and beautiful with high breasts that bulged out over the top of her bikini, and wide, rounded hips. Her hair was dark, and hung down over her shoulders, framing her pretty face beautifully. Lia noted that the colour of her outfit was a very dark brown. The hue of each priestess's clothes seemed to be an indication of her status, demonstrating that Charlotte was some kind of novice. Karla's costume was almost white, and Shuna's and Lisbet's were a light tan.

Charlotte stepped forward, her pretty brown eyes wide open. Lia could see from her demeanour that the girl was nervous. She wondered if it was the first time she had been asked to mete out a punishment, and guessed that it probably was.

"Fetch the thong," ordered Karla.

Charlotte crossed the room to a cabinet that hung on the wall, and opened it. Lia caught a glimpse of an array of canes, whips and manacles inside, the sight of which sent a wicked thrill through her. Charlotte reached in and withdrew something from a shelf, then closed the cabinet again. As she returned, Lia saw that she held a small leather strap about a foot long. She handed it to Karla, who slapped it onto her palm a couple of times, making a loud cracking sound as she did so.

Karla motioned to Lia to approach the central divan. The divan was low, but it rose up at one end into a headrest, which was thick and padded.

"Stand with your back to it," she ordered.

Obediently Lia took up the position. She looked about her. The eyes of all the priestesses were on her. Shuna, standing close to her, seemed unmoved at having to witness the punishment that in a few minutes she too would be receiving. The one who appeared the most nervous was Charlotte.

"Bend back over the divan," said Karla.

Lia shuffled backwards until she felt the leather surface of the head rest on her behind. Then she slowly leant back. It was slightly awkward, since her hands were still manacled, but she eased herself down until she was lying with her head on the flat surface of the couch, her backside raised high on the headrest. Without waiting for the inevitable order, she spread her legs wide. In this position she knew she offered a perfect target for the punishment, her inner thighs totally exposed, as was her wide open sex.

"Mmm, very nice," said Karla, as she gazed down at the prostrate girl. "Come forward, Charlotte, and feel how soft her flesh is."

The girl approached nervously, and Karla took her hand, placing it flat on the smooth flesh of Lia's inner thigh. Still holding her wrist, she guided Charlotte's hand up toward the naked captive's sex.

"Feel for her love bud," she said. "Make it hard. I want to see if she really responds to punishment in the way they say she does."

Gingerly Charlotte ran her fingers over Lia's clitoris. Lia gritted her teeth, trying hard not to respond to this intimate touch, but she was unable to prevent a gasp escaping her lips as Charlotte took her love bud between finger and thumb and began to toy with it. The girl was young and inexperienced, and her caresses were rather fumbling, but still it aroused a spark of lust in Lia as she fought hard to stay still.

She looked up and caught the eye of the girl who was caressing her. To her surprise, she realised that the girl's nervousness had disappeared. In its place, Charlotte wore an expression of longing as she gazed down at Lia's nude body, laid out so submissively before her. For a second their eyes met, and at that moment something seemed to pass between them. Suddenly Lia realised she wanted the girl, with a passion she had never felt towards a woman before. She wanted to strip off the girl's skimpy garment, to caress those lovely young breasts and taste her virgin honeypot.

The sensation lasted only a second, and then Charlotte turned her eyes away in embarrassment. Lia, having dropped her guard, gave a small moan as the fingers continued to work on her.

"That's enough," Karla said suddenly. Lia looked up, wondering if she had seen the glance between herself and Charlotte. "She's nice and hard now," went on Karla. "Begin the punishment."

Charlotte accepted the thong from Karla and stood between Lia's legs. She bit her lower lip, and Lia could sense that this was going to be difficult for her.

Charlotte raised the thong, and Lia shut her eyes.

Crack!

The leather came down hard on Lia's inner thigh, making a sound that rang about the room. Lia jumped as the pain hit her, then lay still again.

Crack!

This time her other thigh received the blow, the hard leather cutting into the flesh, leaving a deep red stripe that ran almost to her sex.

Crack!

Lia cried out as the leather snapped down onto her sensitive skin. The pain was excruciating, and with it came that familiar burn in her sex that was so hard for her to understand. She gazed up between her breasts and open thighs at Charlotte, who was raising the thong yet again, and a spasm of lust ran through her as she once again imagined the girl naked and in her embrace.

Crack!

The fourth blow fell, stinging Lia dreadfully. She could see that, despite her apparent feelings, Charlotte was not sparing her. Perhaps it was because she realised the perverse pleasure Lia received from being beaten. She hoped that was the case.

Crack!

Once again Lia's body shook as the leather came down. This blow was very high up her thigh indeed, and the end of the thong slapped against the edge of her sex lips. As it did so, Lia felt an odd cold sensation about her thighs and realised to her chagrin that the impact had released a spray of wetness that had been welling up inside her. Her face glowed red at this betrayal of her desires.

Crack!

The final blow descended, placing another ugly weal across the whiteness of Lia's flesh, and once again she allowed herself a short cry of pain. Then she felt the softness of Charlotte's hand on her flesh again, stroking over the marks that she had so recently placed there. Lia could see that

49

there were tears in the girl's eyes, and she gave her a small smile of encouragement.

"Note that her bud is still hard," said Karla, and Lia squirmed as she felt Charlotte touch her there once more. "Pull apart her lips and show us the inside."

Charlotte put the thong on the couch, then placing a hand on either side, eased Lia's sex lips apart. Lia's face grew redder still as they all saw the evidence of her arousal.

"Hmm," said Karla. "An interesting reaction. Almost unique. This really is a most unusual young lady.

"Now." She turned to Shuna. "Your turn I think."

Chapter 9

During the next few days, Lia's life developed something of a routine in the New Agers' camp. Every morning she would be woken by Delgado, who would supervise her toilet, after which she would be laid out on the table whilst he shaved her sex. This was a duty he continued to carry out, despite her protests that she could do it herself. He would always take the opportunity to excite her clitoris as he worked, enjoying watching the arousal that this awakened in his captive.

Once he had finished, she would be allowed into the priestesses' inner sanctum where she would be given breakfast in a dining room with the women, though always on a separate table.

Her daily duties were varied. Some days she would be put to work cleaning and polishing in the priestesses' living quarters. On others she would work in the kitchens or the washroom, where she would labour alongside the more junior priestesses. Occasionally she would encounter Charlotte. She longed to talk to the girl, but the young priestess was clearly uneasy in her presence. And besides, Lia was forbidden to speak unless spoken to.

Every evening her hands would be cuffed behind her back and she would be led through the village to the temple. She always hated the walk. The people would line the streets and watch her as she passed, their eyes roving over her naked form. Once inside the temple it was no better. The priestesses had placed the wooden phallus on a small shelf set into a plinth about three feet up on the temple wall. Lia would be made to stand on the plinth beside it, her hands stretched above her and fastened to a ring in the wall. Here she would stay in full view of the worshippers whilst the strange rituals of the New Agers were acted out. Throughout the service, she would stare straight ahead, trying to ignore the eyes upon her. Some of the stares of the congregation were disdainful, others wondering. Not a few of the men would eye her lovely breasts and sex with undisguised lust. This she found very disconcerting, as it kindled emotions within her own body, and she would have to fight to avoid giving evidence of her own arousal to the watchers.

During this period she had no sexual contact of any kind, being carefully supervised when she was working and manacled to the bed at night to prevent her masturbating. This was deprival indeed in one so lascivious as Lia, and at night, when left alone with her fantasies, she would imagine Charlotte's body pressed against hers and her sex would burn with a desire to be penetrated.

A week went by, then another and still the routine continued. The time spent with her beloved Thorkil seemed an age away to Lia. She wondered if he was still searching for her. And if Helda was. She shuddered to imagine what it would be like if the woman caught her again, and her dreams were still haunted by the face of the Black Cat's proprietor.

Then one day there came an abrupt change to the pattern of her life. Towards evening Lia was led as usual from her work place, and she stood in the main chamber waiting for the handcuffs to be attached for the walk to the temple. Instead she was led to the door to the courtyard, where Delgado was waiting for her.

"Follow me," he ordered, and led her to the cell block and into the bathroom.

"Two baths today," he said, and indicated the steaming tub.

Lia climbed in obediently. As usual he did not allow her to lie down in the bath, but made her stand whilst she washed, allowing him to watch every intimate detail of her toilet. Normally he was silent with her, only speaking to issue orders, but tonight he began to talk to her as she washed.

"You know what's special about tonight, don't you?"

"No Sir." He had insisted from early on that she refer to him as Sir.

"It's the New Moon."

Lia felt a strange coldness at the words. Ever since the New Moon Gathering had been first mentioned by the High One the thought of it had preyed on her mind. She knew that it marked some sort of test, but she was unsure for what. Now she heard the words again, a sense of foreboding overcame her.

"You know what it means, don't you?"

"No Sir."

"It means that you're going to be found out. And when they discover that you violated their precious Tree of Birth they're not going to be very pleased."

"I - I don't know what you mean."

"Oh yes you do. I heard about the spunk on their precious Tree of Birth."

"Spunk?"

"Don't play the innocent with me, young lady. You know what I'm talking about."

"It was some kind of message from the Spirits. That's what they said."

"Then they're even stupider than I thought. Trees don't produce spunk.

They're just wood and sap. If there was spunk on that tree, then it must have come from inside your cunt."

"But they said..."

"I know what they said. They're just a bunch of gullible idiots. If someone in bright clothes with enough jewellery told them the world was going to end tomorrow they'd believe him."

Lia considered his words. They were probably true.

"But why do they believe these things?" she asked.

"Because they want to believe. Because they want to bring some kind of meaning into their silly little lives. That's why. And that's why they're not going to be very pleased with you tonight when you give your performance."

"Performance?"

"That's right."

Lia felt an odd feeling in her belly. She looked at him nervously.

"What will I have to do?" she asked.

"Screw yourself."

For a moment Lia was not sure whether this was some kind of insulting dismissal. But it had not been said with any vehemence.

"What..."

"They're going to make you screw yourself. With that wooden cock you broke off that damned tree. And they're going to expect to see spunk. But they won't, will they?"

Lia did not reply.

"Will they?" he persisted.

"No Sir," she muttered.

"I thought not. So who'd been fucking you before your encounter with the tree?"

"A Biker. Called Rico."

"A Biker's girl eh? You must have really had the hots for him to wander about starkers like that."

"I'm not Rico's girl."

"Even better. He shares you round does he?"

Lia turned away.

Delgado grinned, enjoying her discomfort. "Still, it doesn't solve tonight's problem does it?"

"No Sir."

"Of course, there is one solution."

She looked at him. He was still grinning, his eyes roving over her young body. She blushed hotly. There could be no doubting what he meant.

"Right," he said, suddenly. "Time we shaved that pretty little mound of yours. Can't have it looking scruffy when so many people are going to get a look at it. On the table with you now."

Lia stepped out of the bath and crossed to the table, where she prostrated herself across it, opening her legs wide for him.

Delgado began to shave her, working the lather over her sex then setting to work with his razor. As he held the lips of her sex apart, his thumb found her clitoris, making her moan quietly as he gently teased it.

"Well then," he said. "What about it?"

"About what Sir?"

"You know."

Lia looked at him, her face scarlet. She knew, of course. And she also knew that she had no choice. The New Agers would expect to see spunk on the wooden dildo, as they had before, and there was only one place to get it from. She took a deep breath.

"Will you fuck me please Sir?" she asked quietly.

"I beg your pardon?" He was wiping the last of the foam from her hairless mound, his fingers gently caressing her love bud as he did so.

"Will you fuck me please?" she repeated.

"Me? Fuck you?"

"Yes please Sir."

He dropped the cloth, but his fingers continued to stroke her sex. "You'd like that, wouldn't you?"

A small whimper escaped from Lia's lips as he penetrated her with his index finger. He had never fingered her so blatantly before, normally contenting himself with a few strokes as he shaved her. Being deprived of sex for so long had made her extremely horny. The constant nakedness always seemed to arouse her, despite the fact that she hated it so much, and being shaved as she was made her doubly so.

"I said you'd like that wouldn't you?" he repeated.

"Mmm," she mumbled, her eyes closed.

Whack! He brought his hand down hard on her inner thigh, making her jump with pain and surprise."

"Yes Sir," he said.

"Y-yes Sir," she stammered.

"That's better. You're enjoying this, aren't you?"

"Yes Sir."

"Tell me."

"I'm enjoying having your fingers in me."

"In where?"

"I'm enjoying having your fingers in my cunt."

"And what do you want?"

54

"I want you to fuck me."

It was true. She did desperately want him to fuck her. His touch had brought on her arousal almost at once, and she longed to feel a hard, thick cock inside her. He swivelled his fingers in her and she rewarded him with a groan of pure lust as she thrust her hips up at him.

"Would you like to suck my cock?" he asked suddenly.

"Yes please Sir." There was an unmistakable eagerness in Lia's voice as she replied.

"On your knees."

Lia scrambled off the table, feeling a trickle of moisture escape onto her thigh as he withdrew his fingers. She dropped to her knees before him, gazing expectantly up into his face.

"Suck me," he ordered.

Lia reached for his fly, fumbling with his belt, then yanking down his zip. She reached impatiently into his pants, her hand closing around his stiff rod. When she freed it it sprang to attention, jutting out into her face.

Lia didn't hesitate for a moment. Opening her mouth she took him inside at once, sucking greedily at his great member. She wanted him badly now. More than she would have thought possible. Her pussy was soaking as she imagined his firm manhood inside her and she licked hard at his cock as her sex lips convulsed with the thought of it.

Suddenly he grabbed her hair and pulled her face away from him. She gazed up at him, the saliva dripping from her chin.

"On your hands and knees," he ordered.

Lia obeyed at once, turning her back on him and crouching down, her lovely young backside thrust up at him, her legs spread wide apart so that her cunt was open and available to him.

He reached down to her, running his fingers over her anus and sliding them into her vagina.

"Oh!" She gave a little cry of delight as she felt him probe her wetness once more. She widened her legs in an unambiguous gesture of submission.

Then he was kneeling behind her, and she felt the rock-hard tip of his cock brush against her behind. She pushed back at it, willing him to penetrate her.

"Guide me inside," he said.

Lia reached back gratefully, her fingers closing about his massive knob. She pulled on it gently, giving a little start as it touched the wet lips of her pussy. She pressed it against her, at the same time rocking her body backward towards him. For a second her flesh resisted. Then he was inside and sliding deeper and deeper into her dripping sex.

"Ahhh," she groaned, ecstatic with the sensation of his mighty organ, which was filling her completely. Lia was almost beside herself with pleasure. It didn't matter that he had not bothered to ask her consent. It didn't matter that she was being forced to kneel on the hard floor of a bathroom. It didn't matter that she was being held virtually a captive by the man. All that mattered at that moment was that she was being fucked. That her lascivious desires were being satisfied by the cock inside her.

"Mmm." She gave a low moan as he began to move, working his hips gently back and forth, sliding his member back until it was halfway out, it's shaft glistening with her juices, before ramming it home once more, almost toppling her over such was the force of his thrusts.

Delgado gripped Lia's hips in his hands as he fucked her, holding her tight whilst he thrust his cock into her. Lia tried to respond to his rhythm, pushing back as he pressed forward, willing him even deeper inside her. Her body shook with his onslaught, her dangling breasts quivering as she struggled to maintain her balance. Her head was down, her hair hanging over her face as she shook it back and forth, little cries escaping from her lips. She knew she couldn't hold back for much longer, such was the exquisite pleasure that Delgado's cock was bringing her.

She didn't have to. With a grunt Delgado shot his load into her, making her come instantly, her cries echoing round the bathroom as she milked the spunk from his balls. Wave after wave of pure pleasure washed over her as her orgasm filled her. And still he didn't stop, his hips pumping back and forth spurting the last of his seed deep into her. For a while she thought the pleasure would never end. Then he was slowing, his breathing becoming more easy as the passion ebbed away.

At last he was still, sliding his cock from her as she slumped forward onto the floor, gasping for breath.

He flung the flannel down beside her.

"Better wipe yourself clean," he said. "But make sure you leave some in there."

Ten minutes later a manacled Lia was being led from the fortress by the priestesses whilst Delgado watched from across the courtyard. Once the gate was closed he turned away, back into his own quarters.

As soon as he was safely inside he turned the key in the door, then crossed to a writing desk. He opened a drawer and extracted a glossy document which he laid it down on the desk. It was in the format of a magazine, and across the cover were emblazoned the words 'The Black Cat. Prospectus'. He opened it to a well-thumbed page. There, filling the whole of one side, was a photograph of Lia. She was totally nude, leaning back on a table, her legs spread wide apart so that her sex was open. Delgado studied the picture for a few moments, then gave a slight smile and closed the magazine, slipping it back into the drawer.

Chapter 10

There seemed to be more New Agers about than ever in the village as Lia was led down the street. All around were people, dressed in their most brightly coloured clothes and festooned with jewellery. It made the naked girl feel very conspicuous indeed, especially since her hands were trapped behind her, leaving her no means at all of covering her body.

The crowd was in festive mood, dancing and singing and taking long swigs from the jugs of liquor that many of them carried. Clearly the New Moon Gathering was a time of revelry for them, and the air was full of laughter and gaiety.

Lia made her way through the people with her escort, her head down, trying to blot from her mind the comments of the people as they passed. She had expected to be led to the temple as usual, but clearly today's plan was a different one. Just before they reached the square, the priestesses turned away down a side alley. It was a route with which Lia was not familiar, and her puzzlement deepened as she saw that it led out of the village and into the wood. They led her down a path that was lined on either side by New Agers. As they passed the people fell in behind them, so that Lia found herself leading an ever lengthening procession through the trees.

The route twisted and turned for some distance before eventually opening out into a large clearing. In the centre a bonfire had been lit, and Lia could make out the shapes of people as they danced round it. The whole area was lit by flaming torches stuck in the ground, so that despite the gathering gloom, it was bright as day in the centre of the circle.

A cheer went up as Lia appeared, and the crowd ran to greet her, laughing and pointing. There were many faces that Lia had not seen before and she guessed that more than one village was gathering for the festival. As usual the people were in awe of the priestesses and stood apart as they approached, ogling the girl they brought with them.

In the centre of the circle, close to the bonfire, was a wooden platform, and it was to this that Lia was being led. She sighed as she saw it. All the time these people seemed to want to put her on display whilst what she wanted was to hide herself away from their hungry eyes. She longed to be able to cover her breasts and sex. To hide her modesty, like other girls could. But she possessed no clothes, and with nobody willing to give her any she was condemned to display her nakedness to anyone who wanted to see it.

Sure enough, Shuna and Lisbet led her up the steps and onto the platform. She was reminded of the public whipping she had received from Miss Goram all that time back at the depot. She had been caught sucking off a truck driver in his cab whilst his companion fucked her from behind, and had been punished for her wantonness in front of the whole depot. Now it was not punishment she faced, but something equally humiliating, and it was with an air of foreboding that she stepped onto the platform.

Projecting from the floor was a thick post. with a cross-member attached at the top, at shoulder height. Shuna released Lia's hands, then she and Lisbet took a wrist each and stretched them out at either side, lashing them to the cross member so that she stood with arms outstretched, gazing down at the crowd. They left her feet free, but Shuna made her spread them wide apart before they left her there. Lia leaned back against the post, resigning herself to a long evening.

For the next hour the frolics continued, with Lia left to watch, standing like some pagan idol, staring down at the revellers below. There seemed no particular ritual to their revels. They would run round and round the fire, shrieking with laughter before collapsing at the foot of the stage, gazing up at the captive. Many shouted lewd remarks at her, but Lia remained silent.

As time went on, Lia began to become aware of a sense of tension in the air. Everybody seemed expectant, their eyes drawn to the path down which she had been brought. There was no doubt that they were waiting for something, and Lia was not at all sure she was in a hurry to find out what it was.

Suddenly a shout went up, and fingers pointed down the track. Lia squinted in the direction they were indicating, but at first could see nothing. Then, far in the distance, she discerned a light. It was almost night now, and the light appeared like a flickering beacon among the trees.

At once the people went silent and began slowly to make their way towards the edge of the clearing. The mood was eerie. The people did not speak, their actions almost trance-like as they drifted towards the source of the light. In a few minutes Lia found herself alone in the centre of the field, apart from Shuna and Lisbet, who remained at the foot of the stage.

There was a strange sound, almost like a low moaning, and Lia glanced about her, trying to locate its source. Then she realised that it was the crowd. They were chanting some kind of mantra in low voices, the sound carrying through the air like a droning hum that grew louder as she listened. The light was much closer now, and as she strained her eyes, Lia could discern figures moving through the trees towards them.

And all the time the strange chant continued to echo through the wood.

It took fully ten minutes for the meandering light to reach the clearing. Long before that Lia had lost sight of it amongst the flaming torches of the waiting crowd. She knew it was close though, as with every minute the volume of the chanting increased. The people were almost shouting when finally she saw them begin to part, allowing the new arrivals to pass between them.

The procession, when Lia eventually saw it, was a small one. In the lead was one of the priestesses bearing the flaming torch that had been visible from so far away. Behind her marched Kieran, who carried before him a cushion on which lay the wooden phallus. Lia eyed the object with consternation. It signalled that she was soon to become the centre of attention.

Behind Kieran were four more priestesses, bearing a sedan chair, and on the chair sat the High One. He wore a gold robe, with the crown on his head, and he was waving lazily to the crowd, who held up their hands to him, still yelling out their strange chant. Behind the High One marched Karla, her head held high, staring straight ahead, apparently oblivious to the throng around her.

The strange procession made its way to the centre of the clearing and finally drew to a halt in front of the stage. The High One's chair was lowered to the ground and the others flanked themselves on either side of him.

The High One raised a hand, and suddenly the people were silent. Lia shook her head in amazement. It was as if someone had flicked a switch, and her ears were left ringing with the crowd's cries. Then, slowly, the High One rose to his feet and raised his hands skywards.

"See!" he shouted. "The new moon. The Spirits are favouring us."

At this a cheer went up. Looking up with the rest, Lia was just able to discern the thin sliver of the new moon, low down on the horizon. She turned her attention back to the crowd, who were all staring in silent wonder into the sky. They remained watching it for another five minutes. Then Lia saw the High one turn to Karla and nod to her. Almost at once she began to chant in some strange language that Lia did not understand. After every sentence the crowd would reply with something equally incomprehensible.

The service went on for more than an hour. Lia looked on in bewilderment as they chanted, sang and danced about the fire. To the girl, none of it seemed to make sense. One thing was for certain though. At the centre of attention was the phallus, which had been deposited at the feet of the High One.

All of a sudden Lia became aware that the atmosphere had changed. Once again an air of expectancy seemed to prevail and she realised with a shock that all eyes were turned in her direction. She looked down to see that Karla had picked up the cushion on which rested the phallus, and was making her way up the steps of the stage where Lia was tied, with Shuna and Lisbet behind her.

When they reached the platform, Karla moved round in front of Lia, with the other two priestesses on either side. She placed the cushion on the floor at Lia's feet, then stood facing the young captive. Once again Lia was painfully aware of the long flowing robes that covered the priestesses' bodies, whilst she was forced to remain naked, her firm young breasts jutting conspicuously forward.

Karla seemed to sense Lia's thoughts, for, as the crowd watched, she stretched out a hand and cupped Lia's left breast, running her palm over the nipple and feeling it stiffen beneath her touch. She slid her fingers down Lia's smooth skin, pausing to stroke her hairless mound before delving even lower, into her most private place. Lia gave a moan as the woman's fingers found her clitoris, and she realised with surprise that her sex was already wet. The bondage and the exposure among all these people had seen to that. She was apprehensive though, afraid that Karla would delve too deep, and discover the fluid that Delgado had deposited in her earlier that evening.

"Is she ready?" called the High One from below.

In answer, Karla held up her fingers. They were shiny and wet, and glistened in the firelight. A murmur of assent rose up from the crowd.

Karla held out her fingers to Lia. For a second she hesitated. Then she protruded her tongue and licked them clean. Once again the crowd rumbled its approval.

Shuna and Lisbet began undoing the ropes that held Lia's wrists and in no time she was free, rubbing the red marks where her bonds had been. As soon as they had released her, the three priestesses retreated back down the stairs, leaving the naked girl alone on the platform.

"Now must you show us whether you are indeed blessed by the Spirits," said the High One in his shrill, whining voice. "In the Sacred Place it is said that you managed to evoke the very seed of the Tree of Birth with your lustful ways. Now we wait to see if you are indeed the one we await."

Lia stood silent as he continued to speak. She wasn't listening now. Here eyes were on the thick, curving length of wood that lay at her feet, and she felt a warmth rise in her belly as she contemplated what they were about to make her do.

"Pick up the piece of the sacred tree," called the High One.

Lia took a deep breath. Then she stooped and took hold of the thick shaft. She straightened up again, holding it in her hand.

"Now use it," said the High One. "Let the Spirit of the Tree of Birth penetrate you and take his pleasure in you. Give yourself to him."

There was complete silence now as the crowd stood, watching Lia. She glanced down at the object in her hand, and as she did so she felt the lips of her sex twitch involuntarily. She knew that the crowd had seen this, as a low murmur had gone up momentarily. She fingered the object, running her fingers over its rough surface, feeling the bulbous end. She raised it to her mouth and licked the tip, letting her saliva dribble down its length.

All at once Lia was aroused. Standing here, exposed and naked with the stiff phallus in her hand, she suddenly wanted it inside her. And she wanted the crowd to watch as well. Just what perverse trait of her character gave her these lascivious desires she did not know. Most girls of her age would be overcome with shame, hiding themselves away and refusing to perform such an outrageous act. But Lia wanted to do it. She wanted to expose herself to this crowd. And most of all she wanted to feel the thick, hard object inside her, to satisfy the desire that was already welling up in her.

She took the object from her lips. It's end was shiny now, and she rubbed it against her erect nipples, making streaks of saliva across her creamy flesh. Then she was moving it lower, down over her belly and on towards her hot, wet sex.

Lia spread her legs, bending her knees slightly and leaning back against the post. The pink of her sex was wide open, the wetness within visible to the crowd, who jostled for position below the stage, their eyes wide with anticipation.

Lia held the object so its end was pointing downwards and ran it slowly over her mound until its tip touched her clitoris. She whimpered quietly at the sensation, rubbing the rough surface back and forth over her erect love bud. Holding the knob in her right hand, her left went to her breast, feeling for the nipple, which puckered and hardened almost at once. She squeezed her teats gently between finger and thumb, all the time stimulating herself down below. Her body was on fire with lust now and all pretence of decorum had been discarded as she abandoned herself to her pleasures.

She cast her eye over the crowd below, imagining the men's cocks hardening in their pants at the sight of her, and she felt a drop of love juice escape from within her onto her thigh.

"By the Spirits, look at that."

"She's really horny."

"I wish it was me, not that phallus."

Lia heard the comments, a new thrill of pleasure running through her as she imagined the sight she was making, standing naked in the firelight and caressing her body openly.

She began to move the phallus downwards, sliding it over the open lips of her sex until the tip was rubbing against the entrance to her vagina. She turned it, so that it was pointing upwards towards its goal. Then, with a final glance out over her audience, she began to press.

She was so wet by now that her flesh offered no resistance at all, and with a cry she felt the rough wood penetrate her. She pushed again, sliding it deeper and deeper into her, revelling in the feel of the wood as it forced apart the walls of her sex and filled her completely. The phallus was all the way in now, and she let go of it, her latent exhibitionism dominating her desires as she stood, her hands behind her head, her hips thrust forward, allowing the crowd to see how intimately she was pierced by the knob. Its dark wooden shaft projected grotesquely from her cunt, and she began to gyrate her hips slightly in a lewd and silent dance.

But she couldn't keep her hands off it for long. She was too turned on. Reaching down she took hold of it once again. Slowly, her eyes fixed on the crowd, she began to move it, working it gently back and forth inside her, holding it only in thumb and forefinger as she delicately pleasured herself.

"Mmm," she moaned softly as the wood rubbed over her sensitive flesh. The sensation was incredible, and her body was aglow with lust.

She began moving it faster, working it in and out of her with a new urgency, her other hand once more caressing her breasts as she did so. She was almost shaking with desire now, trying desperately to hold herself back, to prolong the pleasure that the dildo was giving her.

"Ahh!" A sudden wave of lust ran through her, and with it all self control was lost. She took hold of the wooden shaft in her fist and began ramming it hard into her vagina, every thrust bringing a hoarse grunt from her throat as she did so.

Lia was a picture of wantonness, standing as she was, her legs wide apart and bent at the knees as she worked the thick wooden object in and out of her, grasping it in her fist, as if she were a man wanking his own cock. Her thighs were spattered with her juices, and more ran down the shaft of the phallus onto her fingers. The wetness caused a sucking sound as she worked it in and out of her, and her breasts bounced up and down with every stroke, much to the delight of the onlookers.

Lia could feel her orgasm coming close now, and her hand began to work back and forth even harder. Her teeth were gritted, her body hunched and tense, her eyes tight shut.

Then it hit her.

"Ahh! Ahh! Ahh!" She threw back her head and screamed aloud as waves of pleasure washed over her, the roughness of the wood taking her to new heights with every stroke. The orgasm was loud, blatant and public, but Lia didn't care. She was slumped back against the post, ramming the thick phallus into her vagina for all she was worth, still crying aloud. Her head shook from side to side, her long mane of dark hair waving back and forth as she lost herself in her pleasure.

Lia wanted the sensation to go on forever, but already her motions were slowing and she began to return to reality. Gasping for breath, she let her head drop forward, watching her fingers as they pumped the glistening phallus back and forth, the urgency gone now, but the pleasure still there. Gradually though her actions subsided until the only movement was the twitching of her sex lips.

For a second, Lia remained motionless, still staring down at the wooden object that projected from her sex. Then, slowly, she began to pull it out, easing it gently from her with both hands. As it emerged, the crowd could see the wetness that now coated it, so that it positively shone in the firelight.

With a gasp, Lia finally pulled it free. She held it close to her face, inspecting it, then gave a little cry of triumph and held it up to the crowd.

The end was sticky with sperm.

Chapter 11

Lia's life at the New Agers' commune changed considerably after the New Moon Ceremony. No longer was she kept in a cell, but allowed to sleep in the priestess's inner sanctum, where she was provided with a room of her own. She was still chained to the bed at night, but during the day she was free to wander about the sanctum and even in the courtyard if she wished, though she tended to avoid anywhere outside the domain of the priestesses, for fear of meeting Delgado. She felt that the incident before the Gathering had somehow given him a hold over her, and his knowing grins when they met were something she found unnerving.

During the days, therefore, she tended to keep to her room, emerging only for meals. These were now sumptuous affairs, served to her by the junior priestesses at a high table in the dining room. It seemed that no luxury was too good for her now, and she was bathed in the sweetest smelling perfumes, usually attended by a junior priestess.

Despite these luxuries, though, she was still aware of being a prisoner, and of being allowed little or no free will. Requests to be allowed out of the fortress were always greeted with a polite refusal, and even her trips to the temple ceased. All the time she continued to be forbidden clothes, despite her most desperate entreaties. Her life became a strange one, in which she felt totally alone, despite being surrounded by fellow human beings. She would often wonder about Thorkil, and whether he was still searching for her. She was desperate to get word to him of where she was, but could think of no way to do so. In order to contact him, she would have to get word to an outsider, and there was nobody.

Except Delgado.

The dilemma tormented her. She deeply mistrusted the man, and feared the power that he held over her. But he was the only one to see the antics of the New Agers for what they were. Just silly superstitions. She knew that if there was any chance at all of getting word to Thorkil it must be through Delgado. At last, after much soul-searching, she resolved to approach him.

It was not as easy as all that. Whilst she had not been forbidden contact with him, she knew that spending any length of time in his presence might arouse suspicion. To be completely safe she had to speak to him in secret. And to do that, she had to choose her moment carefully.

She took her chance in the middle of the day, when most of the priestesses were at the temple and she knew she was certain to find him in his room. Once the fortress was quiet, she slipped out of her room and made her way to the main anteroom, which she was relieved to find deserted. From there she found her way to the outer door, which led into the courtyard. She opened it a crack and peered out. There was nobody in sight.

She slipped into the open, looking about her. As she had hoped, the fortress was completely silent. Up on the turrets she could discern the figures of the duty guards, but they were facing outwards toward the village, so that she was able to cross to the cell block unnoticed. She tiptoed up to the door of Delgado's door and knocked softly.

"Who is it?"

"It's me, Sir."

"Who?"

"Lia Sir."

There was a pause, then footsteps and the sound of a bolt being slipped back. Delgado's face appeared. He eyed her up and down.

"What is it?"

"May I come inside please Sir?"

He hesitated, and for a moment she thought he was going to refuse. Then he gave a shrug and opened the door wider, beckoning for her to enter.

She stepped into the room. It was simply furnished with a low bed, a dresser and one or two chairs. The walls were decorated with girlie calendar shots and motorcycle posters. He beckoned to her to sit down on one of the hard chairs and she did so gingerly, the wood feeling cold and unyielding against her bare backside after the sumptuousness of the priestesses' furnishings. He did not sit, but remained standing, looking down at her.

"To what do I owe the pleasure of this little visit?" he asked.

"I..." Now she was here, Lia found it hard to begin. "I need your help."

"My help? But surely you're living the life of Riley now that the nutters all think you're some kind of messiah?"

"I'm a prisoner here. You know that."

"In a gilded cage."

"I want you to get a message to someone."

"A message? How?"

"There must be some way. After all you're free to come and go as you please."

"Yes, but it's miles to the nearest civilisation."

"But there must be a way," she insisted.

"I might be able to get hold of a horse for a few hours. But what if I did? How am I going to find this friend of yours?"

"You have to try. It's my only hope."

"Who is this friend of yours?"

"He's a Biker. His name is Thorkil."

Delgado gave a low whistle. "Thorkil eh? Of Depot 29?"

"You've heard of him?"

"Certainly I've heard of him. He's a pretty high powered chap. You mean you're his girl?"

Lia nodded.

"Hmm, Thorkil eh?" he mused. "It wouldn't be easy. I'd be taking a hell of a risk."

"I - I'd make it worth your while," said Lia quietly.

"How?"

"Thorkil has money."

Delgado snorted. "Money! What do I want with money? Besides how could I be sure you'd keep your word?"

"But I would."

Delgado shook his head. "No, I want something in advance."

Lia stared long and hard at him, then dropped her eyes.

"You can do anything you want with me," she said.

Delgado grinned. "Nice idea," he said. "But I had my heart set on more forbidden fruit."

"What do you mean?"

"Well," he said. "You know that gorgeous young priestess? The little brunette?"

Lia looked at him in surprise. "You mean Charlotte?"

"That's her. Gorgeous little filly. I'd love to see her out of that bikini of hers."

"You want to have sex with Charlotte?"

"That's the idea."

Lia was silent for a moment. She thought about the request. Ever since her punishment, she had held the girl in some affection. The thought of Delgado getting his hands on the young virgin appalled her. Besides, she knew it would destroy her position as a priestess, and despite Lia's scepticism, she knew that such an occurrence would destroy Charlotte's life.

"I'm sorry, I can't do that," she said. "It wouldn't be fair."

"Then there's no deal," he replied.

For a moment, Lia was devastated. Her last chance to find Thorkil seemed doomed. Then a thought struck her.

"There is one thing I can do," she said.

"Tell me."

"Well, you said just now you'd like to see Charlotte naked."

"That's right."

"What... What if I had her punished?"

"How?"

"What if I had her bare behind thrashed for you?"

A slow grin began to cross Delgado's face. "Hmm," he said. "That sounds interesting. But how would you arrange it?"

"The other day, during their fast, I saw her take a bread roll from the kitchen. That's punishable by six strokes."

"For you and for her, I understand."

Lia looked away. "Yes."

"The only trouble is that watching the two of you get thrashed will make me pretty horny."

Lia blushed. "My offer still stands," she muttered.

Delgado was silent for a moment. "All right," he said at last. "When can you do it?"

"Tomorrow morning," she replied. "Be at the door to the sanctuary at eleven. They'll all be still at prayer then, before the lunchtime service, so I can smuggle you in."

"You've got a deal," he said.

Lia rose to her feet. "I'd better go."

He walked across to the door with her. As she reached for the door handle he grabbed her hand, twisting her arm and pressing her against the wall. He reached up with his other hand and grasped her breast, squeezing it roughly.

"Now you won't let me down will you?" he growled.

"No Sir," whispered Lia.

He reached down between her legs, and she gasped as he penetrated her with two fingers.

"I'm rather looking forward to having you again," he said, twisting his fingers inside her so that she gasped once more. "Are you looking forward to it too?"

"I... Yes Sir," she said, trying desperately to control her body as it responded to his touch.

He worked his fingers back and forth a few times, enjoying the reaction he received from his wanton young companion. Then he withdrew and reached for the door handle.

"Till tomorrow then," he said.

Once he had closed the door behind her, he slipped the bolt across, and once again a grin crossed his face. He crossed to the dresser, and pulled out the Black Cat prospectus, turning as always to the page where Lia's naked charms were displayed. He thought about what she had asked of him. Silly little bitch! She was playing right into his hands. And finally giving him an opportunity to escape from this dismal place.

Delgado was not at the New Agers' commune by choice. Like Lia, he was an exile from the Bikers. From Helda in fact. Three years before he had been employed at the Black Cat. He had had a good job, been well paid, and had every opportunity of becoming a Biker himself one day. But he had been too greedy, too impatient.

He had begun filching money from the takings. Small amounts at first, but then, as he became bolder, larger sums. They had set a trap for him, and caught him red-handed. His escape had been a desperate one, diving through the window and stealing a motorcycle. Ever since he had been holed up here, where he felt safe from discovery.

But now he had the chance to return. He knew Helda was seeking Lia still, he had heard of it weeks before during a rare visit to a service area. If he could be the one to hand her over, then surely it would put him back in favour with her. Possibly even gain him a reward. He grinned once more as he stared down at Lia's photo. He would restore her to the Bikers all right. But not to Thorkil.

Chapter 12

The next morning, after breakfast, the priestesses retired to their room for private prayer, as they did every day. Lia waited until all was quiet in the sanctuary, then went to the door. Delgado was waiting by the cell block opposite, and he crossed the yard quickly.

Lia put a finger to her lips. "Don't make a sound," she whispered.

She led him into the main anteroom, and he looked about at the decorations with interest. It was the first time he had ever seen the inside of the place. He knew that to be there was a risk. But the thought of seeing the lovely young Charlotte beaten made it all worthwhile.

In one corner of the room was a large cupboard, in which brooms and cleaning equipment were kept, and it was to this that Lia led him. She opened the door. It had holes cut into it, about an inch in diameter and positioned at eye level. Their purpose was for ventilation, but they were ideal spy holes.

"In there," whispered Lia.

Suddenly he grabbed her, pulling her to him and placing his lips over hers. He held her close, his tongue probing her mouth whilst his fingers found her bare sex. Lia tried to resist him, but he was too strong for her. His fingers slid into her, and she felt herself go weak at his touch once more, her body responding in a manner that was at odds with her mind.

He kissed her long and hard, enjoying the feel of her bare flesh pressed against him, and the way her cunt pulsated round his fingers. When at last he released her she was panting slightly, and her legs felt weak.

"Just a little appetiser my dear," he said, grinning. Then he stepped into the cupboard and allowed her to shut the door.

It was barely five minutes later that the priestesses filed in through the door and took their places. Some lay on their couches, whilst others gathered together in small groups, chatting quietly together. This was a rest period for them before the service began at noon, and they generally spent it here. In the corner Lia spotted Charlotte talking to another of the novices. She seemed deeply involved in the conversation, but Lia noticed that she was darting frequent glances across at her as she always did. Lia took a deep breath. She was not looking forward to what she had to do next.

"Please, Sereneness," she said, her voice unnaturally loud, so that conversations ceased and eyes turned in her direction.

"What is it?"

"I'm sorry to have to tell you this, Sereneness, but I have to report a misdemeanour."

"A misdemeanour. Tell me?"

"During the fast the other day. I saw a priestess take a bread roll from the kitchen and eat it."

As she spoke she saw Charlotte's eyes open wide, and her face grow pale.

"Who was it?" asked Karla.

"It... It was Charlotte."

"Charlotte!" There was an air of strict authority in Karla's voice as she barked the name.

"Yes Sister?" Charlotte's voice, in contrast, was small and meek.

"Is this true Charlotte?"

"I was only a little roll," she protested. I'm sorry Sister. I was hungry. I..."

"Silence!" snapped Karla. "Did you eat during the fast or not?"

"I did, Sister."

"And you know the punishment?"

"Yes Sister."

"What is it?"

"Six strokes Sister."

"Then it seems we have two young ladies to punish." She turned to Lia. "I'm sure you haven't forgotten our custom of chastising both the miscreant and the accuser."

"No, Sereneness."

" Step out into the middle, Charlotte."

Slowly, hesitatingly, the girl crept across the room to stand beside Lia. She stopped in front of her, staring uncomprehendingly into her eyes, then turned to face Karla.

Lia felt desperately sorry for the girl. She wished that there was some other way, but she could see none. She had to get word to Thorkil, and if this was the only way, then so be it. Still her heart went out to the young priestess. She resolved to hide her own fear as best she could, in the hope that it would give the girl some encouragement.

"Fetch the belt, and two pairs of cuffs," ordered Karla. "We haven't had a proper double punishment for ages. Now Charlotte, remove your clothes."

The girl stared fearfully around the room, obviously deeply embarrassed at the suggestion. Lia knew how she felt. She was constantly aware of her own nudity, and had still found it impossible to come to terms with

71

baring her breasts and sex to complete strangers. She would have given anything for one of those brief bikinis.

Slowly the girl reached for the knot that secured her top. She fumbled with it for a few seconds, then pulled it undone. The skimpy garment fell away, leaving her naked to the waist. Charlotte's breasts were exquisite. Not too large, but rounded and full, the small brown nipples slightly oval in shape. Lia was surprised to feel an intense thrill as she contemplated sucking them.

Charlotte's hands were at her waist now. The brief skirt was also held up with a single knot and it came undone easily. For a second the girl held onto it, then she let it fall away, leaving her totally nude. Lia found herself transfixed by the bush of dark hair at the girl's crotch and by the thick pink lips that ran between her legs. Her body was tanned a rich brown except where the bikini had been, and the patches of white flesh around her breasts and sex only served to accentuate her nudity. She thought of Delgado, watching from his hiding place. From where she stood, Charlotte offered him a full-frontal view of her lovely body.

"Bring the belt," ordered Karla.

Lisbet stepped forward. In her hands she held a thick brown belt, all around the surface of which were brass rings. Lia was puzzled by it. It seemed too thick and unwieldy to be used as an instrument of punishment. She was soon to discover that the belt had a different purpose altogether.

"Stand them face to face."

Suddenly Lia felt her arms grabbed from behind and she was turned to face Charlotte. At the same time Shuna had grasped Charlotte's arms. The two naked girls stood barely six inches apart, staring into each others' faces.

The woman who had been holding Lia stepped back and Lisbet took her place. She wrapped the belt about Lia's back just above her bottom, then handed the two ends to Shuna. Before Lia knew what was happening, the girl pulled on the belt, and she found herself pressed hard against Charlotte.

The two young women were forced together in the most intimate manner. Their breasts were squashed firmly against one another, so that Lia could feel Charlotte's nipples against her own soft flesh, and the roughness of the girl's pubic hair rubbing against her bare mound. The closeness of the other woman was extremely arousing to Lia, and even before the punishment began she knew she would have difficulty disguising her passions.

Behind Charlotte, the priestess was slipping the end of the belt through

72

the buckle and pulling it tight. Lia felt the breath squeezed out of her as the belt closed about her, the hard leather biting into her flesh. Despite the pain, though, Lia was still unable to suppress the eroticism that being forced so hard against Charlotte's warm, soft young body kindled inside her. The sensation of the girl's flesh on hers was extraordinarily arousing and her senses were alive with the closeness of her fellow miscreant.

Once the belt had been cinched as tight as it would go, Lia felt Shuna reach for her hands, pulling them round behind Charlotte's back. Then a pair of cuffs were snapped together on her wrists and she realised with surprise that the short chain between them had been somehow attached to one of the brass rings on the belt, so that her hands were trapped behind Charlotte. Moments later Charlotte's wrists were fastened behind Lia in a similar manner.

Lia glanced across the room to a large mirror that hung below one of the murals. It reflected the pair of them beautifully and she guessed that that was precisely its purpose. The sight it offered her was at the same time thrilling and frightening. The two girls were as one, their slim young bodies pressed together tightly, their legs intertwined, their bare backsides presented perfectly for the punishment that was to come. They looked for all the world like two naked lovers embracing, the golden brown of Charlotte's flesh a sharp contrast to Lia's much fairer skin tone. Lia thought again of Delgado, who could see everything, and a strange thrill ran through her as she considered what a sight they must make.

Lia rested her chin on Charlotte's shoulder, her cheek pressed against her companion's. The girl smelt of lavender water, but beneath that was another, far stronger odour and Lia felt a pang of excitement as she realised that it was the smell of arousal. It excited her greatly to realise that Charlotte too was becoming turned on by their closeness. She wanted badly to kiss the girl, but feared that the two of them would receive an even worse punishment for such a misdemeanour.

She watched as Shuna and Lisbet both selected canes from the cabinet. The canes were made of bamboo, and gave a swishing sound as the two women made practice strokes through the air. Charlotte heard the sound too, and a faint whimpering escaped her lips as she anticipated what was to come. Lia hugged her close, trying to alleviate her trembling.

The two priestesses took up their positions behind the naked girls, and Lia shivered as she felt the hard, cold wood of the cane tapping against her backside.

"Begin," said Karla.

Swish! Whack!

The two canes came down with perfect synchronisation on the pair of behinds so beautifully presented. Lia felt a sting of pain as the weapon bit into her, whilst at the same time her hips were thrust forward against Charlotte's in an almost sexual gesture as the girl reacted to the stroke across her own backside.

Swish! Whack!

Once more it was impossible to distinguish between the sounds as the twin canes lashed down on their hapless victims. Charlotte gave a cry of pain, whilst Lia bit her lip, determined not to betray how much the punishment was hurting her.

Swish! Whack!

Again the two girls' bodies slammed together as the canes descended on their behinds. The stroke stung terribly, but the proximity of Charlotte's body, and the knowledge that she too was being punished was beginning to have an erotic effect on Lia. Her nipples were in direct contact with Charlotte's and she felt them pucker to hardness as a wave of passion swept through her. Then, to her surprise, she realised that Charlotte's teats were responding in a similar manner, the sensation of her hard little brown buttons against her own redoubling the sensation.

Swish! Whack!

With every jolt Lia could feel her own lascivious passion rising. She glanced at the mirror. Charlotte's behind was bright red, with four obvious stripes criss-crossing it and she knew that her own must look the same. She imagined the effect the sight must be having on Delgado, and the thought of the fucking that must inevitably follow her punishment sent a wave of lust through her. She could feel the wetness of Charlotte's tears on her cheeks, but at the same time she could feel the pressure of her pubic mound as she pressed it against her own in an unambiguous gesture of sexual arousal.

Swish! Whack!

Shuna and Lisbet were striking with a deadly accuracy, their blows perfectly in time, and the two naked girls made an extraordinary sight, their bodies writhing against one another in a dance that suggested carnality rather than pain. They were both bathed in sweat now, and their bodies glistened as they hugged tightly together.

Swish! Whack!

The stroke cut into Lia's behind and Charlotte's cry of pain confirmed that her final blow had been equally vicious. But the main sensation Lia felt now was desire for the young woman she held in her arms. Despite her smarting behind, or possibly because of it, she wanted nothing more than to posses this girl. To taste the juices that she could sense flowing in her sex. To suck those succulent nipples and to bring her to orgasm under her fingers.

"Release them."

Lia felt hands on her wrists, undoing her handcuffs. At the same time Charlotte's hands were being released from behind her own back. Then the belt was undone, and for a few seconds the two of them stood hugging one another, though no longer joined. Then Charlotte broke away and collapsed onto one of the divans, her head buried in her hands.

Lia stood where she was, resisting the temptation to rub her stinging backside, staring across at the cupboard where Delgado was still concealed.

For a moment there was silence. Then Karla spoke.

"Right Sisters. Time we were at the temple." She stooped where the prostrate Charlotte lay. "You are excused today's service," she said quietly. "When you're feeling better, perhaps you will assist the preparation of lunch."

With that, the priestesses filed out of the room, leaving Lia alone with Charlotte and the concealed Delgado.

Chapter 13

The moment the door closed, Lia knelt down beside Charlotte. She ran her fingers over the girl's backside, feeling the cruel red stripes, aware that her own behind bore similar marks.

"I'm sorry," she whispered. "Believe me I had a very good reason to do what I did. Are you all right?"

Charlotte turned her face toward Lia. She stared quizzically at her. "But why me?"

Lia kissed her on the cheek. "It had to be you, that's all." She continued to run her hands over the firm young flesh of Charlotte's bottom, trying to ease the pain of the beating.

"Does that feel any better?" she asked.

"Mmm!"

Lia leaned over the girl's body and kissed her warm behind, planting light, delicate kisses on both cheeks. Charlotte lay where she was, but Lia sensed that she liked the feel of her lips on her skin, and continued to press them against her companion's behind. Charlotte lay with her legs slightly parted, and Lia could see the pink lips of her sex, like some precious flower bud, not yet opened, but showing promise of blooming into something extraordinarily lovely. Tentatively she reached her fingers into the crack and stroked them gently along it. Charlotte gave a little start, but said nothing.

Lia looked across at the cupboard, where she knew Delgado was watching her every move. She imagined how hard his cock must be as he observed them both, and she felt a sudden thrill as she remembered her promise to give him relief once she was able to release him.

Charlotte gave a little moan, and Lia suddenly felt a dampness seep through onto her fingers. She looked down at the lovely young virgin. She had her eyes closed and her mouth slightly open. He bottom was starting to move slightly in time to the rubbing of Lia's fingers. Lia touched her shoulder.

"Roll over onto your back," she whispered.

The girl hesitated for a moment, lifting her head from the couch and gazing guiltily about her. What would she think if she knew she was being watched by a man? Then her attention was back on Charlotte again as the girl rolled over, revealing her firm young breasts and dark thatch to both Lia and the secret watcher.

The sight of her succulent globes was too tempting for Lia to resist.

At once she lowered her head over them, taking one of the large brown nipples between her lips and sucking on it. As she sucked she felt it grow hard in her mouth, and she flicked her tongue back and forth over it, enjoying its firm, rubbery texture. At the same time her hand crept down over Charlotte's belly, seeking out her furry little love nest.

"No," murmured Charlotte as Lia's fingers found her slit. But her protest turned into a little sigh of pleasure as Lia took her clitoris and rolled it between her finger and thumb, making it harden almost at once.

Lia licked and sucked at Charlotte's breast, whilst squeezing the other with her left hand. Her right hand remained buried between the open legs of the young priestess. The girl was panting slightly now, her hips moving back and forth as she responded instinctively to the touch of her companion. Suddenly Lia was overcome with a desire to taste the girl's cunt. She knew Delgado was watching her every movement, and what a sight it would make to see her lapping at the sex of another woman, but she didn't care. What mattered now was Charlotte's pleasure.

She took her lips from Charlotte's teat. It stood out hard now, glistening with saliva. She transferred her mouth temporarily to Charlotte's lips, kissing the girl hard, their tongues licking at one another whilst her hand went on teasing her companion's hard little love bud. Then she began sliding her head downwards, pausing to kiss both her breasts and her belly before staring directly into the wide wet slit of her sex.

She put out her tongue and lapped at Charlotte's hard little clitoris, eliciting a gasp from the prostrate girl. Then she had the flesh between her teeth, sucking hard at it, her hands clutching Charlotte's hips as the girl writhed beneath her. Her fingers resumed the work on Charlotte's button whilst her tongue moved lower, savouring the taste of the girl's juices, which were flowing freely now. She delved her tongue deep into Charlotte's vagina, making her cry aloud with the sensation. Charlotte was panting with excitement now, and Lia sensed that she was close to orgasm. She licked still deeper, tasting the girl's arousal, holding tightly to the girl's hips as she thrust her cunt hard into Lia's face, urging her on.

All of a sudden Charlotte's body stiffened, and Lia knew that the time had come. She stuck her tongue as far into Charlotte's gaping hole as she was able as she felt the juices flow into her mouth. Charlotte cried aloud as her orgasm overcame her, her limbs completely rigid, her legs held wide apart, her sex pressed hard against the mouth that fed on it so exquisitely. She gave a little mewing sound, her breasts vibrating slightly as she arched her body. Then she was moving again, thrusting herself lewdly against her lover's face, her breath coming in harsh grunts as she allowed her climax to flow through her. Lia clung doggedly to her, lapping at her juices as they flowed from her, intent on giving her all the pleasure she had to give.

Then, with a sigh, Charlotte relaxed, sinking back down onto the couch, her eyes closed. Lia carried on her stimulation until the girl's sex lips ceased to twitch. Then she straightened up and wiped her mouth on the back of her arm, leaving a silvery trail of saliva and love juice across her skin. She reached for Charlotte's breasts, and the girl positively purred as she stroked them.

Charlotte blinked her eyes open, as if awakening from a deep sleep. She stared at Lia for a second, then gave a little cry, folding one arm across her breasts and covering her sex with the other. She shrank back to the end of the couch.

"What is it?" asked Lia, gently.

"We... we shouldn't have done that."

"Why not?"

"Because it's wrong."

"You enjoyed it didn't you?"

"No. Well, yes but..."

"But what?" Lia moved closer to the girl, stroking her hair. "You're so beautiful," she said, "I just couldn't resist it."

"But what if someone were to find out?"

"Who could possibly find out? There's only the two of us." Actually there were three, Lia thought. But there was no way that Delgado would admit to having been in the inner sanctum.

"I must go." The girl rose to her feet and began searching for her clothes. "I must get to the kitchen before the Sisters return."

She made for the door, but Lia took her by the arm, swinging her round to face her. She took the girl in her arms, holding her close, their bare breasts pressed together. She placed her mouth over Charlotte's and kissed her, forcing her tongue into the other girl's mouth. For a second Charlotte's body was stiff with resistance. Then she relaxed and fell into Lia's arms, returning the kiss with equal enthusiasm.

The embrace seemed to go on for ever, the two girls locked together passionately, their bodies pressed hard against one another as their tongues intertwined. At last Lia pulled away, gazing into her young lover's eyes.

"OK now?"

"Yes," said the girl.

"Back to the kitchen then," said Lia, patting her behind.

The girl tripped off toward the door. Just before she went out she turned to Lia.

"I loved that," she said.

78

"I know," said Lia.

Then the girl was gone.

Lia stood, gazing at the empty doorway, her heart still beating strongly with the passion of her love making. The girl was the most beautiful thing she had ever seen, and she longed to have her for her own. She resolved that, if her escape was successful, she would return one day to make Charlotte a Biker's girl like herself.

Then Lia's thoughts returned to the present, and to unfinished business. She turned to the cupboard.

It was time to let Delgado out.

She crossed to the cupboard, and paused there for a second, her hand gripping the handle. All of a sudden a thrill passed through her as the reality of the situation hit her. She was about to be fucked, whether she liked it or not. With mild surprise she realised how much she wanted it, and there was a genuine eagerness about her as she turned the door handle.

When Delgado emerged, his pants were undone and his cock was sticking up stiff as a ramrod.

"Jeez I'm horny," he gasped. "I'm going to fuck the arse off you you sexy little slut."

"Not here..." Lia began, but he was already pushing her to her knees and forcing his swollen cock between her lips.

His urgency was infectious, and Lia suddenly realised that she too was anxious to have him inside her. She sucked hungrily at him, reflecting that this was the second person she had had in her mouth in the space of a few minutes. But what a contrast between the soft, quiet compliance of Charlotte and the rough insistence of Delgado.

"On the couch," he barked suddenly. "And get your legs open. I want to squirt my spunk into that hot cunt of yours."

Lia hurried across to the couch and prostrated herself on her back, her legs splayed wide apart. Delgado wasted no time on foreplay. He simply fell on her, thrusting his cock into her offered hole and pumping away hard. Lia bit her lip to stop herself crying aloud. She had never experienced such urgency. He simply fucked her for all he was worth, shaking her body with his powerful thrusts, his hands grabbing at her breasts.

Lia knew he wouldn't go on for long, and she was right. Suddenly a hoarse cry escaped his lips and he was coming, filling her with his hot spunk and triggering her own shuddering orgasm as he did so. She held him close, her hips pumping back and forth against his as they both savoured the release of the moment. Then they collapsed onto the couch, both limp and exhausted.

It was Delgado who moved first, pulling out roughly and stuffing his cock into his pants.

"Back to my room," he said. "I haven't finished with you yet."

And with a sharp whack on the backside, he propelled her to the door.

Chapter 14

The days leading up to the Solstice Ceremony were busy ones in the colony. Talk seemed to be of nothing else and there was a tangible air of excitement amongst the priestesses as they prepared special dishes and cleaned and sewed their ceremonial garments. Lia was almost ignored amid the frenzied preparations, a fact that she rather welcomed. She had something else to occupy her.

Since the punishment, Delgado's demands on her had been almost non stop, and she had lost count of the number of times he had pulled her into his room and fucked her on the bed, the floor, the chair, wherever took his fancy.

She acceded to his demands without complaint, for all the time she knew the day of her escape was drawing closer. Her only fear was that the priestesses would find out about their sessions, but all seemed too preoccupied with the ceremony, and scarcely a day passed without Lia finding herself bent across Delgado's bed with his cock rammed into her vagina.

Then one morning, as she knelt on the floor of his room, wiping the spunk from her chin after sucking him off, he told her of his plan.

"It'll be during the Solstice Ceremony," he said. "It's the ideal time, because you'll be out of this bloody fortress. I've got word to a couple of friends of mine, and they'll be helping."

"What's going to happen?" asked Lia.

Delgado ignored the question at first, taking a candle from a drawer and tossing it to her.

"Use that," he said, shortly.

Lia examined the object. It was thick and smooth, about nine inches long. She ran her fingers along its length, stroking it as she would an erect penis. As she did so, she felt the familiar heat kindle in her belly. She knew what she had to do with the candle. She was growing used to Delgado's tastes by now.

She stretched herself out on the floor and spread her legs wide. Reaching down, she worked two fingers into her slit, easing the lips apart. Then, her eyes fixed on her companion, she positioned the tip of the candle against the entrance to her vagina and pressed. It slid in easily, sliding over the walls of her sex and disappearing deep into her love hole, until only the very end was visible, protruding between her soft, pink nether lips.

"How does that feel?" asked Delgado.

"Mmm," she replied.

"Wank yourself," he ordered.

Lia began to gently masturbate, working the candle in and out as she lay on the floor, staring up at him.

"T-tell me about the plan," she muttered through clenched teeth.

"It's simple really." Delgado sat down in the chair opposite Lia, his cock still stiff, massaging it slowly as he watched her. "We're setting up a small diversion. A couple of sticks of dynamite."

"You're not going to hurt anyone?" For a second Lia ceased her movements a look of alarm crossing her face.

He kicked her foot.

"Get on with it."

Lia's hand began to move once more, working the candle in and out of her sex with a steady rhythm. The thick, phallic object was having its desired effect now, and he could see her backside begin to move as her arousal grew.

"Don't worry," he said. "Nobody's going to get hurt. The explosions will be some distance from the ceremony. Play with your tits."

Obediently Lia took one hand from the candle and reached for her breasts. She began to caress them, squeezing and kneading them, making the nipples stand erect, whilst all the time frigging herself with the makeshift dildo. To Delgado she made a delightful sight, stretched out on the floor of his room, her body naked and alive with passion. He began to wank, his own desires now rekindled.

"You... You still haven't... Oh! You still haven't explained..."

Delgado smiled. He liked it when she began to lose control like this. He had never known a girl so easily turned on, and such a slave to her desires. And to his.

"The explosions will be to the east of the site, about a quarter of a mile away. The idea is that when they go off, everyone will be looking in that direction, whilst we ride in from the west."

"Ride?"

"Lift your arse off the ground. Thrust your cunt forward. Offer it to me. That's right."

Lia did as she was told, planting her feet on the floor and raising her backside high off the floor, till the rest of her body was supported by her shoulders. She was working the candle in and out with a new urgency now, her breath coming in short gasps.

"Now tell me you're a slut."

"I... Oh!"

"Tell me."

"I-I'm a slut." she gasped through clenched teeth.

"And a fucking little whore."

"I'm a fucking little... Oh Jeez!" Lia's body gave a sudden lurch as a spasm of pleasure ran through her. "I'm a fucking little whore!"

Delgado grinned again. He had risen to his feet and stood, looking down at the prostrate girl as she pleasured herself, his hand still working his foreskin back and forth.

"I think I'm coming," she whimpered.

"Don't. Not yet. You'll come when I give permission."

"But I can't..." Lia's body was on fire now, and she desperately needed the release of orgasm. But she knew she must obey. She must hold herself back.

"Wh-what are you going to be... Ahh! What are you going to be riding?" She tried to turn her mind back to the subject of the rescue, in order to take her thoughts off the fiery pleasure that was threatening to consume her.

"Horses of course. You've just got to be ready for us to pick you up."

"But I've never ridden a..." Her voice trailed off into a moan of pleasure. Her hand was working harder than ever, ramming the candle eagerly into her vagina whilst her breasts bounced up and down with every stroke. "I've never ridden a horse."

"Don't worry, I'll do the riding. Tell me how you feel."

"L-like I'm being fucked."

"And you like being fucked don't you?!

"I... Yes."

"Say it."

"I like being... Oh! I like being fucked. Oh please..."

Delgado moved closer until he was standing between her legs, gazing down at the girl as she masturbated frenziedly, her head rocking from side to side, her hair flapping about wildly.

"Look at me."

She gazed up at his thick cock. The sight of him wanking it sent a new thrill through her and she almost screamed with frustration. She had to come soon or she would go mad.

"At the Solstice. Listen for the explosions," he said. "Understand?"

"Yes."

"Don't stop now," he said. He had noticed that her motions had slowed in an effort to regain control.

"But I can't... Oh! I can't stop myself." Lia's body was bathed in sweat, and her breasts shone in the light from the window as they bounced back and forth.

"Don't look toward the explosions when you hear them. Look the other way. That's where we'll be coming from. Have you got that?"

"Yes. Look the other way. Oh please let me come!"

"Come when I do," he said

She looked up at him. He was wanking hard now, and she watched anxiously as he worked his foreskin back and forth. She wanted to scream aloud such was her arousal and she watched his face pleadingly for some sign of his climax.

All of a sudden a great spurt of semen sprang from the end of his cock. It flew in a high arc and splashed hot and sticky onto Lia's up-turned face. In a second her orgasm exploded through her, her mouth wide open in a silent scream. Another spurt escaped from him, carefully aimed to land inside her mouth. She swallowed it greedily, offering her face for more as her body writhed beneath her.

He continued to shoot his thick come onto her. As his passion slowed, so it travelled less far, leaving great gobs on her breasts and belly until the last of it dribbled down onto her open cunt. And with every splash a new wave of pleasure filled her as her orgasm seemed to go on and on, the sight of his rampant organ covering her with spunk spurring her to new heights of pleasure.

When at last he had shot his load, he tucked his cock back into his trousers and stood gazing down at Lia. She was still lying prostrate on her back, her naked skin covered with white, sticky sperm that dribbled down from her face and breasts. Her vagina was still filled by the candle, although she had released it now, as she lay panting beneath him.

He grinned. "You'd better have a bath before those priestesses see you," he said.

Chapter 15

The day of the solstice dawned warm and bright, and Lia found herself caught up in the preparations for the ceremony. There were hampers to pack and things to be carried here and there. It was as if they were preparing for some gigantic party. Dozens of people came to the door of the fortress to collect bags and boxes and other strange objects that Lia guessed were part of the ceremony.

All the time there was no sign of Delgado. The priestesses tut-tutted at his absence at such a time, and there was no doubt that had he shown · his face he would have received a severe ticking off. But he didn't appear, and Lia's excitement grew as she thought of where he was and what he was planning. Who could say how soon she would be back with her beloved Thorkil?

At last, all seemed ready, and Lia was summoned to Karla.

"Time to prepare you for the ceremony," she said. "After all, you will be a very important guest."

Shuna and Lisbet led Lia away into the depths of the fortress. There were some parts of the building that were still forbidden to the young captive, and she was surprised to find herself taken through a door that had previously always remained locked. They led her down a corridor, and at the end was another door, through which she was taken. The room behind the door was small. Some kind of store room she guessed. In the centre was a table, on which lay a collar, with a long metal chain running from it about the thickness and strength of a dog's lead. The collar was about two inches thick, fastened by a pair of buckles, one above the other. Around its circumference were shiny studs, as well as a ring to which the lead was attached. Beside the collar lay a pair of clamps. These were small, with sharp metal teeth, and they too had chains attached, although these were smaller and much more delicate than that on the collar.

Lia stood patiently as the collar was attached to her neck. It fitted snugly, just tight enough not to restrict her breathing. Shuna fiddled with the adjustment for some time before finally pronouncing herself satisfied, leaving the lead dangling down in front of her.

What happened next came as a surprise to Lia.

Shuna made her stand in the centre of the room, with her hands by her sides. As soon as she was in position, the priestess reached for her breasts. Apart from her encounter with Charlotte, none of the priestesses had ever made a sexual advance to her before, and Lia gave a gasp as the woman began to fondle her there, rolling the nipples between her fingers so that they responded immediately, hardening to tight firm buds.

Once Lia's teats were fully erect, Shuna lifted the two small clamps from the table. With a shock Lia realised what they were for. She shrank back from the priestess, but all at once she felt her hands trapped behind her back and there was a click as a pair of cuffs closed about her wrists. She watched in fascination as Shuna squeezed the clamp. making the jaws open wide, then extended it towards Lia's breasts.

"Oh!" Lia gave a little cry of pain as the cruel teeth closed over her erect nipple, biting deep into the flesh so that for a second she feared they might pierce her. She gritted her teeth as the second one was fastened in the same way to her other breast. The pain was excruciating, bringing tears to her eyes. But with it came a sensuous pleasure she had never experienced before. To have such a tender and sexual part of her body clamped in this way was strangely arousing, and she felt a hot flush pass through her body even as the clamps bit into her young flesh.

Shuna stood back to admire her handiwork, cupping Lia's breasts in her palms and tugging at the chains to ensure they were secure. Lia had to bite her lip to prevent herself from crying out as she did so.

Shuna made a sign to Lisbet and she took hold of the lead that dangled between Lia's breasts. She gave a little tug, indicating that Lia was to follow her from the room. They led her back through the ante room and into the courtyard. There the priestesses were assembled, all looking smart in their skimpy uniforms, their hair adorned with flowers and their spears shining. Lia felt very embarrassed to be naked when they all looked so fine, doubly so because of the shining clamps, that she knew served to draw attention to her nipples.

In the middle of the courtyard was an object that resembled a large stretcher, about six feet long and three wide, with handles at either end. It was covered by a red cloth, and towards the middle was a small stool, raised about ten inches above the surface. Lisbet pulled Lia across to the stool and motioned her to sit down. Lia lowered her backside gingerly onto the stool. As she did so her ankles were grabbed and pulled back behind her, so that she was almost in a kneeling position, her knees and shins pressed against the cloth. A pair of shackles were attached to the base just beside her ankles, and these were locked in place. Then the manacles on her hands were secured to the stool behind her.

Once she was in position, Shuna and Lisbet each took hold of the thin chains attached to the nipple clamps. They pulled them tight, making Lia wince with pain. She tried to lean forward to ease the pressure, but was prevented by the cuffs at her wrists. The two priestesses pulled the chains as taut as they could, then fastened them to the front of the platform. The clamps stung terribly as Lia's breasts were stretched forward.

At last the Shuna and Lisbet were satisfied with their charge, and four priestesses gathered, one at each corner of the stretcher. On a command from Karla they lifted the poles onto their shoulders. Then the order was given to open the gates.

Lia felt dreadfully exposed, and she blushed scarlet as she thought of the sight she must make, with her bare breasts stretched out as they were, and her legs pulled wide apart in a deliberate effort to make the gash of her sex visible to onlookers. And onlookers there were. Dozens of them, lining the street as she was carried along. This was the first time Lia had been permitted to leave the fortress since the New Moon Gathering, and the New Agers jostled with one another for a sight of her.

The strange procession made its way through the streets of the town, Karla leading, followed by Shuna and Lisbet, then Lia's litter, with the junior priestesses bringing up the rear. All around were people, pointing and chattering. Lia stared straight ahead, unwilling to meet their glances.

They were heading toward the temple, and as they approached it another group of people appeared through its wide doorway. It was the High One, once again resplendent in his robes and being carried in his sedan chair. He too was surrounded by a large escort, and Lia's group joined behind his as they set off into the woods.

They weaved their way on through the pathways, Lia's litter swaying back and forth, so that the tension on her nipples became unbearable at times. They seemed to travel a very long way, the marchers chanting as they went, the hot sun beating down on them. The path twisted this way and that, and the bearers were occasionally obliged to lower the litter to waist height to avoid Lia being swept off by the lower branches of the trees. Glancing behind her, Lia saw that the procession stretched as far as she could see. It seemed as if the entire village had come out to see the ceremony.

All at once, Lia saw something she recognised. Standing by a pool of water was the unmistakable shape of the Tree of Birth, the strange plant beside which they had found her all those weeks before. Its branches were still adorned with fruit, the strange elongations in the trunk looking even more like stiff cocks in the bright sunlight.

In front of the tree was a large table, set out like an altar and draped with coloured cloths. They placed the High One's chair down before this, with Lia's litter alongside it. As soon as they had set him down, the High One rose, and went to the altar. He bowed low before it, then turned to the crowd and shouted something that Lia could not understand. The crowd evidently did, though, for they chorused a reply that was equally incomprehensible.

As always, the call and response session went on for some time. This seemed to be an essential part of all their rituals. Occasional phrases were just understandable, but most of what was said was just gabble to Lia. She closed her eyes, trying to forget the throbbing pain in her nipples, and the heat in her groin that the pain was engendering.

At last, the first phase of the ceremony came to an end. The silence caught Lia by surprise. She had been almost dozing, the strange rhythm of the mantras dulling her senses. She looked up, just in time to see the High One make a sign to the priestesses. At once they gathered round her, and she felt the shackles being removed from her wrists and ankles.

They took the clips from her nipples. Since the movement of the litter had ceased, they had become almost numb with the pressure, but now they stung anew as the blood coursed through them once more. Lia longed to rub them, but feared what the priestesses might do to her if she did.

Shuna and Lisbet helped her to her feet. Her legs were stiff with the confinement, and at first she was unsteady, but she managed to stay erect. The two priestesses led her to the altar.

"Stand on it," ordered Shuna quietly.

Lia turned her back and levered herself into a sitting position on the table, then climbed to her feet. Without waiting to be told she spread her legs and placed her hands behind her head.

The priestesses gathered round the altar, standing shoulder to shoulder on all four sides. Lia glanced round at them, wondering what would happen next. She was extremely tense, now, listening all the time for the explosions that would herald her release. All at once Karla barked an order and Lia realised with a shock that the priestesses had all raised their spears, and were aiming their points towards her.

Lia stood perfectly still, not daring to move an inch as she felt the cold steel of the spears against her body. They were all touching her at about waist height, forming a belt of pinpricks about her middle. As they held their weapons against her, a low chant went up from the priestesses.

For a terrible second Lia thought she was about to be run through, killed like some barbaric sacrifice on this pagan altar. Then came another order from Karla and they lowered their spears once more and stood back from the altar.

What was to happen next, Lia never found out, for at that very moment an ear shattering explosion rang out from the woods just beyond the altar. The sound took her completely by surprise, and for a second she forgot Delgado's instructions and looked across to where a great column of dust rose up above the trees. Almost simultaneously a second blast occurred, even louder than the first, and Lia remembered her instructions. She surveyed the crowd. All eyes were on the site of the explosions, and some people were running toward them.

Lia looked out to the west. At first she saw nothing, just a dense screen of trees. Then she spotted a movement, and as she watched, her rescuers broke clear of the undergrowth. There were three of them, riding hard toward her. In the front she could make out Delgado, though the other two were strangers to her. They were galloping towards her for all they were worth, and Lia felt sure that one of the New Agers must hear their approach soon. But even as she watched a third explosion rang through the woods, its echoes drowning the sound of the approaching hoofbeats.

With the crash of the third blast Lia took her chance. In a single, graceful movement, she leapt down from the altar and began running out to intercept the horsemen. As she did so she saw Karla glance in her direction. It took the priestess only a matter of seconds to understand what was happening, but seconds were all Lia needed. Already she was clear of the crowd and heading towards her rescuers.

Behind her she heard shouts, and she glanced over her shoulder to see Shuna and Lisbet running after her. Delgado was very close now, his arm outstretched, and it was to his horse she ran for all she was worth.

Even as Delgado reached down to grab her, Lia saw Shula unleash her spear. But it was too late. The weapon clattered harmlessly to the ground as she was hoisted onto Delgado's horse.

He dragged her up so that she lay face down across his mount just in front of him. Then, with one hand on her back to steady her, he was off, galloping away from the spot, leaving the New Agers to watch helplessly as he bore Lia away.

Chapter 16

Lia hung helplessly across the saddle as the horses galloped on, twisting and turning down the narrow woodland paths. It was all she could do to maintain her balance. She had never been on a horse before, and the roughness of the ride took the wind out of her. She was lying face downwards, and all she could see was a blur of green as the ground rushed by. The pounding of the horses' hooves rang in her head, but she didn't mind the discomfort. The important thing was that she was getting away, every second putting more and more distance between her and the dreaded New Agers. Closer and closer to Thorkil

They rode on for more than an hour, heading ever further into the forest and putting many miles between themselves and the New Agers. When at last they did come to a halt it was an exhausted Lia that was lowered to the ground.

The three men dismounted and gathered around her. For the first time, Lia was able to take a good look at Delgado's companions.

The first of the men was small and swarthy looking, he had a thin, drawn face and wore a black droopy moustache that seemed to give him a permanent scowl. His eyes were narrow and sly and he looked her up and down with a knowing leer. Delgado introduced him as Mex.

The second man was called Chet. In contrast to Mex, he was tall and broad shouldered, with short brown hair and a broken nose. Lia guessed that he had been a boxer in his time. He too stared at the naked girl with undisguised interest.

"Shit Delgado," he said. "You didn't tell us she was gorgeous."

"Yeah," put in Mex, "and where's her fucking clothes?"

"She hasn't got any," replied Delgado with a laugh. "You're always flashing that bare cunt of yours, aren't you darling? Even keeps it shaved to give us a better look."

Lia said nothing, her eyes cast down.

"Come on girlie," said Delgado. "Let's see you standing properly. You may not be with those nutters any more, but we still expect you to know your place."

Slowly, reluctantly, Lia took up her submissive stance, her hands behind her neck and her legs apart. For the first time she was beginning to feel a little uneasy with her rescuers. This was not quite what she had expected.

Mex and Chet both grinned as they saw how subservient she was, their eyes roving over her bare breasts.

"That's better," said Delgado. "The boys and I expect a little respect from you. Understand?"

"Yes Sir," she replied quietly.

"Jeez those tits are gorgeous," said Mex.

"Go ahead and have a feel," said Delgado. "She won't stop you."

Mex reached out and took Lia's breast in his hands. He squeezed it, his fingers caressing the already hardening nipple. Lia stared ahead of her, not wishing to catch his eye.

"We gonna have a little fun with her before you give her to Helda?" asked Chet.

"Helda?" Lia pulled away from Mex and turned to stare at Delgado.

"Wassamatter," said Delgado. "Something bothering you?"

"He said you were going to hand me over to Helda!"

"So what?"

"You're supposed to be taking me to Thorkil! You promised!"

"Thorkil, Helda, what difference does it make? You'll be back with the Bikers."

"But you can't turn me over to Helda. She's a dreadful woman. It was her I was running away from."

"Do you think I didn't know that?" said Delgado. "Take a look at this." He turned to his saddlebag and pulled out a magazine. Lia recognised it with a shock as the Black Cat's prospectus.

"Where did you get that?" she gasped

"I've had it for a long time," he replied. "I recognised you the first time I saw you."

"Show me," said Mex.

Delgado opened it to the page featuring Lia's naked body and read some of the text out to them.

"Gee," said Mex. "You sound like quite a girl."

"Listen," said Lia, pleadingly. "You mustn't send me back there. If you return me to Thorkil I'm sure he'd pay you well."

"After I've been fucking his girl at every opportunity during the last couple of weeks? I doubt it somehow."

Lia blushed. "You wouldn't have to tell him," she said.

"Yeah, but you might."

"I wouldn't. I promise. Please take me back to Thorkil."

"Nope," said Delgado. "It's got to be Helda. I owe her a favour, and you're it. Meanwhile Mex and Chet here are looking forward to having a bit of fun."

"Yeah," said Mex, groping her breasts once more. "Let's get it together baby."

For a second Lia was stunned as the extent of Delgado's trickery sank in. All this time she had given herself to him in the belief that she was to be returned to her beloved Thorkil. And now those hopes were dashed. Worse than that, she was actually going back into Helda's clutches. She stared at the three faces, Delgado grinning, Chet eyeing her and licking his lips whilst Mex's hands were all over her.

Suddenly something in Lia's brain seemed to snap.

With a heave she brought her knee up into Mex's groin, catching him squarely in the balls. He doubled over in pain, groaning loudly. Before anyone had a chance to react, Lia swung round and disposed of Chet in the same way, this time kicking out with her foot and striking him in his most sensitive area.

Delgado, realising at last what was going on, made a lunge for her, but she was too quick for him, side-stepping at the last second and tripping him up so that he fell heavily, striking his head on a rock as he did so. All three were now prostrate on the ground, two of them clutching their groins and moaning in unison whilst the third lay still, a trickle of blood running from his forehead.

Lia knew she didn't have much time. She ran to the horses, but realised when she reached them that she had no idea even how to mount, let alone to ride one. In an instant she knew what she must do. With all the force she could muster, she slapped them on their rear quarters, making them kick their hind legs in the air and gallop away in panic. Having disposed temporarily of the three men's transport, Lia was off, plunging into the woods without a backwards glance towards her erstwhile captors.

She ran with all the speed she was able, turning down one path after another in an effort to confuse them. Her heart was pounding in her chest, but she dare not slow down for a moment, leaping over fallen trees and stumps in her desperate effort to put as much distance between herself and the men as she could.

At last it all became too much, though, and she slowed her pace, first to a trot, then to a walk. She tried her best to calm her nerves. After all, even if they were following her, they were a long way behind. It seemed impossible that they could have traced the zig-zag path she had taken through the trees. No, she was certain that she was well away from them now.

She walked on, trying to keep going in the same direction, in the hope that she might soon find some kind of landmark. She came upon a wide, bubbling pool, and she bent down and drank from it gratefully, splashing some of the water onto her face and breasts to cool her. Nearby grew a bush covered with berries, and she tasted one. It was sweet and juicy, and she picked a handful and sat down beside the pool to eat them.

Evening was coming on, and she felt strangely relaxed in this peaceful spot. For the first time in weeks she was free, although still lost and totally naked. Even so it felt good to be out of her shackles for a while. She lay down on the soft grass, intending only to rest for a moment. But before long she was in a deep sleep.

Chapter 17

Lia was woken by the rays of the early morning sun as they fell on her upturned face. For a few seconds she couldn't think where she was, and sat up, blinking wearily. Then it all came back to her. The rescue, the ride through the forest, her escape from her captors. And now here she was, lost and alone in the middle of this great forest. Somehow some of her optimism of the day before had ebbed away overnight, and this morning she felt very lonely indeed.

She rose to her feet, stretching herself, making a lovely picture in the early light, her lithe young body arched so that her breasts were thrust invitingly forward. Lia seemed to sense the erotic sight she made there in the clearing, and her hand strayed to her sex, feeling for her clitoris and exciting it briefly.

She bathed in the pool. The water was cold, but she didn't care, her flesh standing up in goosebumps as she splashed it over herself.

She climbed out of the pool feeling considerably refreshed, brushing the droplets of moisture from her body. The warmth of the sun soon dried her, and she settled in the grass to eat some more berries and consider her position.

She had to keep moving, she knew that. But she also needed to know in which direction she should be travelling. In a forest as thick as this one she could wander for days without finding a way out. She had been in this position once before, and had climbed a tree to ascertain where to go. This time the land was too low, and no tree stood out far enough to make it a viable plan. Her only hope would be to follow one of the game paths, After all, the animals ought to know which way they were going.

She found the path she wanted almost at once. It was wider and straighter than the others, and led directly away from the water hole. She set off along it at a brisk pace. She kept her eye on the sun at all times, to make certain that she wasn't doubling back on herself. Progress seemed good, and she felt a new optimism as she stepped out.

Lia had been walking for almost an hour when she came across the wall. It was a brick wall, about twelve feet high, and it seemed to stretch for miles in both directions, cutting a swathe through the wood. At the top were strings of barbed wire, designed to prevent it from being climbed. It was almost as if it surrounded a prison, or some other secure institution. The path ran alongside it, so the naked girl had no choice but to follow it, gazing up at the unfriendly edifice beside her.

For a further fifteen minutes the wall was unbroken, just a monotonous red-brown sheet, stretching endlessly on. Then, Lia's eye was caught by a door in its side. It was green in colour, though the sun had long since faded it, and the paint was old and peeling. Lia stopped before it, wondering what could possibly be on the other side. On an impulse she tried the handle, and was surprised to find that it swung open when she pushed.

She hesitated, the handle still held in her hand. The wall had clearly been built to exclude interlopers and she was reluctant to be taken as an intruder. On the other hand it held a promise of security, something behind which she might be able to hide her nudity and escape those she was convinced were still hunting her. Taking a deep breath she stepped through the opening, allowing the door to slam shut behind her.

On the other side of the wall the landscape was somewhat different. There were still trees, but they were scattered more sparsely, and the grass was cut shorter. The whole impression was of a park rather than wild forest, and the openness made Lia feel exposed and nervous. The further she walked from the entrance, the more vulnerable she felt. Far from allowing her to hide her body, the landscape here made her feel even more visible than before, and she found herself covering her breasts and sex with her hands and glancing nervously about her. She walked a few yards more, then turned and stared back at the door. Perhaps this had been a bad idea.

All at once she found herself quickly retracing her steps to where she had come in. When she reached the door, she snatched at the handle, turning it quickly. But to her surprise it refused to open. She tugged at it hard, but it seemed to be locked and would not move an inch. After rattling it frantically a few more times she stopped trying, and collapsed against the wood, gazing about her in dismay. She had no choice now. She had to stay inside the wall.

There was a well-defined path leading away from the wall, and having no better plan she decided to follow it. The track led deeper into the park. Somehow leaving the wall increased her sense of insecurity. It had seemed like a sort of shelter to her as she had followed it, and in her state anything that gave her the slightest cover was welcome. Here, in this well-tended park, there was very little in the way of shelter, and the more she walked the more open the scenery became.

She began to consider where she might be. This was clearly no natural place. To produce a park like this one and keep it cultivated would take a number of people. But who would bother to keep such a wide stretch of land so well? Then it struck her. She must be on the estate of one of the Aristos.

It was an odd thing that there were still some landed gentry amid the chaos of the current landscape. Whilst the cities had degenerated into lawlessness and the highways had been taken over by the Bikers, most of the upper classes had either fled or had their properties taken over by the likes of Helda, to be turned into service depots or pleasure houses such as the Black Cat. But a few had survived, generally by making pacts with the Bikers. Some of these people still exercised a good deal of authority over the local people and the Bikers had been shrewd enough to exploit this, striking deals whereby a percentage of their profits went to the lords of the manor. They in turn assisted in keeping the peace amongst those that lived in the nearby villages. In time they became known as the Aristos, and they tended to live secluded lives in their large houses.

And this, Lia was convinced, was an Aristo's park. Nobody else could possibly afford such a large acreage. The realisation made her more nervous still. The Aristos were rich and proud. What would they make of a waif like herself trespassing on their property? She had to get out of this estate as soon as she could. But how? Certainly not through the entrance she had come in by.

Suddenly Lia's imagination began to conjure up mental pictures of what might happen if she was caught. She saw herself dragged before the lord of the manor and prostrated before him. She imagined the sort of punishments that might be meted out on her for trespassing on this private land. She saw herself strung up and whipped before the powerful owner.

But Lia's was no normal imagination, and as these images passed through her brain, an odd feeling of arousal began to fill her. She gazed down at herself, at her jutting breasts, the nipples bare and prominent, already hardened by her lascivious thoughts. She took in her bare mound, an open invitation to anyone who saw it. And suddenly a powerful heat began to well up in her groin.

Slowly, almost without thinking what she was doing, she let her right hand creep down to her sex. In the fortress she had been forbidden to masturbate, though what they would have made of her sessions with Delgado she could not think. Here there was nobody to prevent her pleasuring herself, and she toyed with her clitoris as she walked along, sending thrills of pleasure through her as her fingers circled round it.

She moved her hand still further between her legs, sliding her fingers into her vagina, feeling the heat inside her as she rubbed herself. She was still walking, but her steps had become awkward now as she thrust three fingers inside herself, frigging herself gently, her breath rasping slightly as she worked her hand back and forth.

All at once she desperately wanted an orgasm. It was something to do with her exposure, naked and helpless in a place where she might be discovered at any minute. It was almost as if she wanted to be caught. She looked about her guiltily, but could see nobody. Nearby was an old tree, its bark twisted and gnarled. Still masturbating she made her way across to it.

The tree's surface was covered in knobbly lumps of rough wood, and she ran her hand over it. In a way it reminded her of the Tree of Birth, and a spasm passed through her as she remembered being tied to that tree and whipped. Taking her hand from her cunt she embraced the tree, wrapping her arms about its thick trunk. They barely reached all the way round, but were sufficient to steady her as she spread her legs wide and pressed her hips against the bark so that one of the more prominent nodules on the surface was rubbing against the hard little nut of her clitoris.

She gasped at the sensation, twisting her shoulders so that her nipples brushed against the roughness. She began moving her hips back and forth, as if she was fucking the tree, the sensation on her love bud causing a wet trail to leak down the tree's trunk.

She released her right hand, which she had been using to hug herself against the wood, and reached behind herself, sliding her fingers down her backside and penetrating her vagina from the rear. She gave a grunt as her fingers slid inside her, thrusting herself still harder against the wood, her eyes closed, her breath coming in short gasps as wave after wave of pleasure shot through her.

"Well, well, well."

Lia froze as she heard the voice behind her, snatching her hand from inside her. She knew it was too late. It must have been obvious to whoever owned the voice that she had been sexually stimulating herself on the tree. She felt the blood run to her cheeks as she thought of what her discoverer had seen. Slowly she began to turn, but the voice barked again.

"No! Just stay exactly as you are."

It was a man's voice, and it held a note of authority that made Lia obey instinctively. She stayed still, her body pressed against the tree, her mind in turmoil. Who had found her? And what must they think of her wanton behaviour, naked and masturbating in the open air? She felt her face grow more and more crimson as she pressed it against the rough bark of the tree.

"What's going on?" a second voice said.

"Come and see what I've found."

"Jeez. who the hell is she?

"Bloody trespasser."

"What's she doing there?"

"You may well ask. When I found her she was rubbing herself up on the tree and frigging herself at the same time."

"You're joking."

"No I'm not. Just look at that wet patch on the trunk. That's from her cunt."

"Wow!"

All the time the two were talking Lia didn't move, her head pressed against the trunk, her eyes closed. She cursed herself for not having had the sense to walk past that door in the wall. Now she was in trouble again. She wondered how they treated trespassers around here, and once again her mind was filled with powerful images of punishment.

She felt something hard press against the skin of her backside.

"Put your hands on your head and turn around."

Lia obeyed, her eyes cast down as she exposed her breasts and shaven sex to the guards. There were indeed two of them, both dressed in khaki uniforms, with green berets on their heads. Each was carrying a long truncheon. It was one of these that she had felt on her behind. Both men were tall and rough looking, Their menacing appearance was enhanced by the fact that their heads were almost shaven. Their eyes were cold as they surveyed her.

"Why were you trespassing?" asked the first, sternly.

"I didn't mean to."

"How did you get in?"

"Through a door in the wall. It wasn't locked. But then, when I tried to get out, I couldn't open it."

"That'll be that damned east door," said the other guard to his companion. "The electronic lock's been playing up for a couple of weeks now. I've been meaning to fix it."

"Well you'd better get it done before Her Ladyship finds out. You know how tough she is on security."

"Shit yes. Do you reckon we'd better turn this bitch over to her?"

"Might not be a good idea. She's bound to find out how she got in. And that'll put us in the shit."

"What the hell do we do with her then?"

"Let's just thrash the little slut then throw her out again."

"We could have a bit of fun with her first," the other man grinned.

"You mean fuck her?"

"Why not? After all she wants it. She must do if she was frigging herself."

Lia had been listening to their conversation with some alarm. Her greatest fear was that they hand her over to the authorities. Being simply thrown out was the best she could hope for. But then there was the thrashing. And what was to follow...

She barely had time to ponder that though, when the two men closed in on her. One of them took a pair of handcuffs from his pocket.

"Hands behind you," he ordered.

Lia obeyed at once, and felt the familiar coldness as her wrists were clamped together. A second pair of cuffs was then fitted just above her elbows, leaving her quite unable to move her arms. She was becoming familiar with this method of bondage, and she was unable to suppress a slight thrill as she realised how vulnerable she now was.

One of the men produced a length of rope, and this was secured to her cuffs. Then the other end was thrown over one of the branches of the tree against which she had been pleasuring herself. The man pulled the rope tight, and she found her arms being dragged up in the most awkward manner, forcing her to bend her body forward. He continued to tighten the rope until she feared her arms might break. Then he secured it to a lower branch.

Lia was quite helpless, her naked body stooped forward so that her breasts dangled freely. Her head was down, making her hair drop over her face, obscuring it completely. She stared at the ground, her body trembling, partly with fear, partly with anticipation of what was to come.

"Right young lady," said a voice at her ear. "It's time you learnt your lesson. Trespassing is a pretty serious offence round here, and I'm going to leave a few marks on that pretty little backside of yours to remind you of that. And to remind you not to wander about bare-arsed in public. Do you understand?"

"Yes Sir," whispered Lia.

Thwack!

Lia's body lurched forward as the blow hit her square on the rear. It had come more suddenly than she had expected and she gave a little yelp as her flesh burned. She craned her head round to see that the man had removed the thick leather belt at his waist, and was using that to thrash her.

Thwack!

Once again the belt came down on Lia's perfectly offered behind, making a wide red mark across her flesh.

Thwack!

"What the hell's going on here?"

The voice was a woman's, though Lia could not see her face from the position she was in. The beating stopped immediately and she heard the two men's boots snap together. Clearly the new arrival was someone important.

"I said what are you doing? Who's she?"

"Trespasser, Your Ladyship."

"What have you done with her clothes?"

"She was like this when we found her Ma'am. Not a stitch."

"And," said the second man, "she was, er, working herself."

"You mean masturbating?"

"Yes. She was rubbing herself up against that tree, with her fingers inside her."

"A sex starved trespasser eh?" Lia felt a hand take hold of her hair and swivel her head round so she was looking up at the new arrival. It was a young woman, about twenty-five years old, She wore a cotton shirt, beneath which were outlined large and shapely breasts. She also had on a pair of faded blue jeans, that hugged her slim figure tightly. She had a mane of long blonde hair, that hung down her back in tresses. She stared intently at Lia with bright blue eyes.

"Is it true what he just told me?"

"Yes Ma'am."

"How did you get in?"

"I ... I came through the door."

The woman turned on the guards. "Which door?"

"The east door, Your Ladyship. The lock's faulty."

"Then why the hell hasn't it been repaired?"

"I'll see to it Ma'am."

"You make sure you do. Anyone could have come wandering through that door. Just consider yourselves lucky it was only some local village tart on the lookout for business."

Lia wanted to shout out a denial of this, but felt it prudent in the end to remain silent. She was still feeling very uncomfortable, suspended as she was, and her backside was stinging from the ministrations of the belt.

"Right," said the woman, dismissively. "Give her a good thrashing, then chuck her out, though I suspect you'll want to screw her first. I'm going into the house now to prepare for this evening's..."

She broke off and turned back to Lia again.

"Wait a minute though," she murmured.

With a shock Lia felt the woman's hand cup her breast, feeling it's firmness. Then her other hand slipped through Lia's legs from behind, and Lia gave a sharp intake of breath as she felt herself probed.

"She's certainly sensitive," said the woman. "How many strokes did you give her?"

"Just three Ma'am."

"Three eh? It seems to have turned her on. Just look at the way she's responding to my finger."

She twisted her finger in Lia's vagina, and once more was rewarded by a gasp from the tethered girl.

"I think I've changed my mind," said the woman suddenly. "Bring her to the house. She'll be an invaluable addition to tonight's little party. Hand her over to the housekeeper, and tell her to get her cleaned up, then deliver her to my room, just as she is. Get on with it now."

And with that she turned and strode away.

Chapter 18

The two men marched Lia along in the direction the woman had gone, holding the rope that was still attached to her manacles and shoving her forward in front of them. Lia progressed with her head down, trying to ignore the lewd remarks the men made as they eyed her lovely behind. The pair were obviously disgruntled at having missed their fun, and they grumbled on about someone they called the Countess. Lia surmised this to be the young woman who had stopped her punishment.

The park seemed vast to Lia as she trudged along, and it was some time before the house came in sight. It was very large indeed, with turrets at the corners and mock battlements running along the top of the walls. It was surrounded by a wide green lawn across which the men took her. The grass felt soft under her feet after the hard path she had been following.

They led her up to a rear entrance to the building. Even here the door was large and imposing, with a short flight of stone steps leading up to it. Lia climbed these and was made to halt on the doorstep whilst one of the men tugged on a huge brass bell pull.

The woman who came to the door looked none too friendly. She was in her fifties, short and overweight, with a menacing gleam in her eye. When she saw Lia, her jaw dropped.

"Who on earth is this?" she asked in astonishment.

"Just a trespasser," said one of the men.

"What, walking about like that? She should be ashamed. Why have you brought her here? She's no concern of mine."

"The Countess said to."

"Her Ladyship?"

"That's right. Said you were to give her a bath, then take her to Her Ladyship's room, just as she is."

"What, with no clothes on?"

"That's what she said."

The woman shook her head.

"I don't know," she said. "The goings on in this house. It never would have happened in her grandfather's day. At least he was discreet."

"Look," said the man. "Are you going to take her or not? Only we've got work to do."

"I suppose if Her Ladyship said so I'll have to. Where are the keys to those handcuffs?"

"Here," said the man, handing them over. "But be careful. It's my guess she'll try to escape."

"Not from me she won't," said the woman sternly. She turned to Lia. "Now come inside at once. Don't stand around on the doorstep where everyone can see you."

She took the rope and dragged Lia through the door, slamming it shut in the faces of the two guards. Then she led Lia down a short corridor and into a kitchen. Here half a dozen maids were sitting at a table drinking tea. When they saw Lia they stared in astonishment, then burst into peals of laughter.

"What on earth..."

"Who's she?"

"What's going on?"

"Never you mind," barked the housekeeper. "Ellie, take her up to the bathroom. You'll have to manacle her to the pipes whilst she's washing. Apparently she's liable to try and run away."

"What, like that? She wouldn't dare. Why the guards would..."

"That's enough," said the housekeeper firmly. "Just do as you're told. Flora, you'd better go too. And hurry up now."

Still giggling, two of the girls rose to their feet. They were both identically dressed in black maids uniforms with small white hats tied to their heads and white aprons about their waists. Lia estimated they were no more than seventeen years old.

The one called Ellie took the rope from the housekeeper. As she did she saw the stripes across Lia's behind.

"Look," she said, pointing. "Someone's been thrashing her behind."

"Best thing for her in the circumstances," said the housekeeper. "When she's had her bath I want you to bring her straight back to me. Understand?"

"Yes Miss Strong," chorused the girls, and they dragged Lia with them out of the kitchen.

Lia was taken down a series of narrow hallways and up a flight of stairs into what she took to be the servants' quarters. They led her into an old fashioned bathroom, full of brass pipes and fittings, with a bare wooden floor. Once she was inside, they shut the door behind her and slid a bolt across. Flora began filling the large bath, whilst Ellie saw to Lia's manacles, releasing her right wrist momentarily before clamping the cuff round a sturdy pipe that ran beside the bath. Only then did she release her elbows and take off her collar, which they discarded in a bin.

Once the bath was full, Lia was ordered in. The water was hot, and smelled of lavender, and Lia lay back. It felt wonderful to be relaxing at last after her long ordeal since escaping the New Agers, and she stretched her body luxuriously, feeling her aches and pains melt away.. She was not allowed to rest for long, however. A bar of soap and a bottle of shampoo were handed to her, and the two maids stood back to watch as she began to wash herself.

As she was completing her toilet, Lia noticed that the two youngsters were whispering and giggling again. After much discussion, Flora nudged Ellie to her feet, and the girl went to a cabinet on the wall. She extracted something from it and handed it to Lia. It was a can of shaving foam and a razor.

Her face burning, Lia raised herself until she was sitting on the edge of the bath. She spread the foam over her pubic mound and sex lips, and began gingerly shaving off the layer of stubble that had grown there. All the time the two maids sat watching, occasionally lapsing back into fits of giggles.

At last Lia was done. She rinsed herself carefully, then placed the shaving implements on one side, looking up expectantly at her keepers. The two maids went through the process of manacling her again, first the elbows, then the wrists. Only then did they unbolt the door. They need not have been so careful. Lia had no incentive to escape just at the moment, especially with the two guards still patrolling the grounds.

They sat her on a stool and towelled her hair. Flora produced a hair dryer and began drying it off, running a brush through Lia's flowing tresses as she did so. Unexpectedly, Lia found herself rather enjoying their attentions, the brush having a soothing effect as it ran through her locks.

Once they were satisfied that that the job was complete, they pulled her to her feet and led her out of the bathroom and back down to the kitchen. There the housekeeper inspected her minutely, before at last pronouncing her presentable and fit to be taken to the Countess's room.

"Though how I can use the word presentable when she's completely nude like that I don't know," she complained. "Well, I suppose you'd better take her to the Countess. Hurry now!"

At once Lia was on the move again, this time to a quite different part of the house. This was clearly where the owner of the house lived. The hallways were thickly carpeted and lined with oak panels. Large oil paintings hung from the walls, and the furnishings were all antique. Lia padded along, her feet sinking into the plush floor coverings.

They walked all the way through the house. The building seemed deserted apart from a few domestic servants, who stared at Lia as she passed, their jaws open. They reached a wide reception room, and she was guided up a sweeping staircase to an upper floor. Here there were more hallways down which to trudge. At last they reached a door, where Ellie knocked timidly.

"Come." Lia recognised the voice as that of the lady she had encountered in the garden, and who she now knew to be the Countess.

The maid opened the door. "Please Your Ladyship..." she began.

"Yes, all right Ellie. I see you have our new house guest with you. Leave the keys to her cuffs with me and be off with you."

"Yes Ma'am."

Ellie ushered Lia into the room, then placed the keys on a table and she and Flora retreated, closing the door behind them. Lia stood, glancing round her uneasily. Like the rest of the house the room was sumptuously furnished, with a large four-poster bed at one end and a suite of comfortable chairs set beside a window which overlooked the green lawns outside. The Countess was sitting in one of these chairs.

"Come over here," she instructed Lia.

Obediently the tethered girl crossed the room and stopped in front of her.

"Do you always stand with your legs apart like that?"

Lia blushed. It was pure force of habit that made her stand as she did. She had been well trained by both the Bikers and the New Agers to keep her cunt open and in view at all times. She made to close her legs.

"No!" said the woman sharply. "Stay as you are. I rather like you like that."

She rose to her feet and began to walk round Lia, who remained rooted to the spot.

"Such a pretty little thing you are," she murmured. "What gorgeous breasts. You're quite right to leave them bare like that. And that arse. Those red stripes across it look exquisite. Tell me, where are your clothes?"

"I haven't any, Your Ladyship."

"What?"

"I lost them."

"When?"

"I can't remember. It was months ago."

"Months? Where have you been since then?"

"I was captured. By the Bikers. Then the New Agers got me."

"I think you'd better tell me the whole story."

So Lia recounted the full tale of her adventures, starting from the incident with the warden at her hostel, and going on to tell how she had run away, lost her clothes whilst swimming and been picked up by the Bikers. She told the story in full, leaving out no details under the woman's close questioning. She glowed red as she described the incident in the diner, where she had brought herself off with a bottle in front of the truck drivers. She described the sale of her indenture at auction, and her life at the Black Cat. She went on to tell of her short-lived rescue, and her times with the New Agers. Finally she brought the story up to date, with her second rescue and subsequent escape. When she had finished the woman sat back and gave a low whistle.

"Well! You have had an interesting time! And this Biker, the one you're in love with. What was his name again?"

"Thorkil, Your Ladyship. He's from Depot twenty-nine."

"Thorkil eh? Yes I know of him."

Lia's eyes opened wide. "You do?"

"It's not so surprising. He's quite well known among the Bikers. He's not one of our local men, though I know where to find him."

Lia stared in disbelief. For the first time since Helda's Bikers had attacked them in the forest, there was news of Thorkil. Her heart beat fast. She wanted to ask more, but her training taught her to remain silent unless addressed. What she heard next though, made her want to shout aloud with joy.

"I'll put in a call to his depot in the morning. See if he wants to come and get you."

"Thank you Mistress." In her excitement and happiness Lia reverted to her old form of address.

"Mistress?"

"I'm sorry Your Ladyship. It's what I used to call my superiors."

The woman smiled. "Don't worry, I rather like it. Perhaps we should find you some clothes before your Thorkil arrives."

Lia blushed. "Thorkil keeps me naked," she mumbled.

"And I can see why," laughed the woman. "Now, young lady, I didn't ask you to stay here just to find your kinky Biker friend. I've got plans for you tonight."

"Your Ladyship?"

"I've got some friends coming for a little party this evening. Just some other girls. And you're going to help me entertain them. We need a man to liven things up."

"A man, Your Ladyship?"

The woman moved closer, so that Lia's breasts were almost brushing against the fabric of her shirt.

"That's what I said."

"But..."

The woman held up a hand. "Listen, little Biker's girl," she said. "Around here I'm known as the Countess, but to you, from here on I'm your Mistress, and if you want to see your beloved Thorkil tomorrow, you'll have to obey me utterly. All right?"

"Yes Mistress."

"Good. Behave yourself, and I think you're going to find it as much fun as I am."

The Countess rang a bell, and shortly afterwards Ellie and Flora presented themselves at the door.

"Come in here," she ordered, leading them into a small dressing room just off the main bedroom.

The three disappeared inside and the sound of low voices drifted out, punctuated by drawers slamming and occasional squeals of laughter. When the three finally emerged, Flora was carrying a black bag, and her face was bright red.

"Take her away with you," ordered the woman. "And prepare her for tonight."

Once again Lia was led through the house by the two young maids. But this time they did not take her back to the kitchen. Instead they led her to a small room on the ground floor. It appeared to be some sort of study, with a large leather topped desk in the centre.

Once inside they locked the door, then Flora set about undoing Lia's cuffs. It felt good to have her arms free again, and Lia stretched them up above her head.

Ellie dipped her hand into the mysterious bag, and produced two thick leather wrist straps. She ordered Lia to hold out her hands and strapped them tightly onto each wrist. Lia noted that they had rings attached to each, and she guessed at once that their purpose was for bondage. She felt a surge of excitement at this realisation. Why was it that this sort of treatment always brought out the more wanton side of her nature?

More straps were applied to her ankles and a collar, not unlike the one used by the New Agers, was placed about her neck, though there was no lead attached. There was a mirror on the wall, and Lia eyed herself in it. Somehow the dark brown of the straps seemed to enhance her nudity. They reminded her of the straps worn by slave girls in a film she had once seen, only those slaves had been allowed short ragged dresses. As a naked slave, she seemed far more erotic, and she felt the stirrings of arousal as she contemplated the evening ahead.

They sat her down on a chair and Flora began to work on her hair once more, though this time the styling was to be quite different. She began pulling the long tresses back behind Lia's head and plaiting them together into a thick rope. Once this was complete she curled it round on top of her head, pinning it there with a series of hair clips. Then she produced a cap and put it on her, so that the plait was completely hidden beneath it. The whole affair was very puzzling to Lia, and staring into the mirror, she barely recognised her reflection.

"On your feet," ordered Ellie suddenly. Lia jumped up at once.

"Over there. Sit down on the desk and lie back."

It seemed strange to be taking orders from one so young, and whose position in the household was obviously so servile, but Lia was accustomed to obedience and did not question the command. She crossed to the desk and sat down on it, the leather feeling cold and hard against her bare behind. She leant backwards until she was prone, her legs still dangling. Then, without waiting to be told, she spread her thighs apart.

"Good," said the maid.

She reached into the bag again and pulled something out. Lia stared at it in surprise. It was like nothing she had ever seen before.

The object was a sort of double dildo. Two enormous rubber cocks, perfectly shaped and joined at the base so that they formed a vee shape. From the base of one of them dangled a pair of balls, looking extremely realistic. The two maids began giggling once more as they examined it.

"How does it work?" asked Flora.

"The two ends are connected," replied Ellie. "Look, when I squeeze the end of one, the other one's end swells up."

Lia watched, her stomach full of butterflies, as Ellie demonstrated the thing to her friend.

"Just feel the shaft," went on Ellie. "It's got like a sheath on it that moves backwards and forwards, and when it does so the other one does the same."

"What's that little lever for at the base?" asked Flora.

"Whenever you move the sheath up and down or squeeze it, the lever moves. It even does it when you squeeze the balls. Watch."

Ellie demonstrated, and Lia saw the little projection that curved back from the base of one of the dildos did indeed move back and forth in response to the manipulation of the other one. The whole thing was the most elaborate sex toy she had ever seen, and she felt a growing warmth between her thighs as she realise that it was intended for her.

There were a series of thin pink straps hanging from the object, and Ellie spent a few seconds undoing them. Then she approached Lia with it

"Hold her lips apart for me whilst I put this in," she said to Flora. Her tone was so matter-of-fact that she might have been talking about filling a sack, but Lia felt a thrill as she heard the words.

Flora approached Lia. She could see the maid was nervous. She guessed the girl had never touched another woman's sex before, and her hand shook slightly as she placed it on Lia's leg. She ran her hands up Lia's thighs, pausing as she reached her crotch.

"Go on," said Ellie. "It won't bite."

Slowly Flora moved her hands higher, sliding her fingers into Lia's sex, stretching the lips apart.

"Look, she's wet inside," she said to her companion in surprise. "She must be turned on."

"Takes all kinds, I suppose," sniffed Ellie. "At least it'll make it easier to slip this thing into her."

It was all Lia could do to keep herself still as she felt the end of the dildo press against her already gaping sex. At first the inexperienced girl had trouble penetrating her, despite Lia's own efforts to spread her thighs as wide as she was able.

"Give it a twist," suggested Flora.

Ellie tried again, turning the knob back and forth as she pressed, and at last it slipped into Lia's vagina, making her gasp as it stretched her love hole.

Once Lia had been penetrated, the wetness of her sex meant that Ellie was able to force the great cock into her more easily. She pushed hard on it, still twisting it as she did so, ramming it deeper and deeper inside until it was completely buried within the prostrate girl. In this position the moving lever was resting against Lia's clitoris, and every time Ellie touched the dildo the lever would oscillate, rubbing against her sensitive love bud and making her groan aloud.

Ellie took the straps and began to fasten them. One was cinched tight round Lia's waist, with two more straps running down diagonally over her bottom cheeks and between her legs to attach at the base of the balls. Two more ran down in a vee in the front, fitting to small rings on either side of the dildo, leaving her bare pubis exposed.

Ellie fussed with the straps, making them as tight as she was able, then stood back.

"There," she said. "I think that'll do. Take a look at yourself in the mirror."

Lia found it slightly awkward to walk, her legs forced apart by the thick rubber cock that filled her so completely. She waddled across to the mirror and stared at her reflection. What she saw was extraordinary.

It was as if she really did have a cock. A stiff, erect rod that rose from her groin like a flagpole, the balls dangling between her legs indistinguishable from the real thing. Lia stared at herself in astonishment. So this was what the Countess had meant about needing a man at the party. It explained the way they had made her hair look short, as well. The only thing they couldn't hide were her luscious firm breasts, looking totally incongruous above the erect cock. She had been turned into a kind of hermaphrodite, and she felt a sudden thrill of lust as she realised what an erotic sight she made.

Even the maids had ceased their giggling as they took her in, standing wide-eyed. For a full minute nothing was said as they circled the naked girl, taking in every inch of her.

The sound of the door handle turning brought them back to their senses, and they swung round guiltily as the mistress of the house entered.

"Oh yes," she said, ignoring the maids, her eyes fastened on Lia. "That's perfect. You look absolutely gorgeous."

Lia glowed red, and did not reply.

"Come here," ordered the Countess.

"Yes Mistress."

Once more Lia's gait was less than elegant as she crossed to where the woman stood. She stopped in front of her, her face reddening even more as she contemplated the massive cock that separated them.

The Countess reached down and gave the end of the dildo a squeeze, causing the end deep in Lia's vagina to swell and the lever to rub against her clitoris. Lia gasped at the sensation, her sex giving an involuntary spasm that caused the end in the Countess's hand to swell. The reaction was not lost on the woman, who smiled.

"I see it's giving you some pleasure too," she said.

Lia dropped her eyes.

"Right." The woman turned to her maids. "Take her into the party room and get her ready. My guests will be here soon."

Chapter 19

The voices of the Countess's guests increased Lia's nervousness as she waited for the party to begin. They seemed so close, yet she was unable to see the speakers. She tugged at her bonds, but they held her fast. She had no choice but to wait for the guests to be introduced.

The party room was smaller than she had expected, though in this house even the small rooms were large enough to host a banquet. Lia was standing against the wall, her wrists chained to rings on either side of her, stretching her arms wide apart and high above her head. Her ankles too were trapped, secured to more chains attached to the floor, so that her body was held in a great X. She made an extraordinary sight to anyone who encountered her, the stiff pink penis jutting from her groin like a permanent erection.

The maids had secured her behind a pair of curtains that hid her from the rest of the room. Then they had left her there to await the party. She had heard the sound of The Countess's guests as they arrived one by one. Now they chatted and laughed together on the other side of the curtain, their conversation punctuated by the occasional pop of a champagne cork. The party had been going for nearly an hour, and still she remained chained where she was, waiting with apprehension for the curtains to be opened, and for her to be exposed in all her naked glory, penis and all.

She estimated there to be four guests, all women of a similar age to their hostess. They conversed like old friends, and even at this early stage she could tell that the drink was beginning to have an effect on them, the laughter growing louder as the evening went on.

Suddenly she heard the words she had been anticipating with a mixture of dread and suppressed excitement all evening.

"Hey, Amy, what's behind the curtains?"

Lia froze, her heart beating fast, wondering if the others would take up the theme. They did.

"Yeah," came another voice. "They weren't here last time we came. What is it Amy?"

"It's a little secret," replied a voice that Lia recognised as her new mistress for the evening.

"A secret! I love secrets. What is it, some new stud you've found to fuck the arses off us?"

"It's better than that. This stud isn't going to lose his erection after a few screws."

"What do you mean?"

"Yeah, go on Amy, show us."

Lia's apprehension grew as she listened to the conversation. The women were curious now, and she knew that in a few moments she would be exposed to them. She looked down at herself, at her firm breasts, the nipples made hard by the thrill of her bondage, and at the heavy dildo that filled her vagina, that forced her legs apart even without the chains that held her spread wide for all to see. She felt a deep sense of shame at her situation, but at the same time enormously aroused, and the cock twitched like a man's as her vaginal muscles contracted around it.

The room was quiet now, and the ring of the Countess's shoes echoed from the walls as she made her way across to where Lia was hanging. The curtains shook, and Lia knew that her mistress was holding them. There was a long pause, during which she held her breath, then with a swish the curtains were pulled aside.

"Wow!"

"My god, Amy, that's incredible."

"Who is she? It is a she isn't it?"

"Look at that cock!"

Lia stared out at the four women, blushing furiously as she was exposed to them. They were all in their mid twenties, beautiful to look at and expensively dressed. What must they think of her, naked and chained and filled by this grotesque sex toy?

At once the guests gathered round her, chatting excitedly as The Countess explained where Lia had come from.

"A Biker's girl?" said one. "Lucky Biker."

"Just look at those gorgeous tits," said another.

"And the way you've tied her. It's so sexy."

"But what a cock! Can I touch it?"

"Of course you can," their hostess replied. "For tonight her orders are to do whatever you wish. And she's very obedient, as I think you'll find."

One of the women reached for Lia's breasts, running her hands over them and feeling the hardness of her nipples, which were fully erect and protruded invitingly.

Another reached for her cock.

"Ahh!" Lia let out a cry as the woman squeezed the bulbous tip and the clitoris stimulator rubbed against her love bud. The woman turned to her hostess, her eyes wide.

"She's acting as if it's really her cock."

"That's right. Every time you touch her there she gets stimulated

112

inside. And she's a randy little thing. I've never seen a girl so easily turned on. She used to work at the Black Cat, you know."

"Not the one called Lia?" asked one of the women, licking her lips. "The one who was always kept naked?

"That's the one," replied the Countess. "And she's ours for tonight."

"Wow! I was told she took on a whole roomful of guys one night, and was ready for more in the morning."

"Yeah, I heard that too,"

Lia stared at the women, astonished that they could know her name. It was obvious that the fame of the Black Cat spread wider than she had imagined. The next words she heard surprised her even more.

"Oh shit, Amy. I've just got to have her. Where's the key to these chains?"

The woman who spoke was blonde, with sparkling green eyes. She wore a tight mini dress that hugged her figure like a second skin. She was braless, and her nipples were clearly outlined against the clinging material. Lia felt a spasm of excitement as she heard the words. She looked across expectantly at her mistress.

"Have her now if you like, Barbara."

The Countess tossed a bunch of keys across the room.

Lia's body was alive with excitement as Barbara undid her bonds. She could sense that the woman was equally aroused, barely able to insert the keys in the locks such was the trembling of her hands. It took an age, but at last Lia was freed, and Barbara dragged her out onto the dance floor.

"Put on some music," she shouted. "I wanna dance with my new fella."

Somebody touched a button, and all at once the room was filled with a throbbing beat. Barbara began to dance, her body shaking to the rhythm of the music. For a few seconds Lia watched her in fascination, unable to take her eyes off her lithe body.

"Dance, girl," ordered the Countess, shouting above the music. "You're here to entertain my guests remember."

Obediently, Lia too began to move, placing her hands behind her head and gyrating her hips, so that the phallus that projected from her groin rotated provocatively. To Lia the dance was totally instinctive, like some primitive tribal ritual. She closed her eyes, allowing the beat to carry her as she swung her hips back and forth. The other guests looked on with fascination at the naked girl, watching the muscles in her backside contract as she thrust her pelvis forward at her partner.

Suddenly Barbara's emotions seemed to overcome her. She moved closer, pulling Lia towards her. Lia melted into the arms of her partner like a lover, their breasts pressed together, the great pink cock trapped between them.

Barbara placed her lips over Lia's and Lia opened her mouth eagerly, allowing the woman's tongue to enter it. She held her close, grinding her hips against her, making small mewing sounds as her sex was stimulated by the dildo.

Barbara stood back for a moment, and Lia gave a small cry of disappointment.

"It really turns you on when I touch your cock, doesn't it?" asked the woman in surprise.

"Yes Ma'am."

"Is that right, Amy?" Barbara asked.

"I told you. That thing is designed to give her as much pleasure as if it was a real cock," replied the Countess.

"Wow!"

At once Barbara reached down to Lia's crotch and began playing with the balls that dangled between the girl's legs. Each squeeze brought a wave of pleasure to Lia as the lever rubbed against her hard little love bud.

"Jeez she's turning me on," gasped Barbara. "I gotta have her on my own."

"Go ahead," said the Countess. "She's all yours."

Barbara grabbed Lia's hand. "Come on," she said. "It's time to give Barbara what she wants."

So saying, she dragged Lia off behind her into the room next door, the office where Lia had been prepared for the party.

As soon as the door was closed, Barbara moved in on Lia.

"Unzip me quick," she ordered. "I just gotta have my tits sucked. Come on, get a move on."

Lia slipped down the zip that held the woman's dress closed. Once it was undone, the garment dropped to the floor, to be kicked aside by its owner. Lia stared at her companion. Barbara's breasts were large and shapely with big brown aureoles surrounding her nipples. All she wore now was a pair of black briefs and a matching black suspender belt that supported her stockings.

"Suck my tits," she ordered quietly.

Lia leant forward and placed her lips about Barbara's nipples. She began to suck gently As she did so the nipple swelled to hardness in her mouth, the teat thick and rubbery. Lia slurped greedily at it, at the same time toying with the woman's other nipple with her fingers. Barbara's breathing became heavy as the young girl stimulated her, and she pressed her chest forward against Lia's face.

"That's it," she whispered. "Suck me you gorgeous, randy little bitch."

Lia responded by sucking even harder, eliciting a groan from Barbara, whose hand reached down almost automatically for the dildo. She squeezed its tip, making Lia squirm with the exquisite sensation of it.

Lia transferred her lips to Barbara's other breast, nibbling gently at the protruding tip whilst her tongue worked back and forth over it. The taste of this woman's flesh was extraordinary and she found herself tingling with the prospect of what was to come.

"My knickers," murmured Barbara suddenly. "Pull them off. Do it now."

Lia dropped to her knees at once. She grasped the waistband of Barbara's panties on either side and dragged them all the way down in a single movement, lifting the woman's feet and pulling the flimsy garment off. She stared at her companion's crotch. Her pubis was covered in short, dark hairs, trimmed to a perfect triangle. Beneath, her sex lips were pink and thick. Hesitantly Lia reached up for them, prising them gently apart and feeling for Barbara's love bud. She found it almost at once, bringing a low moan from her companion as she felt the hard little nodule.

"Oh fuck!" moaned Barbara. "Lick me, for goodness sake."

Lia moved her face closer, her nostrils filling with the woman's arousal. She protruded her tongue, sliding it between the pink lips, and Barbara gave a sharp intake of breath as Lia found that sensitive spot only just vacated by her fingers.

She protruded her tongue still further, sliding it down between those soft lips and seeking out the entrance to Barbara's vagina. She slid her tongue inside, darting it back and forth. Barbara grabbed hold of Lia's hair, forcing her head further down, pressing her face against her sex as she writhed in the ecstasy of the girl's kiss.

"Over to the desk," she whispered suddenly. "Come on."

She dragged Lia across the room, to the very desk where just a short time earlier she had had the dildo fitted. Barbara placed her backside on the edge, then lay back, her open sex framed between her black suspenders. She reached out and grabbed the end of Lia's cock, making her gasp with pleasure once more.

"Stick it in me," ordered Barbara. "I want to be fucked properly. Do it standing up so I can watch those delicious tits of yours."

Lia had never experienced the male's dominant position before, but she knew what to do. Taking the tip of the rubber tool in her own hand she guided it towards Barbara's vagina. Barbara was thoroughly turned on now, and the end of the phallus shone with moisture as it brushed over the woman's sex. Lia rubbed it back and forth a number of times, teasing Barbara's clitoris so that she almost cried aloud with the sensation.

"Fuck me little boy-girl," she said, through gritted teeth. "Stick that fucking cock in me and give me a good rogering."

This time there was no hesitation on Lia's part. She positioned the cock at the mouth of Barbara's vagina and shoved her hips forward. The two girls cried out in chorus as the object slipped into Barbara's sex. Every sensation felt by Barbara was transmitted with equal intensity to Lia. It was as if the dildo was being inserted anew, and she thrust it in with renewed effort, revelling in the sensation it gave her.

Lia buried the phallus all the way into Barbara, so that the balls were brushing her companion's backside. Then she began to fuck her, her hips pumping back and forth as the glorious sensation filled her too. Her clitoris was so stimulated she felt it would burst as the secret lever rubbed back and forth, bringing her to new heights with every stroke.

All the time she was being fucked, Barbara kept her eyes on Lia, watching her lovely young breasts bounce up and down with the rhythm of her thrusts. Lia's mouth was wide open, gasping for breath, a small trickle of sweat running down between her breasts as she rammed the dildo home. Lia glanced across at the mirror on the wall. The sight was extraordinary, the two beautiful women, both naked apart from Barbara's suspenders and stockings, joined together by their cunts, the shaft of the dildo gleaming with wetness as it moved in and out of Barbara's gaping hole.

Suddenly Barbara lifted her backside clear of the desk, thrusting it up at Lia, and she knew the woman's climax was upon her. She redoubled her efforts, her backside pumping back and forth as she felt her own peak approaching.

The two women came together, both screaming aloud, oblivious of the fact that they could be heard in the next room, Lia thrusting the cock into Barbara for all she was worth as they both drowned in the pleasure of the moment, the dildo making a sucking sound with the copious juices that flowed from both of them

When they were finally spent, Lia slid the cock out of her companion, who was stretched out across the bench, her eyes closed now, a blissful smile on her face. She blew a kiss to her young companion

"Mmm," she murmured. "That was lovely."

"Hey Barbara," shouted a voice from the next room. "Don't hog her. Let's have her back out here. We need her."

Barbara waved a hand to Lia. "You heard them," she said. "Get back in there."

Lia left Barbara where she was and re-entered the party room. What she saw there made her stop short. Where she had been shackled to the wall, one of the other women had taken her place. She was dark and petite, with hazel brown eyes and pouting lips. Quite how they had got her to the wall was not clear, as she was evidently not happy to be there, struggling with her bonds and cursing her companions. As Lia entered, The Countess was approaching her with a pair of scissors.

"Don't you dare, Amy," shouted the trapped woman. "This dress cost me a fortune."

"You can afford it, Mandy," laughed her hostess.

Mandy was wearing a long slinky gown that was slit all the way up to her thighs on one side. A thin strap ran round her neck, and the neckline of the dress plunged deeply, revealing a large part of a pair of small but beautifully formed breasts.

Mandy gave a shriek as the Countess slid the jaws of the scissors into the top of the dress's slit and began to cut. Lia forgot for a moment her own extraordinary appearance, her eyes wide as she watched the scene unfold.

Mandy was struggling for all she was worth, but there was no hope for her. The manacles held her fast. All she could do was watch in dismay as the scissors snipped their way up the dress until they reached her underarm.

The dress fell open, revealing the brief panties and bra that Mandy wore underneath. A final snip at the neckband and the dress was just a pile of useless material on the floor. Mandy stared down at it in dismay, then up at her grinning hostess.

"You bitch," she shouted. "That was brand new."

"Bitch am I?" said The Countess, still grinning. "I'm afraid that remark just lost you your underwear."

"No!" shouted Mandy. "Leave me!"

But it was already too late. With three quick snips her bra was rendered useless, falling to the ground beside the dress. Mandy's naked breasts were a sight to behold, firm and round like large ripe oranges, the nipples small and hard. Mandy gave another squeal as The Countess set about her briefs, and in no time at all the woman was totally naked, pinned to the wall like some biological specimen, whilst her friends surrounded her, shrieking with laughter.

"You rotten cows!" shouted Mandy. Somehow her anger made her seem even more lovely, standing there with her legs forced apart, so that her thick black pubic curls and the pinkness of her sex were revealed for all to see. Lia licked her lips. For the first time she could see why others found her irresistible when chained, and the thought of it sent a spasm through her that made the penis twitch visibly.

"Look," said one of the other two women. "Our little boy-girl is turned on by the sight of Mandy's cunt. I just saw her cock move."

"Then it shall have what it desires," said their hostess, a wide grin spreading across her face. "Young lady, I want to watch you fucking Mandy."

"No!" shouted Mandy. "You mustn't. Not in front of everybody."

But she was helpless to resist as Lia was led forward.

The Countess took hold of the end of the phallus, and once more Lia felt herself stimulated. She looked at the beautiful naked body in front of her, and again the cock bobbed up and down.

The woman guided the tip of the knob towards Mandy's open sex, ignoring her protests.

"No Amy. You mustn't. You mustn't ... Oh!"

The tone of her voice changed suddenly as Lia pushed the dildo deep into her, pressing it up inside as far as it would go until her face was just inches from Mandy's, their hard nipples brushing against one another in a way that Lia found deliciously stimulating.

She began to move her hips back and forth, quickly finding a rhythm. The session with Barbara had already taught her something of taking on the man's role, and her hips moved smoothly back and forth as she screwed the protesting woman.

But the protests were already becoming more and more feeble as the sex began to have it's desired effect on Mandy. Where she had been shouting, she was moaning now, and beginning to match Lia's thrusts with her own. Suddenly she brought her head forward.

"Kiss me, you disgusting little minx," she said quietly. "Kiss me like you kiss that Biker of yours. Kiss me like you really mean it."

Lia responded at once, wrapping an arm round the back of Mandy's neck and pulling her close, so that their breasts were squashed together. She placed her mouth over Mandy's and forced her tongue deep into Mandy's mouth, increasing the strength of her thrusts as she did so, making Mandy's bare backside slap against the wall behind her. Lia glanced at the other women out of the corner of her eye. The Countess and her two companions were watching intently, the smiles that had been on their faces replaced by expressions of total arousal. Then a moan made them all glance towards the door. Barbara was leaning back against the door post, her legs spread wide. She was still wearing only stockings and suspenders, and her fingers were jammed in her vagina, masturbating hard. The sight of her served to spur on Lia, who redoubled her own efforts, her mouth still locked over Mandy's.

Mandy's orgasm was loud and long, and her cries were matched by those of Lia and Barbara as the three women climaxed together. Lia held Mandy close to her, continuing to ram the dildo deep inside her until she felt the captive relax in her chains. Then she withdrew, leaving the woman hanging spread-eagled where she was, and turned to the others.

"Right, who's next?" asked the Countess.

But one of her companions was already sliding her knickers down her legs and beckoning to Lia.

Chapter 20

Lia rolled onto her back and opened her eyes. For a second she couldn't think where she was. Then she remembered the Countess. She looked sleepily about her. She was lying on a sun lounger beside a large swimming pool. All about were empty bottles and glasses, and lying on the terrace beyond she could see the double dildo, now discarded. She was alone. The rest of the revellers seemed to have gone inside, leaving her where she slept.

She had no idea what time the party had ended, but by the finish she had been utterly exhausted. She had been made to fuck all five women in turn, a task which she had carried out gladly, sharing their orgasms on every occasion. Then they had come out to the pool terrace, where the antics had continued, the women all stripping naked and diving into the water before returning to Lia to be fucked again in every possible position. Lia soon lost count of the number of orgasms that had swept through her as she continued her male role, pandering to the whims of her lustful mistress and her companions.

At last, when she could go no further, they had let her rest, unstrapping the phallus from her and sliding it into themselves. Lia had fallen asleep to the groans and shrieks of the women as they pleasured themselves.

And now she was alone. She gazed dozily up at the starry sky, thinking of the following day, when she would finally get her Thorkil back. With a sigh of contentment she rolled over once more and fell asleep.

"Wake up."

Something hard was prodding Lia in the ribs and she shifted uncomfortably.

Whack! This time it was a stroke across the backside with something long and hard that stung her into wakefulness.

"Wake up I said."

Lia gazed up into the morning sunlight, still not fully comprehending what was happening.

"Tie her and gag her. We don't want her alerting anybody."

Lia felt her hands seized and trapped behind her at the wrists and elbows. Then she felt something being forced between her teeth. It was a large rubber ball, that filled her mouth so she was unable to speak. A pair of straps went round her head and fastened at the back, holding it in place.

Rough hands grabbed her and hauled her to her feet. She stood uncertainly in the early light, trying to focus her eyes. Then she recognised her captors. It was the two security guards.

The taller of the two men eyed her up and down. Having her arms trapped as they were caused her breasts to be thrust forward, and he took one in his hands, his coarse fingers sliding over her soft white skin. For the first time she noted that he had three stripes on his arm, whilst the other had only two.

"Right," he said. "You're coming with us."

Lia tried to protest, but with the gag in her mouth it was impossible. She wanted to run away, but already one of the guards had attached a lead to her chains and was pushing her forward.

"March," he said. "And get a move on or you'll feel my truncheon on your behind again."

Lia had no choice. She set off across the lawn with the men close behind her. She couldn't understand what was happening. She had been convinced of the Countess's sincerity in promising to reunite her with Thorkil, so where were they taking her?

"Get a move on," said the man with the sergeant's stripes. "And don't make a sound."

All at once it dawned on Lia that the men were acting against the Countess's will, and that they had some other purpose in mind. She thought of the whipping they had begun on the previous day, and her apprehension deepened. She gave a despairing glance over her shoulder at the house, but all was quiet. And whilst the Countess slept, she was being carried off once more.

They made an odd sight as they marched on through the park, the two men in their military uniforms, preceded by the naked girl, still wearing the collar and straps fitted for the party, her lovely breasts thrust forward, the hard nipples indicating that the bondage was arousing her, despite herself.

"You sure we'll get away with this Sarge?" It was the first time either of them had spoken since they left the house, and her heart sank as she heard her fears confirmed. They were definitely not obeying the orders of the Countess.

"Don't worry," came the reply. "We simply say she escaped. After all, they left her out on that terrace all night. What did they expect? She just found her way back to the east door. Her Ladyship knows that lock is faulty."

"I guess so."

"Well let's face it, she's just some slut as far as they're concerned.

They'll have forgotten about her in a couple of days."

Ahead of them, Lia could see the wall looming up, and in it the small blue door through which she had entered the day before. She wondered why she was being taken there. At first she had thought that maybe the two men had just wanted to fuck her. To take the pleasure they had been denied the day before, but there seemed to be more than that. What could they possibly want?

They reached the door, and the sergeant opened it. He pushed her through onto the dusty path outside.

"Well, well, well. Look who's here."

Lia gave a gasp into her gag. There were three men standing outside the door.

It was Delgado, Mex and Chet.

Delgado moved forward, taking the lead from the sergeant and dragging her close to him.

"I bet you weren't expecting to see us again, you crafty little bitch," he growled. Lia wouldn't have been able to find an answer even if her mouth hadn't been filled by the gag.

Delgado turned to the guards. "You've done well," he said. "She give you any trouble?"

"Came quiet as a lamb," the sergeant replied.

"Good. I'll see to it that you get rewarded for this. Probably end up with a security job at the Black Cat. Good money, and a few perks, like this little one."

"You're gonna hand her over to Helda then?"

"Sure, just as soon as we can."

"We've got a little score to settle first, though, haven't we?" put in Chet.

"We certainly have." Delgado made a sudden grab for Lia's hair, pulling her face up to his. "That little escape plot of yours caused me and my pals a good deal of pain."

"As well as the trouble of finding you again," put in Mex.

"You gonna thrash her?" asked the sergeant.

"Too bloody right we are," said Chet. "Wanna watch?"

The sergeant grinned. "Certainly do," he said.

Lia glanced fearfully from one to another. From the moment she realised she was back in the hands of Delgado and his friends, she had known she would be punished. After the way she had escaped it was inevitable. She would have preferred it to happen without the guards watching, but it was clear that Delgado held all the cards. When they ordered her to stand under a branch of a nearby tree, she did as she was told. It was most unlikely they would give her another chance to escape.

The sergeant released her arms, and at once her wrists were seized by Mex and Chet, who bound each one with rope, tying it tightly. Then they made her raise her arms up to the overhanging branch. At full stretch she could just touch the branch, and they tied her hands there a shoulder's width apart, hauling her almost onto tiptoes to do it, leaving her body taut, her breasts elongated slightly by her position. Once they were sure she was secure, Delgado removed her gag, tossing it to the sergeant.

Lia felt very vulnerable hanging there in front of the three men, naked and helpless. Delgado took full advantage, stroking her firm breasts. He slid his hand down and slipped a finger into her sex, twisting his hand as he did so. Lia closed her eyes, trying to suppress the emotions that his touch aroused in her.

The sound of cracking wood made her look over Delgado's shoulder. Behind him she could see that Mex had cut a cane from the undergrowth. It was thin and whippy and he was swishing it through the air. She knew he would soon be using it on her bare backside, and the thought sent a strange thrill through her that caused the muscles of her sex to contract. Delgado felt this, and his grin broadened.

"I think she's looking forward to it," he said. "Her cunt's fairly throbbing."

"Let me feel," said the sergeant. Delgado stood aside as he too fingered Lia crudely. This time she could not suppress the sigh that escaped her lips as his fingers probed her.

"I reckon you're right," said the sergeant. "The bitch is positively on heat."

"Let's get some heat into that arse of hers," growled Chet.

"Good idea," said Delgado. "Four strokes each guys. That should teach her who's boss around here."

Lia watched with apprehension as Mex approached her. She knew she made the perfect target, her lovely rounded behind completely unprotected. She gave a start as she felt Mex tap her there with the cane as he took his aim. Then he drew the cane back.

Swish! Whack!

He brought the weapon down on her backside with all the strength he could muster, making her grunt with pain as it cut into her tender flesh. She saw the corporal lick his lips at the sight, and she knew he was enjoying the show.

Swish! Whack!

Down it came again, this time on the underside of her bottom cheeks, making her body sway forward with the force of the blow.

Swish! Whack!

"Ah!" she cried as the cane sliced across the top of her legs, leaving yet another read streak in her otherwise flawless flesh.

Swish! Whack!

Mex's final blow fell almost precisely where the first had done, making the mark sting anew. Lia was breathing heavily now, her backside on fire. She wondered if she could possibly survive a further four blows from the other two. She looked about her audience. They were all standing, their eyes fixed on her naked body, and she felt a sudden surge of excitement, the combination of her bondage and the pain of the beating bringing on the perverse pleasure that she could never understand, but was unmistakably there.

Delgado had taken the cane from Mex, and now it was his turn to move in closer to her. He ran his eyes over her helpless body, a smile playing about his lips.

"Such a lovely body," he murmured. "Especially those delectable tits. Let's see what they'd look like with a couple of stripes across them."

Lia was astounded. Surely he wasn't going to cane her breasts? Even Helda had not allowed that, though she had threatened it on a number of occasions and had often slapped her there. She gave a sharp intake of breath as she felt him lay the hard weapon across her firm young globes.

"Put your head up," he ordered. "Shoulders back. Present your tits to me."

Lia obeyed as best she could, thrusting her chest forward to allow him the target he required. She watched anxiously as he raised the cane in front of her face.

Thwack!

He brought it down hard across the top of her twin mounds, causing them to quiver deliciously. He used none of the force that Mex had done on her behind, but still it left a cruel red stripe across her creamy flesh.

The blow had another effect, though. Almost at once Lia's nipples began to pucker and harden. She glowed red as she realised what was happening, powerless to control her own body as her brown teats swelled until they were solid and protruding, pointing stiffly outwards and upwards.

Delgado gave a short laugh.

"Look at that, guys. I reckon she likes it."

To illustrate the point he laid the cane down across her nipples, and it remained where it was, supported by the erect flesh. Lia looked down at the weapon of punishment, wondering at the recalcitrance of her body.

Delgado picked up the cane again and once more took aim.

Thwack!

This time it came down across the front of Lia's mounds, catching her just above the nipples, the blow marking her soft skin once again. She gave a little whimper as the stinging pain hit her, but at the same time she felt a spasm in her vagina.

Delgado seemed to have sensed the effect the blow had had on her, for he reached down between her legs and felt the heat in her sex. He grinned knowingly at her.

"Want some more?" he asked, shoving his fingers deeper into her so that she moaned aloud.

"That's enough on your tits," he said. "After all, there's no sense damaging the merchandise."

He slid his fingers out of her sex and moved behind her. Once more she felt the tap on her glowing backside.

Swish! Whack!

This time he showed no restraint as he brought the cane down on her behind, rocking her forward with the force of the blow.

Swish! Whack!

The second blow fell quickly, catching Lia unawares so that she gave a cry as it landed. Her backside was on fire now, and she wasn't sure she would be able to stand the four blows still to come. Sweat was trickling down her naked flesh, making her lovely young body glisten in the sunlight, and she was panting hard with arousal as she watched Chet take the cane from Delgado.

Swish! Whack!
Swish! Whack!
Swish! Whack!
Swish! Whack!

Chet's blows fell with such rapid succession that she barely had time to think. He struck her with deadly accuracy, leaving a row of four stripes in a parallel line across her buttocks, the first one still white even as the final one fell so that the men were able to watch them darken to red together. Lia's body fairly jumped as the blows fell, a shout of pain issuing from her lips as each one struck her. But now, at last, her punishment was over, and she hung there in her bonds, her backside and breasts striped with the cane's marks, her nipples hard and her sex visibly throbbing, small drops of moisture trickling down her thigh having been dislodged by Chet's blows.

"OK," said Delgado. "Cut her down. We've got to be moving."

Mex stepped forward, but the sergeant moved first, shoving him aside. He produced a large knife from his belt, which sliced easily through Lia's bonds. She staggered slightly as her weight came back on her feet, but he caught her, placing one arm behind her back beneath her armpits. Then with the other he began to grope her, running his great hand over the tender flesh of her breasts, then reaching down for the wetness of her sex.

"You wanna fuck her?" asked Delgado.

The sergeant nodded.

"I guess that's OK by us."

Lia looked at him, wondering at the power he assumed over her, just casually giving her to the sergeant to be screwed with no attempt at gaining her assent. The thought of it sent a new surge of lust through her as she realised how she loved to be dominated, to be tied up and beaten, then turned over to a man who's name she did not even know, but who was about to perform the most intimate act possible with her.

The sergeant wasted no time, shoving her onto her back and reaching for his fly. Lia licked her lips as his rod sprang into view, stiff and thick, a drop of his own moisture shining on the tip. He knelt down between her legs and she spread them for him, offering her open cunt to him in an unambiguous gesture of abandonment.

He sprawled over her, his heavy body pressing down on her. For a second she felt a stab of pain as he brushed her still smarting breasts, but the pain was instantly forgotten as she felt his cock against her sex.

"Ahh!" Lia cried out with pleasure as he shoved his penis into her, ramming it home so that her body was jolted with the force. He began fucking her at once, his hips pumping hard, taking her breath away as he forced himself down on her. Lia moaned and writhed under the onslaught, her body alive with unbridled passion, the arousal triggered by the beating spurring her to new heights.

The sergeant came quickly, his hot semen spurting out suddenly, catching Lia by surprise. His cock was still spitting out thick creamy gobs of spunk when he pulled it out, spattering it over her belly. Lia gave a whimper of frustration as she realised he had finished. She was still burning with desire, writhing about on the ground, her hips pumping back and forth, her cunt lips opening and closing as her sex convulsed about empty air.

Then, with a gasp of relief, she realised that the corporal was undoing his pants. He stood over her, his cock rising erect from his flies, watching as she thrust her sex up at him.

"You want it?" he asked.

"Yes, please."

"How bad?"

"Really bad. Oh please fuck me. I really need it."

"Get on your hands and knees."

Lia did as she was ordered at once, scrambling up onto all fours.

"Open your legs wide, and push your tits down."

Lia obeyed, pressing her chest downward so that her nipples brushed the ground, raising her striped behind up to him and pushing backwards so that the pink lips of her sex lay open before him. Even now she was barely in control, and her hips continued to move back and forth as if against some imaginary lover.

The corporal delayed a little longer, enjoying the sight of the totally aroused girl, so anxious to be penetrated, her red behind beautifully presented to him. Then he knelt down, grasped her hips and without further ado, thrust himself into her.

Lia gave a cry of joy as he impaled her on his stiff weapon and began fucking her hard. He too showed no finesse at all, treating her roughly, simply as a receptacle for his rampant tool. But Lia didn't care. This was how she loved to be fucked. Treated as no more than a pleasure object. It was a wonderful feeling to her to be owned and used, to be the plaything of anyone who wanted her, and she felt her orgasm build within her as the realisation of her total wantonness filled her mind.

Like the sergeant, the corporal did not last long, but this time Lia was ready for him, and as she felt his body tense she let go, the force of her orgasm wracking her body as she thrashed about, screaming aloud at the sensation of a second helping of spunk pumping into her vagina.

She tightened her sex about him, milking his balls dry, holding him inside for as long as she was able, so that when he finally withdrew she flopped contentedly on the grass, her legs still wide apart, the semen oozing from her as she gazed up into the faces of her captors, a slight smile of satisfaction playing about her lips.

Chapter 21

Once the Guards had satisfied their lusts in the young captive, Delgado, Mex and Chet set off through the forest once more. Lia rode in front of Delgado, her arms secured behind her. She sat astride the forward part of the saddle, her sex pressed against the hard pommel, so that all the time they rode her clitoris rubbed against the leather, keeping her constantly aroused. Her condition was made more acute by Delgado's habit of frequently feeling her up, Rubbing her breasts to keep her nipples hard and occasionally penetrating her with his forefinger, so that by the time they had been going for an hour she was panting once more, much to the amusement of the other two.

They rode on for hours, only stopping twice in the day to water the horses and partake of a small meal. When night fell they halted and set up camp in the woods beside a river. The first thing Delgado did was to make sure that Lia was secure, shackling her leg to a stout tree with a thick chain. The chain was long enough to allow her to wander round the camp, but prevented any possibility of escape.

They lit a campfire and Delgado prepared a meal. After dinner they set Lia to work washing the dishes and packing them away whilst the men sat around the camp fire, talking, smoking and drinking. Once she had finished they summoned her to the fireside.

"Stand properly now," ordered Delgado.

Lia placed her hands behind her head and thrust her hips forward, her heart beating fast with anticipation. Delgado stretched his arm out and ran his fingers over her backside. She winced as he felt the weals so recently deposited there.

"You really do look exquisite with stripes across your behind," he said, smiling. "And as for the ones on your tits. Quite irresistible, don't you agree?"

"They sure are," said Mex. "Real cute."

"Come over here," ordered Chet suddenly.

Lia moved warily closer to him, placing herself in front of him. He reached out a hand, running it up her inner thigh, his fingers lightly touching her skin. His hand rose higher, just barely brushing her sex lips, but enough to make her draw breath sharply. He let his fingers stray further upwards until they found the underside of her breast. Here they paused momentarily. Lia stood as still as she was able, hardly daring to breathe. For one with so powerful a physique, Chet was remarkably gentle, and despite her reluctance, her flesh tingled with anticipation as she waited for his hand to move again.

After what seemed an age, it did begin to move, his palm closing over her breast and caressing it.

"Very nice," he murmured.

"Come on Chet," called Mex impatiently. "You gonna fuck her? If not pass her over here."

Lia's stomach turned over at these words. It was not just what was said, it was the casual way the words were spoken. Once more there was no question of consent from her. She was simply a slave to their whims, a realisation that sent a powerful spasm of lust through her. Why was it, she wondered, that her body acted this way? What was it that gave her the taste for the beatings, the bondage and the humiliation? All she knew was that they aroused her such that it was impossible for her to resist. And now, as Chet's fingers drifted down towards her sex, she knew she must surrender.

Chet took her there and then, stretched on her back by the fire, gasping and moaning as he filled her with his stiff cock.

Once Chet had spurted his seed into her, Mex took over. He draped her face down across one of the saddles and took her from behind, his heavy thrusts making her grunt loudly with every stroke, grunts that turned into cries of pleasure as she felt his sperm pump into her.

Finally it was Delgado's turn. He made her suck him, kneeling before him in the dust and slurping at his cock whilst wanking the shaft vigorously until he shot his load down her throat.

Before retiring for the night they hammered four stakes into the ground and chained her spread-eagled there. Lia slept soundly, exhausted by the rigours of the day. She was wakened at first light by Mex, who crawled onto her whilst she was still tethered and screwed her hard, followed in rapid succession by Chet and Delgado. Lia, as usual, responded enthusiastically to the treatment, the bondage heightening the sensation so that her orgasms were loud and long. To have three cocks inside her before breakfast was an extraordinary experience and once again she wondered at her own wantonness.

At last they freed her arms and legs and she was allowed to bathe, her leg iron still in place, whilst Delgado prepared the breakfast. Then they were off once more, winding their way through the forest.

It was nearly midday when Delgado reined his horse to a halt at the top of a high ridge. Below, Lia could see a farmhouse, with a number of outbuildings, and a track that led away through the trees.

They began to pick their way down towards the building. The path was steep and narrow, and Lia felt sure the horses would slip and fall, but they were sure-footed beasts and brought the four of them safely to the bottom. Once on the flat again, Delgado spurred the horse on toward the farmhouse.

The buildings, when they reached them, were old and dilapidated and at first Lia thought they must be deserted, but as they pulled the horses up, a door swung open in the farmhouse and a man emerged. He was an old man, about seventy, and he eyed Lia up with some interest.

"You're late," he said. "You said you'd be back yesterday."

A bit of a problem with this young lady," said Delgado. "Don't worry, we'll pay for the extra day."

"Darned right you will," said the man. "You wanna eat something? I got a stew on the stove."

"That'd be good," said Delgado. "Where do you want the horses?"

Just leave them in the yard here. I'll see to them later."

The men dismounted, along with Lia. Delgado pulled the leg iron from his saddlebag, and secured her to the same post as the one to which the horses had been tied.

"Now stand properly," said Delgado.

Lia took up her submissive stance, much to the delight of the old man, who seemed unable to take his eyes off her. At last, though, the men trooped into the house leaving her alone.

About a quarter of an hour passed, then the door opened once again. The old man emerged, carrying a bowl of stew. He looked her up and down, his eyes wide. Lia blushed, but did not move. The man approached her hesitantly, holding out the plate of stew. Lia made no move at first, until he gave a nod of his head. Then she reached out and took the food. The man took a final glance at her, then turned and went into the house.

Lia ate hungrily, scooping the food into her mouth with a spoon. The ride had made her hungry and the stew tasted good. Soon she was holding an empty plate. She placed it carefully on the ground, then clasped her hands behind her head and waited.

The man returned about ten minutes later. he went to pick up the bowl, then paused, his eyes fixed on Lia's breasts. Lia guessed it was the stripes across them that had caught his eye, and once again she felt the blood rise in her cheeks. The man reached out a hand, running his bony old finger along the stripes. Lia closed her eyes at the touch.

"Who gave you those?" the man asked.

"They did."

"Those guys in there?"

"Yes."

"How come?"

"Because I tried to escape."

"So they beat your breasts?"

"Yes. And my behind."

"Your arse as well?"

"Yes."

"Show me."

Lia turned around so he could see the marks on her backside. He gave a low whistle.

"Can I touch?"

"If you want to."

Lia felt the man's fingers tracing the marks of her beating.

"Tell me about how they did this to you," he said.

Lia related to him how she had been tied, and the three men had taken it in turns to cane her. The man listened. his eyes wide open, his fingers still running back and forth over Lia's bare behind.

"What happened next?" he asked when she had finished.

"Nothing."

"Come on girlie. You're not trying to tell me that they just cut you down." As he spoke he slipped his finger down the crack of her behind, and felt her wetness for the first time."

"N-no," she stammered.

"Tell me then."

Lia went on to tell how she had been taken by the two security guards. But the man wanted more, so she was forced to recount her night in camp. And all the time his coarse old fingers were rubbing back and forth over her sex.

"What the hell are you up to now?"

Delgado's voice made Lia start. She hadn't heard the three men emerge from the farmhouse. Suddenly Lia realised what a sight she must make. Almost unconsciously she had bent herself forward over the hitching post, her backside shoved up and back to allow the man unrestricted access to her vagina, her breasts hanging down and quivering slightly under his touch. She snatched her body erect and placed her hands behind her head, but the man continued to finger her, apparently unconcerned by the presence of the others.

"She's certainly a horny little bitch, isn't she?" he said.

Delgado laughed. "She just loves it. That's why she goes around bare-arsed like that. No need to waste time stripping off. Still, we gotta get going I'm afraid."

The old man withdrew his fingers from Lia's sex, wiping the moisture off on her behind, leaving two glistening streaks there. As he did so, there came the sound of an engine starting, and a few seconds later an old van emerged from one of the barns with Mex at the wheel. It was battered and rusting, but the engine still ran and with a squeak of brakes it halted beside Lia.

Delgado pulled two sets of cuffs from his bag, and once again Lia found her wrists and elbows secured. Then he pushed her through the front door of the van.

"In the back," he ordered.

Lia climbed awkwardly over the seats and into the rear of the vehicle. Inside it smelt musty and greasy, but an old piece of carpet had been laid on the floor, which was at least clean. Lia was made to sit with her back to the side of the van, and her cuffs were undone momentarily, then slipped through a metal handle set into the floor. Once she was secure, the three men seated themselves in the front, and with a grinding of gears, they were on the move once more.

Chapter 22

The first part of the journey was very bumpy indeed as the old van rattled along the farm track, and Lia found it quite difficult to maintain her balance. All she had was the handle to which her wrists were attached and she clung to it grimly, trying to keep herself upright. In the front the three men chatted idly as they drove, apparently unconcerned about the discomfort felt by their passenger.

Then the van hit a particularly large bump, and Lia lurched forward. As she did so there was a bang, and suddenly she realised she was no longer secured to the handle. It's attachment points had been so rusted that the weight of her body had been too much and one of them had given way, allowing her cuffs to slip out. She glanced fearfully at the men in the front, wondering if they had heard or seen anything, but they showed no signs of having done so. She braced herself against the side of the van, her heart beating fast. For the first time since she had been recaptured, the possibility of escape filled her thoughts.

For the next few miles, Lia's journey was very uncomfortable indeed. Without the handle to steady her, it was extremely difficult to hold her position. But she knew she must do just that. If the men suspected that she had any degree of freedom they would soon deprive her of it, and would probably administer a beating into the bargain. She dug her heels into the carpet and pressed her back against the van's side, praying that they would not suspect.

At last the van swung to the left, and the bumping stopped. They had reached the highway, and Lia was able to relax as the vehicle gained speed.

They travelled for another hour along the highway. From her position at the rear of the vehicle Lia could see almost nothing, but occasionally she would hear a roar of diesel as a truck thundered past them, so she guessed they must be on one of the major trunk roads.

At last, the note of the engine changed, and she realised they were slowing. She felt the vehicle swing off the main road and stop for a few seconds, then move forward again, but this time much slower. She guessed that they had turned into a service area, possibly even the same one as that to which the Bikers had taken her when she had first been captured.

The van came to a halt, and Mex jerked on the handbrake and extinguished the engine. The three men turned to their naked captive. Lia was exactly as they had left her, stretched out on the floor of the vehicle, her arms secure. She prayed that they would not check her bonds.

"Time for a little refreshment," said Delgado. "I take it you're not coming in with us?"

Lia said nothing, but her thoughts went to the last time she had visited such a place. On that occasion the Bikers had forced her to go inside with them, and had made her serve the drinks at their table whilst naked, the eyes of all the truck drivers upon her. This time she wanted only to be left outside.

"Right," said Delgado. "We're gonna have a couple of beers. But first of all we've got a call to make. Helda's gonna be pretty pleased when she finds her little whore is back in harness. I reckon she can be here in less than an hour. Then we're going to have to part company I'm afraid."

Once again Lia did not reply, but her thoughts were racing. Helda less than an hour away. She had to get as far as possible from this place. But how?

To her relief, her three captors climbed out of the van without checking her bonds, simply slamming the door and leaving her alone. Lia stayed where she was for a full five minutes, not daring to move. Then, when at last she felt that the coast was clear, she got gingerly to her knees and shuffled forward.

She leaned her head over the front seats and stared out. They were, indeed, in one of the service areas. On one side was the diner, with its neon signs flashing on and off, advertising its wares. On the other was the refuelling area, where the mighty trucks drew up to refill their tanks.

As Lia watched, one of them pulled away from the pumps and headed toward the van. Instinctively she ducked down, not wishing to be seen by the drivers. The truck stopped about fifty yards from where the van was parked, and for a second she wondered if she had been spotted. The two men descended from the cab, but instead of heading in her direction they disappeared into a small brick building.

Lia continued her vigil, waiting to see what would happen next. The men were gone for about two minutes, then they emerged together and climbed back into the cab. There was a roar from the engine, a plume of black smoke from the great chrome exhaust and the vehicle was moving again, heading for the exit.

Lia watched as a second truck pulled away from the pumps and was surprised to see that it too halted by the building whilst the men went inside. The same happened with the third to leave. Then Lia realised that the building was a gents lavatory, and that the men were taking the opportunity to relieve themselves before setting out on the open road.

She watched three more trucks pass. Two of the three stopped by the toilet block. There was something else, too. Most of the truckers tended to leave their cab doors open whilst they were inside.

Lia thought hard. This had to be her best means of escape from the service area. All she had to do was board the truck whilst the men were out of the cab, and conceal herself until they were away.

' All, she thought bitterly. First of all she had to cover fifty yards across the car park, in broad daylight, stark naked with her hands tethered behind her. She scanned the parking area. There was a scattering of vans and trucks between her and the lavatory block. It wasn't much, but it was all the cover she had, and time was fast running out. She took a deep breath. She had to try it.

She climbed over onto the front seats of the cab, then fumbled with the door handle on the driver's side. It wasn't easy with her hands tethered as they were, but eventually she managed to undo it, and the door opened a crack. She checked out the windscreen. Two men were making their way across the car lot to the diner. She waited until they were safely inside, then pushed the door open and stepped down onto the tarmac. It felt hot under her bare feet, and the gravel dug into her, but she pushed the pain from her mind.

Her first objective was another van about ten yards away, and she scuttled across the open space as quickly as she was able, crouching down beside it. She made sure the coast was clear, then made a dash for a large truck some fifteen yards beyond. When she reached it she glanced back at the van in which she had arrived. She had burned her boats now, and she knew she had to go on. She felt dreadfully exposed out there, leaning against the side of the truck, and her eyes darted about, fearful that she might be spotted.

She made her way down the length of the truck and peered round the back. Then she froze. A group of four men had emerged from the diner and were heading toward her. She crouched down and slid beneath the trailer of the truck, where she remained, her heart beating fast.

She kept praying that the men would veer from the route they were taking, but still they came on, so close now she could hear their voices. She moved up behind one of the massive sets of wheels on the truck, then kept perfectly still. Two of the men were no more than a couple of yards away now and, to her chagrin, as they came alongside her they stopped.

"You wanna check the load?" said a voice.

"Why, is there a problem?"

"Not 'specially. It's just about time we checked it."

"Nah. It'll be OK."

Lia gave a sigh of relief as the two men moved on. Soon she heard the doors bang as they climbed into the cab.

Lia was in a quandary. She knew that the truck beneath which she was crouching must soon move away, leaving her exposed here. She looked out in the direction of the lavatory. There was another large truck less than ten yards away. She would have to get to it as soon as she could.

Suddenly she saw something that made her give a stifled cry of dismay. There were two men sitting in the cab of the other truck. They must have been the other two of the foursome she had seen leaving the diner. The pair were facing in her direction, and she knew that the moment she broke into the open they would see her.

Then with a shock she heard the engine of the truck under whose trailer she was hiding burst into life. She gave a sob of despair. If it moved away now she would be left in full view of the one behind. She cursed her luck at her bad timing and watched the other cab anxiously. The men inside were chatting and showed no signs of moving. If they saw her they would certainly take her back to the diner, then all would be lost.

The truck's engine continued to rumble, but still it did not move off. Lia was helpless. All she could do was watch the other cab and wait.

Suddenly a plume of smoke issued from the exhaust of the second truck and she heard its engine start. Lia's heart leapt. Maybe there was still hope. She watched the vehicle carefully, willing it to move, but it remained where it was. Through the windscreen she could discern the crew, still chatting. At the same moment she heard the sound of the gears being engaged on the vehicle under which she was hiding. Then the engine note began to rise and all seemed lost. She held her breath and waited for the exposure and capture that must inevitably follow.

All at once, with a gasp of relief, she saw the other truck began to move, swinging out and passing the one she was hiding under. Almost simultaneously the one above her began to move too. She crouched low as the great trailer passed over her. Then she was in the open, and on her feet, running for all she was worth, her thrusting breasts bouncing as she sped across the tarmac.

There was a truck pulled up beside the latrine, its doors open, and Lia made the decision to go straight for it. She sprinted towards it, watching the door of the low building, hoping desperately that the men would not emerge just yet. It seemed to take forever to reach the throbbing vehicle, but at last she was there.

There was no point checking to make sure she hadn't been spotted. It was now or never. The first step up to the cab was very high, and without the ability to grasp the handle that ran up the side it was extremely difficult to climb onto. She placed her foot on it and leapt upwards, only to drop back again. She tried a second time with similar results. Lia gave a sob of despair. At any moment the men would return, or someone else would spot her. It was a miracle nobody had seen her so far. She placed her foot on the step once more, and with an almost superhuman effort managed to jump up, so she was standing on it.

She climbed on, a trifle unsteadily, going up step by step until at last she was level with the door. She fell through onto the seats of the truck. At once she was on her feet. Above the back of the seats was a bunk bed, and it was onto this that she climbed, rolling over the plastic surface as far as she could, then lying still, hardly daring to breathe.

Almost at once she felt the cab shake as the driver and his mate mounted the steps. The doors slammed, and with a jolt they were moving. They travelled at low speed for about half a minute, then they stopped again. For a moment Lia thought the game was up, then she realised with relief that it was just the checkpoint at the gate. They were stationary for no more than fifteen seconds, before she felt the vehicle lurch and they were off down the highway.

Chapter 23

The truck roared on along the highway, gathering speed all the time. Lia remained where she was, her heart still beating fast after her fortunate escape. The driver and his mate clearly had no idea she was aboard, and she could hear them conversing idly below. Soon even the talk died away and they turned on the radio. The strains of country and western drifted up to where Lia lay, and she closed her eyes. Before long she was asleep.

She was woken by the sound of the vehicle slowing. Although she could not see out, the reflection of the headlights on the ceiling of the cab told her that it was dark. She lay listening as the vehicle came to a halt. One of the doors to the cab opened, and someone got out. There was a clank of chains, and they moved forward. Then she heard the bang of a large gate being shut. They were in some kind of enclosure, probably stopping for the night.

Most of the hauliers maintained a number of stopping places along the highways, since it was unsafe to park on the road itself, and she guessed that it was at one of these that they had arrived.

The truck swung round and came to a halt, and almost at once the engine died. The silence was very welcome after the constant roar of the diesel, but Lia had to hold her breath for fear the men would hear her.

She heard the driver's door open, then slam again, and she knew she was alone. Nevertheless she waited a few minutes before sliding to the edge of the bunk and peering over. There was nobody in the cab. Carefully she climbed down onto the seats and glanced out the windscreen. The truck was parked on the edge of a wide parking area, and all she could see was a heavy chain fence, with the highway beyond.

She wondered what she should do next. Despite the fact she had escaped from Delgado, she was clearly not yet safe. Apart from anything else she was trussed, her arms pinned behind her, making her breasts project forward in a most provocative manner. If only there was someone she could rely on. Someone who could contact Thorkil, so he could rescue her.

She considered remaining in the cab. But to do so would mean certain discovery eventually. She wasn't even sure whether the drivers would return to sleep in there. After all, with the seat and the bunk it was perfectly suited to accommodate the pair of them. There was nothing else for it. She would have to get out.

As with the van earlier, operating the door handle was no easy feat, but eventually she managed it. She eased herself backwards onto the steps and climbed down carefully, jumping from the bottom step to land on the hard gravel surface of the parking area. Once she had steadied herself she pressed her body against the trailer and inched along its length, peering round to see where she was. The enclosure was quite small, only a hundred or so yards across. It consisted of an open parking area, with a small building at one end. She could see a light burning inside the building and a plume of smoke issued from the chimney. There were two more trucks parked on the far side of the enclosure, and nothing else.

Lia studied the fence. It was more than twelve feet high. There was no way she could climb it with her arms secured. She had to free herself. She wondered if any of the trucks were carrying tools that could be used to cut through the cuffs. She went to the rear of the truck in which she had been travelling. The back doors were secured with a large handle. Perhaps there would be some tools inside. She turned her back on the truck and fumbled behind her for the handle.

It was then that the light shone in her face.

"What the hell do you think you're doing?"

Lia could not see the man behind the powerful flashlight as she blinked into its strong beam. She cursed herself for being so careless. She should have known that someone would be on watch, despite the security of the enclosure. She remained where she was, like a rabbit transfixed in the headlights of a car.

"I said, what are you doing?"

"I - I was looking for some tools."

"Some what?"

"Some tools."

"Well you won't find any in there. He's hauling cigarettes. What do you want tools for, anyhow?"

"My hands. They're tied."

"Show me."

Slowly Lia turned round, revealing the cuffs to the man.

"I see what you mean," he said. "Who did that to you?"

"Some men. They were kidnapping me."

"And they stripped you as well?"

"I was already naked."

"I see. But how the hell did you get in here?"

"I came in this truck."

"What, Buck and Dan brought you?"

"I don't know their names. I stowed away. I was trying to escape you

139

see."

"Hmm," he scratched his head. "I guess you'd better come inside. I'm sure the boys would be pleased to meet you."

"Please, couldn't you just let me out?" she pleaded.

"What, onto the highway? In that state?"

"I - I just want to get away."

"No chance I'm afraid, baby. You're coming with me."

The man took her by the arm and led her towards the building from which the light shone. Lia tried to hang back, but he was strong and simply pulled her along. As he reached for the handle of the door, Lia felt a pang of apprehension, only too aware of her vulnerability, being led naked and helpless into a room full of men.

The door flew open and the man pushed her through. Inside, the room was warm but smoky, an aroma of food hanging in the air. Opposite the door was a table, at which five men were sitting, playing cards.

"Look what I've found."

The five swung round and their eyes widened. Lia felt the blood rush to her cheeks as they studied her. She wished for the hundredth time that she had some means of covering herself, even if only with her hands. But there was no hope of that, and she was forced to remain where she was as they feasted their eyes on her breasts and her shaven sex.

"Wow!"

"What a beauty."

"Where did you find that?"

"She was outside, sneaking about the back of the trucks. Claimed she stowed away in Buck and Dan's cab."

"Our cab?" The man who spoke was large and burly, his hair cut short. On his massive hairy arms were tattoos of naked women. "Where the hell were you?" he asked.

"On the bunk," said Lia timidly. "I got in at the service depot. I was trying to escape from someone, you see."

"You mean we've had her trussed up like that in the cab all afternoon?" This man who spoke was much younger that the first, and she took him to be Dan. He was thinner than his companion, with long hair and a ring through his nose.

"Talk about a missed opportunity," said another of the men, laughing. Dan shot him an angry glance.

"The question remains, what the hell do we do with her?"

"Well let me know when you decide," said the man with the flashlight. "I'd better get back outside."

He left Lia standing just inside the door, and went out. Lia stared apprehensively from face to face, wondering what they would do with her. She wished her hands were free, so at least she could cover herself with them.

For a few moments there was silence, then the man she took to be Buck rose and crossed to where she stood.

"Where were you headed?" he asked.

"I want to get to Depot twenty-nine," she said.

"Twenty-nine, eh? Why?"

"There's someone there. A Biker. I'm a Biker's girl."

"I should have guessed from those stripes across your tits. They know how treat a girl do Bikers. Have you had your arse thrashed too?"

She dropped her eyes. "Yes."

"Show us."

Slowly Lia turned and raised her arms as best she could to reveal the marks of her punishment, criss-crossing her rear. She could have explained that it was Delgado, and not a Biker that had put them there, but there didn't seem much point.

"Very nice," said Buck. "Very nice indeed. Don't you agree boys?"

The others nodded their assent.

Then Buck said something unexpected.

"You're heading for twenty-nine, aren't you Slim?" The words were addressed to a tall man, who had sat silent until now, watching proceedings. He nodded.

"Fancy a passenger?"

"What's it worth?"

Buck turned to Lia. "Passengers don't travel for free with Slim you know. He'll want something in return. What you offering?"

Lia's stomach gave a little lurch. The question made her more aware than ever of her naked and helpless state. She knew what was being asked of her, and she was shocked at how her body was responding to the request. She dropped her eyes, staring down at herself, aware that her nipples had hardened the moment he had spoken. Then she looked up again at Buck. She did not speak. She did not have to. The gesture had said it all. She was offering all she had. Prostituting herself for the sake of the lift. Her cheeks glowed as she considered her wantonness, and at the same time she felt the thrill of arousal begin to creep into her loins.

Buck placed a hand on her full breast, squeezing it gently.

"We get the message," he said, grinning. "And you get the ride. In more ways than one."

"Let's fuck her now," said Dan his voice enthused. "Come on, who's first?"

"Yeah," said another young man, whom Lia took to be Slim's mate. "C'm on. I wanna be first."

He and Dan rose to their feet and began to converge on Lia. Dan reached her first, his hands grabbing for her breasts. Lia tried to take a step back, but she was already against the door. They pinned her back against it, reaching for her crotch. She gasped as a finger penetrated her, whilst another was running down the crack of her behind. A mouth closed over her nipple and she found herself being pushed and shoved back and forth as the two men fought over her.

Lia began to feel the first stages of panic rising in her as they licked and groped her. She tried to struggle, but to no avail. They were too strong for her.

"Stop!"

The sudden shout caught the two men by surprise and they froze instantly. Lia shook herself free of them, staggering across the room. She turned to look at Slim, who was on his feet.

"Stop fighting over her like a couple of mutts over a bitch," he rapped. "The lady's not going anywhere, is she?"

"Sorry Slim," mumbled the pair.

"Anyhow," said Slim, a faint smile playing about his lips. "I've got a much better idea. Instead of fighting over who's gonna be first, we can all be first."

The others stared at him.

"All?" said Buck.

"Sure. I used to know a whore down south who claimed she could take on five men at once."

"Five?"

"So she said. Never tried it myself, but I always intended to. Lets see how this little lady gets on."

"Yeah, sure. I'm game."

"First of all we gotta get those shackles off her. Len, go and get some cutters."

"Sure thing," said the young man, who had been mauling her with Dan. He shoved the door open and set off at a trot.

Lia stayed silent through all this, her eyes going from man to man. All five! They wanted her to take on all five! Her mind went through the possible combinations, and she felt the wetness inside her increase as the ideas tumbled through her brain.

Buck and Dan moved a bench from the side of the room. It was wide and heavily padded, and they carried it to the centre. The fifth man stirred himself too. He was another driver. His name was Jack and it had been his assistant who had found Lia in the first place.

By the time the bench was in place, Len had returned with a pair of cutters. They were big ones, with long handles and strong jaws. Buck made her face the wall whilst he slipped the blade under her cuffs. There was a loud snap, and the cuff fell away from her wrist. He moved on to the other wrist.

In no time Lia's arms were freed, and she was able to windmill them round, revelling in her new-found freedom. She was not allowed to stretch for long, though. The men were watching her expectantly.

Slim loosened his belt, and opened his pants. His cock was already stiff and Lia stared at it with undisguised interest. He lay back on the bench, then beckoned to her. Lia moved forward hesitantly, her heart beating fast. Her knees trembled slightly as she approached him, but she wasn't sure if it was fear or lust that made them shake so.

She was just able to straddle the bench, so wide was it. She moved up his body until she was positioned just above his jutting weapon. He nodded to her, and she began to lower herself down onto him.

She shivered as she felt the tip of his cock touch her sex. She took it in her hands and guided it into her. She was surprised to find herself extremely wet, and he slipped into her easily. She let herself crouch lower and lower, until he was all the way inside her. He filled her wonderfully, stretching the walls of her vagina and plundering deep into her most private place.

The moment she had settled astride him, he pulled her forward, dragging her down until she was lying on him, her legs stretched wide, her feet barely touching the ground.

All at once Lia felt an odd sensation about her backside. Something cold was trickling down the crack of her behind. She craned her neck round to see Buck standing there. He had a small bottle of oil in his hand and was rubbing it into her anus, his fingers slipping inside her. The sensation this gave her was at the same time both strange and erotic, particularly since her vagina was so full of cock. She dropped her eyes to his groin. Buck's cock was standing proud from his fly, and shining with moisture. She guessed that it too had been coated with the oil.

He positioned himself behind her, the tip of his weapon rubbing up and down between the cheeks of her backside. Lia knew what was coming, and she tried as best she could to relax the muscles of her sphincter. Only once before had she been fucked in the anus, by one of the Black Cat's clients, and she had found it painful. What it would be like with a cock already inside her vagina she could not imagine.

She did not have to wait long to find out. Buck began pressing his rampant organ against her tight little rear hole, twisting it as he did so in order to facilitate its penetration.

Lia gave a cry as it suddenly slid into her, stretching the muscles around her backside as it did so. This time there was none of the pain, just the perverse thrill of being doubly penetrated, of opening her body to admit two men in at once.

Lia felt the rough curls of Buck's pubic hair against her flesh, and she knew he was all the way inside. Still neither man made a movement. Then a hand grasped Lia's hair and she felt her head pulled round to the side. There, just at the level of her mouth, stood Dan's cock. It bobbed up and down before her eyes, the glans exposed and shining. She opened her mouth and took it inside. At the same moment she felt her wrists grabbed from either side and guided to the shafts of two more swollen penises.

Lia's body was alive with arousal. Three of her orifices were filled by rock-hard cocks, whilst she held two more in her hands. She was going to pleasure five men at once, and the idea sent a new surge of moisture rushing through her sex. This was followed almost immediately by another as Slim began to move.

Slim's first thrust was a cue to his companions, and almost at once she felt Bucks cock shove forward in her backside, whilst Dan began ramming his hips forward, his youthful exuberance returning as he fucked Lia's face. She tightened her grip on the two shafts she held in her hands and began to wank them vigorously, making the two men grunt with enjoyment.

Lia could not believe what was happening to her. Just a few minutes ago she had been lying alone in the cab of the truck. Now she was laid out in this seedy little shed, with cocks in her cunt, rectum and mouth whilst she simultaneously masturbated two more. She couldn't imagine any more wanton behaviour, and but for the mouthful of male flesh that was pumping into her open mouth she would have cried aloud with her lust. Her body was being battered back and forth by Slim and Buck, and it was all she could do to hold her head steady as she slurped greedily at Dan's organ. It seemed impossible to establish a rhythm, and in the end she gave up, lying passively among them, concentrating on the cocks in her hands and abandoning her body to the other three.

The first to come was Buck, his hot semen spurting into her rectum as he gasped with pleasure, the pulsations of his organ sending waves of pleasure through Lia's ravaged body as she accepted his seed in so intimate a place. Seconds later it was Dan's turn, his cock unleashing copious amounts of spunk into her mouth and over her face even whilst Buck was still shooting his load into her behind. Lia spluttered and gasped as she tried her best to swallow the thick white liquid. So preoccupied was she that Slim's climax took her by surprise as he too unleashed a stream of semen deep inside her cunt with a hoarse grunt of satisfaction. Even as he was filling her, she could feel Buck withdrawing from her behind, a dribble of warm sperm escaping from her as he did so. And all the time she was vigorously wanking the other two, their cocks twitching in her fingers.

No sooner had Slim spurted the last of his come into her, than she felt herself being roughly pulled from him. The men pulling her were Jack and Len, and she lost her grip from their shafts as they dragged her to the table and lay her back across it so that her backside projected over the edge. She peered down between her breasts and watched as Jack yanked her legs apart, staring down at her open slit momentarily before plunging his stiff prick into her, making her cry out as she felt herself penetrated yet again. As Jack began to fuck her, Len climbed onto the table and sat astride her midriff.

"Squeeze your tits together," he ordered. Lia looked at him quizzically.

"Your tits. I want to fuck your tits. Do as I tell you."

Lia took hold of her breasts, and watched as he positioned his stiff cock in the valley between them. Then she pressed them together so that the hard, protruding nipples were almost touching. Len began to move his hips back and forth, his cock beautifully trapped between her mounds, his face a picture of contentment as he took his pleasure.

Throughout all this Lia had been too intent on satisfying the five men to think of her own pleasure. But now she was able to let herself go she felt her climax rising rapidly, spurred on by the taste of spunk in her mouth and the sensation of it deep in her cunt and trickling from her anus. Jack was pumping hard now, and though she could not see his face, she knew he was close to coming.

This time, when her cunt was filled, Lia responded with her own orgasm, her cries ringing about the room as she let herself go. She couldn't believe how long Jack went on spurting into her, and every drop of spunk sent a new thrill through her. Then, just as she was beginning to come down, Len unleashed a stream of semen onto her face, neck and breasts. She opened her mouth wide, endeavouring to catch and swallow the white gobs that flew from the end of his cock, and a second orgasm swept through her as she felt him throbbing between her swollen breasts.

By the time John climbed off her, she knew she must look a sight, her face, hair, neck and breasts dripping with spunk, her sex red and open, more spunk leaking from it. She gazed round at the men, still panting with the force of her orgasms.

All at once there was a commotion outside. Shouts rang out, and the roar of a motorcycle could be heard. The men turned and stared toward the door, and as they did it crashed open.

A figure stood framed in the doorway. The shiny black leathers, studded with silver, betrayed the fact that it was a Biker. The eyes darted round the room, then alighted on the naked girl, splayed out over the bench. The eyes were cold, and they took in every inch of her, fixing on the evidence of her recent ravishment.

"Still up to your old tricks I see, my dear."

It was Helda.

Chapter 24

Lia stood on the table, her hands clasped behind her head, her legs spread wide, looking down at the faces below her. The truckers had retreated to the back of the room, and were gathered in a huddle looking very uncomfortable. There were six Bikers besides Helda, some of whom Lia recognised from her days at the Black Cat. Delgado was there too, his face a picture of relief. It was clear to Lia that Helda had not been at all pleased to find she had escaped, and there was little doubt that Delgado would have been severely punished had she not been found.

But she had been found. Somehow they had tracked her down, and now she was back in Helda's clutches. She trembled slightly at the feel of the leather tip of Helda's whip brushing her flesh as the Biker walked round her young captive. Lia's body was still spattered with the drivers' sperm, which had grown cold on her bare flesh as it gently trickled down her body. She knew there were creamy white patches on her cheeks and chin, and longed to be able to wipe them off. But for the moment she was still, not daring to move as her captor examined her body.

"Well, my dear," said Helda, in a menacing tone, "you have led us a dance, haven't you?"

Lia said nothing, her eyes staring straight in front of her, her heart beating fast.

"You very nearly gave us the slip again today," Helda went on. "It was most fortunate for Delgado here that a young man at the refuelling bay saw you climb into the cab of that truck. It had to be you that he saw. After all, who else prances about in service areas in broad daylight whilst stark naked? It took us a while to find a witness to your escape, but he told us all we needed to know. Then it was just a case of finding this little enclosure. But I see you haven't been idle. How many of these truckers managed to have you before we arrived?"

"Five of them," muttered Lia, her eyes cast down.

"Five? In your cunt? I would have thought that was fast going, even for you. Tell us how you managed it."

Lia said nothing.

Thwack!

Helda's whip came down hard on her right buttock, making her stagger.

"Tell us."

"Only two in my cunt."

"And the rest?"

"One between my breasts, one in my mouth. And one..." Lia's voice trailed away.

"Yes?"

"In my bottom."

"Your arse? He fucked your arse? Show me. Bend down and show me."

Lia bent her body forward. She took her hands from behind her head and used them to pull the cheeks of her backside apart. She stood, her face glowing whilst Helda felt her anus. The touch made her sphincter contract, and she felt a trickle of semen escape from her and dribble down her leg.

"Fascinating," said Helda. "Maybe we should sell that orifice more often. There are plenty of men who prefer the tightness of a woman's arse. Stand up again."

Lia straightened, and replaced her hands.

"Is there a shower in this place?" Helda asked the Truckers curtly.

"Through there," muttered Buck, indicating a door at the end of the room.

"Well I think it's time you got cleaned up, young lady. We have to be going. And don't even think of escaping. A couple of my guards here will accompany you inside. I think they'd enjoy that. Now move!"

Lia scrambled down from the table and headed toward the shower room, two burly Bikers just behind her. She pushed open the door and found herself in a spartan washroom, with an old-fashioned shower at one side. It consisted of a pipe that rose up from the floor and bent over, with a wide shower head on the top. Halfway up the pipe was a shiny chrome tap.

There was no curtain, but Lia doubted she would have been allowed to use one anyway. The two Bikers leant against the wall, watching her as she struggled with the tap. The water came in a rush, catching her momentarily by surprise. Its coldness took her breath away, and it was all she could do to remain in its stream. There was a piece of soap on a rack on the wall, and she began to wash herself, sluicing the men's come from her flesh, soaping her breasts and belly, then allowing the icy water to wash it away.

Lia cleaned the truckers out of her, scrubbing every part of her body, before finally turning off the tap. There was no towel, so she stepped wet onto the floor of the bathroom, her body covered with tiny goosepimples, her nipples hard. She made to cross to the door, but one of the Bikers placed a hand on her arm.

Suddenly she felt her arms gripped from behind, her shoulders pinned back so that her breasts were thrust forward. Whilst the first Biker held her thus, the second began feeling her up, clutching at her offered breasts and rubbing them, running a hand up her thigh and penetrating her sex with his finger. Lia tried to struggle, but she was held firm, and almost at once the man's fingers began to stimulate her, sending a thrill through her as he frigged her. At her back she could feel the hardness of the other Biker's cock pressing into her flesh.

"Jeez, it's true what they say about her," said the man who was fingering her. "I've never known a woman come to the boil so quickly."

"You reckon there's time?" began his companion.

"Nah. She'd only have to shower again." He tweaked Lia's nipple between finger and thumb. "Some other time, eh baby?" he said, and with a final thrust into her vagina, he removed his fingers, leaving Lia panting for breath.

They opened the door and led her out. The truckers were still standing in an isolated group, whilst Helda was perched on the table. There was a powerful sexuality about the lady Biker, in her tight leather outfit, her full breasts pressing against the jacket, which was open almost to the waist, revealing a large portion of her ample breasts. Her pants were skin tight, showing off the contours of her long, slim legs beautifully. Her boots were black and shiny, with high, narrow heels and bright silver spurs. She rose cat-like to her feet as Lia entered.

"Hmm, that's a little better," she purred. "Quite delightful really. I'm almost tempted to have you myself. I'm sure you're a real accomplished cunt licker."

The words gave Lia an odd sensation in her stomach. Helda was indeed extremely attractive, and the thought of having her naked was one that greatly appealed to her.

"All set to go then?" asked Helda.

Lia bowed her head.

Suddenly Helda took hold of Lia's hair, pulling her roughly forward. so that the unsuspecting girl stumbled against the table. Helda forced her down on it with her left hand.

Thwack!

Thwack!

Thwack!

Thwack!

Thwack!

Thwack!

She brought her whip down hard on Lia's behind, the strokes falling in quick succession. So quick in fact that the hapless girl had no chance to protect herself and she gave a yell of pain and surprise as the blows rained down.

Six blows. Then she stopped.

Helda was panting with exertion as she looked down at her captive, who writhed with the pain that coursed through her burning behind. The Biker grabbed her hair again and pulled her head round to face her. Her eyes were like thunder.

"Don't ever try to escape from me again," she growled. "Or I'll lock you away where you'll never see the light of day again."

She released Lia, who staggered backwards, shocked by the vehemençe of the woman's tone.

"Get her outside," barked Helda. "We're leaving."

Chapter 25

Lia found it hard to think straight as she roared along the highway on the back of Helda's bike. Her ankles were shackled to the footrests and her hands trapped behind her by two metal cuffs at the rear of the seat. Her mind was numb. Too numb even to cry. After all that work she was back in Helda's hands again, with little or no chance of escape. And she had seemed so close.

If only she had not fallen asleep outside the Countess's house the guards would not have found her. She wondered what the Countess had thought. Whether she suspected that Lia had been abducted, or whether she believed that she had run away. Had she called Thorkil? She hoped she had. At least it would have been some kind of contact between them.

And then there had been the truckers. They would have taken her to Depot twenty-nine, and to her beloved Thorkil. She would have had to endure their treatment of her on the way, but that would have been small price to pay for her return to her true master.

But in the end it had been Helda that had won. Surely she would never risk losing Lia again?

The bikes sped on through the night, the other Bikers flanking Helda, using up the full width of the highway. Only Bikers would have dared to travel at night along these roads. The journey seemed to go on forever, the roar of the motorcycle engine and the rush of wind in her ears blotting out all other sounds, so that she felt deprived of her senses, almost as if in a dream.

Perhaps she had dozed. She wasn't sure. Suddenly, though, she was aware of the Bikers slowing. She looked about her. She had absolutely no idea where she was. All around was dark, and there was no sign of any life.

They pulled off the highway and set off down a long, straight road. Despite the gloom, Lia could see that they were well out of the forest. The land about here was very flat, and almost devoid of vegetation. Leaning round Helda she spotted a light ahead. At first she couldn't make out what it was. Then she saw that a barrier had been lowered across the road, and realised it was a checkpoint. On either side was a high fence, not unlike those that surrounded the depots, but taller and stronger looking.

The barrier was manned by men in uniform, who drew pistols from their holsters as the bikes approached. Helda slowed right down, and seemed about to stop. As they came close to the barrier, however, the men appeared to recognise Helda, and there was a scramble to clear the road and raise the barrier. They achieved this just in time, and Helda and her entourage swept through, giving barely a glance to the guards.

They passed two more such checkpoints, and had a similar reception at each. Clearly, whatever the men were supposed to be guarding, it was not from Helda.

Soon after they had passed the final barrier, a huge building loomed into view. It was like some kind of giant fortress, with turreted walls. Watchtowers were visible every few yards. The entire area about the building was lit by powerful floodlights, and the pencil beams of searchlights raked back and forth across the grounds. The Bikers sped along the length of the edifice, then swung round and came to a halt before a great door. This too was bathed in light and, looking up at it, Lia could read a sign across its top.

It read 'Bleakmoor Prison'.

Ever since the breakdown of law and order, the authorities had struggled to retain some semblance of control over the people. In many cases, particularly in the cities, vigilante squads would roam the streets, meting out swift justice to anyone failing to defer to their authority. The Bikers too, ran large sections of the cities, though it was in the countryside that their influence was strongest. In all cases, the security forces played a secondary role, generally acting with the consent of the Bikers.

The prisons remained, though. Many were used for housing the political opponents of the government, or anyone who wrote or spoke out against the authority of the ruling group. But there was still a need to incarcerate those less pleasant members of the criminal classes who threw themselves at the mercy of the authorities in order to escape the summary justice of the unofficial forces. These were the hard criminals. The terrorists, armed robbers, and murderers.

The regimes in these prisons were severe. All attempts at rehabilitation had long since been abandoned. Nowadays they were ruled with an iron fist, and the order of the day was generally breaking stones or digging trenches.

Lia stared up at the imposing face of the building. Why had they brought her here? And how was it that Helda was able to ride through the checkpoints with such ease?

Helda propped the machine on its stand and walked across to the great doors. She reached for the bell push, but before she could press it a small door set into the main one opened, and a man stepped out.

"Yes Madam?" he said, deferentially.

"Tell the governor I want to see him," said Helda shortly.

The man disappeared inside, and Helda turned to her companions. "Bring her," she ordered.

Two of the men released Lia's ankles and freed her wrists from the seat, leaving them still fastened behind her. Then they led her past the gaping guard and into the prison, the other Bikers and Delgado remaining behind with their machines.

Lia felt very self conscious as she was taken into the great building. All about her were male guards, who regarded her naked body frankly, some giving wolf whistles as she passed. She did her best to ignore them, staring straight ahead of her as she padded over the cold stone floors of the prison. Helda seemed to know exactly where she was going, leading the way down dark corridors and up stone steps, penetrating ever deeper into the building.

At last they came to a door marked 'Governor'. Helda shoved it open and stepped inside.

The office was in stark contrast to the rest of the building. The carpet on the floor was thick and the walls were hung with oil paintings. There was a desk at one end with a large imposing chair behind it. Helda strolled across to this and sat down on it, placing her boots on the desk. She nodded to the escorts to undo Lia's cuffs, then they dragged her across beside the desk.

It was only then that Lia spotted the manacles hanging down from the ceiling, looking strangely out of place in this comfortable room. At once the two Bikers made her lift up her arms whilst they clamped her wrists. Then they pulled on a chain that raised her arms high above her head. Lia caught sight of her reflection in a mirror opposite. The glass had clearly been placed there for just such a purpose, so that whichever miscreant stood in that spot they could see themselves and ponder their fate.

Lia eyed her reflection. Her body was stretched beautifully taut, her firm breasts pulled slightly oval by the tension, the hard, brown nipples pointing slightly upwards. She was standing almost on tiptoe, accentuating the slim shapeliness of her long legs. Even so she was able to place her legs apart, so that the pinkness of her sex lips was evident. She looked at Helda, lounging in the chair, and at the two Bikers leaning against the wall opposite and, despite her situation, felt an oddly pleasurable feeling deep within her. She glanced down at the stripes that still marked her breasts, and imagined the similar ones across her backside, so recently renewed by Helda's crop.

All at once the bondage made her feel extremely aroused, her sex moistening with the realisation of her helplessness. She wished she could touch herself, but the cruel manacles prevented that. She closed her eyes, trying to blot the lustful thoughts from her mind.

The door suddenly opened, making Lia start. She glanced over her shoulder at the man who had come in. He was not very tall, with a balding head and glasses. From his appearance he had obviously dressed in a hurry. His tie was askew, and one shirt tail hung outside his trousers. He stared open-mouthed at the view of Lia's behind he was presented with on entering, and her face glowed as he took in the marks of the cane on her lovely bottom.

"Ah, Governor," said Helda. "So good of you to come." She made no effort to rise from his chair.

"It's always a pleasure to see you, Miss Helda," he said nervously.

"Good. and how are those two I brought in last week?"

"Back in solitary confinement. You did an excellent job, catching them. We might have been searching for them for weeks."

"Well, we can't have escaped prisoners wandering about the countryside," replied Helda. "After all, they might go breaking the law. Now, Governor, I have a little favour to ask you."

"Yes, Miss Helda?"

"This pretty little slut here. I expect you noticed her when you walked in?"

"Well yes."

"She is a problem to me. So pretty don't you think so? Turn round my dear and let the Governor see your tits and cunt."

Lia struggled to turn, but could manage only a few inches, since the chains from which she was hanging were set wide apart.

"So silly of me," said Helda sweetly. "Come round here and take a look Governor."

The man walked round the desk to stand beside Helda. He ran his eyes over Lia's bare flesh. As he did so she could see that a slight sheen of perspiration had broken out on the top of his head, making it shine. She wondered if it was the sight of her that made him sweat so, or his nervousness in Helda's presence.

"Very nice," he said hoarsely.

"Yes she is isn't she?" Helda reached out with her riding crop, teasing Lia's nipples and smiling as they came erect almost immediately. "And so sensitive," she murmured. "But unfortunately she has been the bane of my life of late. Would you believe the little bitch escaped from me, and has been on the run for more than two months? And all the time as naked as you see her now. When I found her this evening she'd just had five men at the same time. Totally shameless!"

The Governor nodded, the beads of moisture on his head growing larger.

"What I need, you see, is to take her out of circulation for a time. There are others searching for her, and I need to take the heat off for a while. I have plans for this young lady, but I'm not ready to implement them as yet. That's where you come in."

"Me, Miss Helda?"

"Certainly. What better place to lose someone than incarcerated in here? After all, some of the people coming into this prison are never seen again, for one reason or another."

The governor flushed. "I can assure you..." he began, but Helda raised her hand.

"Never mind that," she said. "The fact is, I want you to take charge of her for the time being."

"But..."

"No buts. She is to be kept here and treated like any other prisoner."

"But she's a woman."

Helda smiled. "I would have thought that was obvious. Now I want a strict regime. She must be kept busy and kept fit. She is to be caned regularly. Do you understand?"

"Yes Miss Helda." At the mention of the caning the Governor had widened his eyes, and Lia felt a strange thrill run through her.

She had been listening to the conversation with growing amazement. So that was Helda's plan. She was to be incarcerated here. She had been expecting to be returned to the Black Cat. The thought of being in the prison filled her with trepidation. How long would she be here? And what would they do with her? She already knew she was to be thrashed regularly, but she had few illusions what else would befall her, held here with all these desperate men.

Helda rose to her feet. She took Lia's breast in her gloved hand, the feel of the leather on her soft flesh making the girl gasp. Helda leaned forward and kissed her full on the lips, her tongue darting into Lia's mouth whilst her hand continued to knead her breast. Lia responded to the kiss at once, her legs going weak at the sensation of Helda's tongue wrapping itself round her own. She leaned on the leather clad girl, raising her right leg and wrapping it round Helda's so that she could rub her sex against the rough studs that ran down her tight pants. Helda broke away, laughing.

"All in good time, pretty one," she said. She turned to the Governor. "See how responsive she is? I'm sure she'll give you lots of fun."

The Governor was watching, his mouth slightly open, his crotch bulging.

Helda beckoned to her companions and made for the door. As she reached it she turned back.

"One other thing," she said.

"Yes?"

"Keep her naked. I think she secretly likes it, and I know I do."

And with that she was gone.

Lia turned to look at the Governor. He was unbuttoning his pants.

Chapter 26

It was three months before Lia left the prison. Three months of hard work, beatings and sex. She was locked in a cell at night and made to mix with the other inmates during the day. To chronicle her adventures totally would take another book, and perhaps one day that will be written. Suffice to say that her naked body was beaten and fucked by staff and prisoners alike, that she spent hour after hour crushing stones, digging trenches and waiting on the staff. And all the time she took a perverse pleasure from her treatment, occasionally reaching orgasm simply from a well-directed touch, or the stroke of the cane across her behind.

But never a day went by when she didn't think about Thorkil, and wonder if he was still searching for her, or had given her up for lost and was even now sharing his bed, and his belt, with some other girl.

On the day they came for her, it was totally unexpected. She had been working outside on a chain gang cutting wood when she was ordered to go straight to the Governor's office. She had knocked on the door with trepidation. Normally such a summons meant a beating, followed by the Governor's cock rammed into her whilst she lay face down across his desk. It was with a start, therefore, that she found Helda sitting in the Governor's chair once more, smiling sweetly at her.

Lia went to the centre of the room, her hands immediately going to the back of her head, and stood silently, waiting to see what would happen. Helda rose to her feet and approached her, walking round her and inspecting every inch.

"Very nice indeed," she said at last. "Prison life seems to have suited you."

Lia blushed. There was no doubt about it, the prison regime had done her nothing but good. Her body had a lovely tan, not too dark, but covering her all over. Her body was even more lithe than before, the hard work and strict diet toning her muscles to perfection. Even her breasts were firmer, as the result of constant lifting of heavy weights. Her pubic bush had grown back too, though she kept it carefully trimmed on the orders of the warders. All in all she was a picture of beauty, the stripes across her behind simply enhancing the effect.

"Good," said Helda, and the Governor beamed, clearly pleased with her response. "Now, young lady. Are you ready to leave?"

"Yes Mistress."

Lia's reply was given with mixed feelings. Though the prison life had been hard and demanding, as with all things she had grown used to the routine. Returning to Helda meant the unknown. She was certain she was not going back to the Black Cat. Helda had intimated as much before leaving her at the prison. So it was with a beating heart that she followed Helda out through the great doors to where the motorcycles were parked.

The journey was a long one, but Lia didn't mind. It felt good to be away from the dark and gloomy fortress in which she had spent the past quarter year and sitting there, manacled to Helda's machine, the wind blowing through her hair, she felt almost carefree.

It was almost evening when the bikes left the highway and headed off down a minor road, that twisted and turned until it ended at a large building. It was a tall brick-built affair, with none of the brooding darkness of the prison. Lia guessed it was an old manor house, not unlike the Black Cat, but a good deal smaller. As they unshackled her from Helda's machine, Lia looked about her, taking in the beauty of the location. In front of the house was a wide lawn that led down to a lake at the bottom. Beyond was a thick forest that seemed to stretch for miles into the distance.

But she wasn't given much time to admire the view. Helda was hustling her into the house.

Stepping through the door, she was surprised by the decor. Despite its rich exterior, inside the building was sparsely furnished, the floors and walls bare, so that the great entrance hall echoed to the sound of the Bikers' boots as they strode in. On one side a pair of double doors were open, and sneaking a glance inside, Lia could see masses of wires and strange shaped pieces of equipment, none of which meant much to her. She had no time to take a closer look, however, as she was taken through the doors on the other side, through an equally bare room, then down a narrow staircase to the basement. Here she was led into a small stone cell. On the floor was a mattress, and everywhere there hung chains. They stood her against the wall, attaching her hands to manacles that hung down from the ceiling. Then, without a word, they left her, closing the door and plunging her into darkness.

She had no idea how long they left her standing there, her muscles cold and cramped, chained to that rough, hard wall. In the darkness the passage of time was impossible to gauge. At last, however, she heard the sound of someone outside the door. A key grated in the lock, then it swung open, the shaft of light from outside illuminating her body as she hung there.

"Hello again."

She recognised the voice at once. It was Delgado. He was standing, his hands on his hips, grinning at her. "So nice to have you back," he said. "Now come on. I've got to get you ready. There's some very important people here to meet you."

He undid her shackles and led her from the cell. They ascended the stairs once more, and he took her into a large kitchen, with a huge old-fashioned range on which pans were bubbling. A woman, whom Lia took to be the cook, was stirring one of these and she eyed Lia with distaste.

"This is her, I presume," she said.

"This is her," replied Delgado. "A plate of your best game pie please, Mrs Barnes."

The woman gave a snort, and bent down to open the oven door. She scooped a generous portion of pie onto a plate, then set it round with vegetables and potatoes. She placed it on a table on one side of the room. Delgado pulled back a chair and indicated to Lia to sit.

Lia ate hungrily, savouring the richness of the food after the spartan fare she had become used to in the prison. Delgado poured her a glass of red wine, and she quaffed it down, enjoying the warm feeling it gave her.

Once she had finished, Lia was allowed to use the bathroom to wash and tidy her hair. Then her hands were cuffed and she was led back through the house.

Most of the building was deserted, and rather gloomy. Clearly it hadn't been lived in for some time. At the end of one of the corridors, however, a light was streaming out from under a door and beyond it Lia could hear voices. She hesitated on the threshold, suddenly shy of exposing herself to whoever was within, but Delgado simply swung the door open and pushed her inside.

The room was brightly lit and smoky. In the sudden glare Lia found it hard to make anything out. Then her eyes cleared, and she realised there were a number of people in the room. Helda sat in a large chair by the far wall. Beside her was an enormous man, wearing the leathers of a Biker. Despite the fact that he was sitting, Lia could see that he was well over six feet tall, with a huge beer gut that hung over his pants. His face was almost completely hidden by a vast bushy beard, and his eyes glittered below thick eyebrows. Beside him sat a number of other Bikers that Lia did not recognise, as well as those that had accompanied her and Helda from the prison that day.

"Ah, here she is," said Helda, a smile spreading across her mouth. "Lovely, don't you think, Horst?"

The fat man licked his lips. "Very nice," he said. Around him the other members of his entourage mumbled their assent.

"But how rude of me," went on Helda. "I haven't introduced you. This is Horst. He's a film producer."

Lia said nothing as Horst studied her body, his eyes roving over her firm, upturned breasts and neat pubic bush.

"Yes, my dear," went on Helda. "We've been making lots of plans for you over the last few months. You see I have an idea that's going to make you very well known indeed, and me very rich."

Helda nodded to the young man next to her, and he threw a pile of magazines and books at Lia's feet.

"Go ahead," said Helda. "Read them."

Lia stooped and picked up the first magazine. She had seen it before. The warden had shown it to her just before her escape from the Black Cat. It depicted her in the diner, on the table, masturbating herself with the bottle. The copy was lucid and lurid. She put it aside and picked up another. This again pictured her in the diner, this time spread-eagled against the mirror, with the officer's fingers firmly inserted in her sex. The look of passion on her face told it all. She picked up a third. This was a popular tabloid newspaper, and the cover picture displayed her bent over a chair at the Black Cat, whilst a man beside her wielded a cane. The headline read 'Where is kinky Lia?' and went on to describe how she had disappeared after her escape from the Black Cat. Inside there were more photos, and detailed descriptions of what went on at the Black Cat.

There were more. A surprising number. It seemed to Lia that her naked body had appeared on the front of most of the newspapers in the land.

"You see," said Helda. "We've made you quite a celebrity. Almost anybody who reads that sleaze knows your name, and that you're missing. There have been some quite interesting theories as to where you've gone. None of them correct of course."

Lia was barely listening. She was staring at the depictions of her naked body that had been circulated everywhere. She wondered what her former colleagues in the factory and the hostel must think, when they saw her baring her breasts and sex so publicly. And yet at the same time there was something erotic about the idea of all those men ogling her, and suddenly Lia had an image in her brain of a young man holding one of the magazines in his hand and studying her body whilst wanking hard. She imagined him coming, his semen splashing across her photo, and an odd thrill ran through her body. She shivered slightly, a reaction that was not missed by Helda.

"See?" she said to her friends. "She's turned on. I said she would be."

Lia said nothing, trying to blot the image from her mind as Helda spoke again.

"Well, now we've got the public interested, we're going to cash in. Horst here is going to make a film. A film about your adventures. And you're going to be the star."

Lia stared at her in amazement. So this was what she had been preparing! Her stomach churned at the prospect. She had little doubt as to the type of film they would make.

"We start shooting tomorrow," went on Helda. "Of course we've had to change the story slightly. Your little mishap being washed away by the river would be too hard and dangerous to film, so we've decided you're going to be caught trespassing instead." She turned to Delgado. "Have you organised the men who catch her?"

Delgado grinned. "No problem. There's a gang of lumberjacks working in the forest about half a mile away. I had no difficulty persuading three of them to take the parts. And they've got their own horses."

"Excellent," said Helda. "Well, my dear, it's time you were back in your cell and chained for the night. You've got a big day tomorrow."

Chapter 27

The scene depicts a pile of clothes lying on the ground. They are a woman's clothes. A singlet and shorts, bra and pants. As the camera pulls back, we see a camp fire, beside which lie a few tins. The camera pans to the right, and a large picturesque lake fills the picture. In the middle someone is swimming, though at present their shape is vague.

The credits roll up the screen as the camera slowly zooms in on the figure. By the time the director's name has come and gone we can see that the swimmer is a beautiful young girl, and as we watch she rolls onto her back, kicking out so that her body rises to the surface.

She is completely naked. Even at this distance we can discern the plump breasts and the darkness of her pubic bush. She is swimming towards the shore.

The camera moves back to the camp fire, and the pile of clothes, with the swimmer still just visible in the background, though out of focus. As we watch, an arm appears from the left of the screen. It is clearly a man's arm, thick and hairy, with a tattoo just above the wrist. We do not see his face or body, simply the arm as it reaches for the clothes.

The hand picks up the panties, turning them over and rubbing the material between the fingers. Then, with a single gesture, it tosses them onto the fire, where they flare up with a bright flame. The bra, singlet and shorts follow in quick succession, each burning quickly. Then the arm is withdrawn and the focus changes to the girl.

As the camera zooms in on her she rises to her feet, and for the first time we see her breasts in all their glory, the nipples hard with the coldness of the water and pointing upwards. She walks toward us, her image filling the whole frame now, and we wait with anticipation for the lower part of her body to be revealed.

We are not disappointed. Her waist is slim, her belly flat, her pubis covered with a layer of short dark hair. Beneath we can discern the pink of her sex. She is almost completely clear of the water now, walking up the beach naked and innocent, unaware of what lies in wait for her.

She reaches the fire, and a puzzled look crosses her face. She looks about her, searching for her clothes. Then her eye falls on the fire, and she gives a cry of dismay. She tries to rescue her garments with a stick, but they are burnt beyond repair.

The camera pulls back, and behind her we see two men emerge from the bushes. They are tall and strong, naked to the waist, their chests bristling with dark curly hair. Like the arm seen earlier, they too are tattooed, and their faces are rough and unshaven.

Suddenly another figure steps into the frame in front of the girl.

"Oh!" She cries, wrapping one arm across her breasts whilst her other hand drops to cover her crotch. The man is similarly dressed to his companions. The three could almost be brothers.

"What do you think you're doing, swimming in our lake?" the man asks sharply.

"Your lake?"

"That's what I said."

"I'm sorry. I didn't know it belonged to anyone."

"All the land round here is ours. Right up to the edge of the forest. You're trespassing."

"I'm sorry," she repeats.

"Sorry's no good. Round here trespassing's a pretty serious offence. We horsewhip trespassers in these parts."

"Horsewhip?"

"Yeah. Now come here."

He takes a step toward her, and she edges slowly backward. She gets no more than two steps when she is grabbed from behind by the other two men. They pin her arms behind her, revealing her breasts and sex once more. She tries to struggle, but to no avail. One of the men produces a coil of rope from his belt, and they force her back against a tree, where her arms are tied behind the trunk. The three men stand back to admire their captive.

"OK, sister," says the first man. "What the hell are you doing here?"

"I was just camping," she replies in a small voice. "I didn't know it was private property."

"Of course it's private. All the land round here is."

"Well, I'll leave then."

"Damned right you will. But not before you've been horsewhipped."

"But you can't!"

The man moves forward. The camera goes into close up on his hand as he runs it over her breast. She makes a small mewing sound, as her nipple hardens. The camera stays close, as his other hand slides down her belly. She clamps her legs shut.

Smack!

He brings his hand down hard on her inner thigh.

"Open your legs," he barks.

She complies, and he slides his fingers into her slit. He moves his hand back and forth, and she groans aloud. The camera moves to her

163

face. Her lips are slightly open, and she is breathing fast. We return to a close up of her crotch. His fingers are wet now, and her hips are beginning to move, shoving forward against his hand. The man turns to his companions and grins slyly.

"Go and get the horses," he says. "We'll run her off the land."

He withdraws his fingers. The girl is panting now, her face flushed. The camera lingers on her crotch, which is pulsating visibly, the wetness on the lips glistening in the sunshine.

He wanders across and kicks out the embers of the fire, stamping them down, then emptying a can of water on them. The water condenses in a cloud of steam, making a loud hissing sound. Behind him the men are approaching with three horses in tow.

One of the men disappears behind the tree, and the girl's wrists are freed. She stares about her, and for a second we think she is going to try to escape. Clearly the man thinks this too, and he grabs her by the arm. In no time her hands are bound in front of her. She stands, her hands over her crotch, staring at the three men as they saddle up their horses. The camera once again moves in, panning down her body, over the lovely young breasts and down to her sex, and we discover that she is touching herself, her fingers teasing her love bud as she waits. The scene moves back to her face, and her arousal is obvious.

Then all at once they are off, the horses at the trot, their captive forced to break into a run behind them.

We follow her through the wood, tripping and stumbling as she struggles to keep up with the horses, her breasts dancing up and down as she runs. On and on they go, pulling her along behind them. Occasionally she falls, but they do not trouble to check their horses, simply dragging her through the grass until she finds her feet again and runs on.

The scene changes to the edge of the wood. We are shown a fence, topped by barbed wire. There is a gate in the fence, above which is a notice that bears the legend 'No Trespassers'. At that moment we hear the sound of hoofbeats and, sure enough, through the trees, we witness the three horsemen approaching, dragging the hapless girl behind them.

They rein the horses to a stop beside the fence, and the men jump down. The camera lingers on the girl, whose exhaustion is clearly not feigned, her breath coming in great gasps as she struggles to regain her composure.

One of the men takes the end of the rope to which she is tied and drags her across to the fence. It is about ten feet tall and is formed of strong metal links, squares of thick wire about an inch and a half across. She is secured to it, her arms and legs spread wide apart and tied to the links. The camera moves outside the wood looking in, and we see her pressed against the mesh, her breasts flattened, the nipples so hard that they project through.

We return inside the fence as one of the men pulls a horsewhip from his saddlebag and takes some practice swipes, the weapon swishing through the air as he does so. The girl cranes her neck round to watch, an anxious expression on her face. She looks the picture of helplessness, her pert behind thrust backwards, a perfect target for the crop.

Swish! Whack!

The whip comes down squarely on her plump, white buttocks, leaving a thin white stripe that almost at once begins to turn red.

Swish! Whack!

Down comes the whip again. This is no simulation. Both whip and backside are real, and the crack of the leather on her bare flesh rings through the trees.

Swish! Whack!

We are outside looking in again, and the anguish on the girl's face is obvious as her body is thrown against the fence by the blows. But then the camera drops, and we are treated to a view of her open sex, which is visibly twitching, and as yet another stripe is laid across her behind, a sheen of wetness is visible about the lips.

Swish! Whack!
Swish! Whack!
Swish! Whack!

The beating goes on, the blows forming a regular tattoo as they crack down on the girl's behind. We watch her from all angles, no part of her body hidden from our view as her punishment is meted out.

At last, though, the beating ceases, and the man throws the crop aside. The girl is hanging limply from the fence now, her chest heaving, her backside bright red from the blows. And yet, when we see her face in close up, the expression is not one of pain, but of passion, so that as the man slides his hand between her legs and feels for her sex, the cry from her lips is one of pure lust.

"Jeez, the bitch really wants it," the man says, staring at the wetness that covers his hand.

They waste no time in cutting her down from the fence. Once free she drops to her knees. At once one of the men loosens his pants and his cock springs out, thick and hard. The kneeling girl does not hesitate, wrapping her fingers round the shaft and pulling it into her open mouth, sucking noisily at it.

The man sits down on the grass and she buries her face in his groin, her head bobbing up and down as she does so. We are presented with the perfect view of her red and punished behind. Her legs are spread wide, so that her sex is temptingly open. Even as we watch another massive cock is probing at her hole.

The camera closes on her sex as the man's great weapon slips into her, and the muscles of her sex close about his shaft. Then he is fucking her hard, shaking her body with his efforts, making her breasts swing beneath her as she continues to fellate his companion.

The sex goes on and on, the three men taking her in every position imaginable, with none of it missed by the camera's probing eye. The girl shouts and screams as she enjoys innumerable orgasms, none of them faked. By the end she is covered with mud and spunk, her breasts shining with the glutinous fluid that matts her hair and trickles from her cunt.

At last they are sated, and they lift the girl up, carrying her through the gate and depositing her on the ground outside. Then they return to their horses and remount, riding off into the wood with barely a backward glance.

The camera lingers on the girl. She is lying on her back, her legs spread wide apart. As we watch, her fingers creep down to her crotch and she begins to masturbate. The shot pulls back from the writhing figure, panning upwards toward the treetops as once again she orgasms, her cries ringing through the trees.

The picture fades.

Chapter 28

The filming went on for four weeks, during which time Lia was made to relive all the adventures she had had between leaving the city and her time at the Black Cat, with a few variations thought up by Helda thrown in. They recreated the scene in the diner, using a real diner with real truckers, who shouted their delight as she brought herself off in front of them. The scene in the truck cab, where she had been sold to two truckers and had taken them both on at once was also repeated. In fact all her sexual encounters and punishments were recreated in detail under the cold eye of the camera lens, up to and including her first night at the Black Cat, with the raffle, the public whipping and the subsequent gang bang.

For Lia, it was a bittersweet experience, her body kept in a state of constant arousal by the succession of fuckings and beatings she received on the film set. By the end of the fourth week, though, she was exhausted, and was glad to see the final shot in the can.

There then followed a period of relative quiet for the girl. She spent her days doing the housework or assisting the cook, and the nights chained in her cell. During this time she saw nothing of Helda, who she felt sure was no longer at the mansion. Occasionally Bikers would stop by, but otherwise her only companion was Delgado, who supervised her, but never touched her. Clearly he was under orders.

The days passed, and Lia fell into a routine that she found quite pleasant after the gruelling time she had experienced previously. She was no longer beaten, and for the first time in ages her backside was free of blemishes. In the afternoons she would be allowed to lie in the garden, always tethered by an ankle to a strong post, and by the end of another four weeks she looked tanned and fit. During all this time she was not touched, and was forbidden to masturbate, not an easy prospect for one of Lia's desires, particularly since she spent her days naked. During the filming she had once again lost her pubic bush and her bare cunt often ached to be touched or penetrated.

Then, almost six weeks after the departure of the film crew, Helda came back. It was quite unexpected. One minute Lia had been relaxing in the sun, the next a shadow had fallen across her face and she opened her eyes to find the woman Biker standing over her.

"So here you are," said Helda. "My, they've been pampering you, haven't they? Have you been looked after well?"

"Yes Mistress."

Thwack!

Helda's riding crop came down hard across her thigh, making her jump with surprise.

"Don't you stand up in your Mistress's presence?" she snarled.

Lia leapt to her feet, cursing herself for allowing her guard to drop so easily. She stood stiffly, hands behind her head.

"That's better," said Helda. "We can't have you forgetting your training. I'll have to have a few words with Delgado. Why, by the look of that backside you haven't been beaten for ages. Has Delgado been fucking you?"

"No Mistress."

"And have you been frigging yourself?"

"No Mistress."

"Good. Give me your cunt."

Lia had not heard the command since her days at the Black Cat, but she remembered only too well what was required of her. At once she thrust her hips forward, bending her knees slightly in a lewd gesture of submission.

Helda reached out a hand, running it between Lia's legs and sliding a finger into her. The reaction was electric, Lia's whole body stiffening, a moan escaping from her lips. She had almost forgotten how delicious it was to be touched so intimately.

"Mmm," said Helda. "Nicely on the boil I see. Well young lady, your little holiday is over. Tonight you begin earning money once more. I'll explain it all to you after dinner."

And with that she turned and strolled away.

All through her evening meal Lia's stomach was so full of butterflies she could hardly eat. What could Helda have meant? A return to the Black Cat? The thought of going back to that place sent a shiver down her spine, as feelings of fear and pleasure ran through her. She thought of how she had been used there as a plaything for anyone who could afford her. Of the humiliation and the beatings. But she thought too of the way she had felt so stimulated, of the orgasms that had filled her, often many times a night, and a warmth crept into her groin.

Delgado came for her soon after she had finished eating, and led her to the room where all those weeks before she had been introduced to the film crew. Helda was waiting for her, along with two other Bikers she recognised from previous visits.

"Do come in, my dear," said Helda. "How was your dinner?"

"Very good thank you, Mistress."

"I'm glad to hear it. We have to keep you strong for what's to come. Would you like to know what's in store for you?"

"Yes please, Mistress."

"You remember all that publicity we'd organised for you? All those magazine and newspaper articles?"

"Yes Mistress."

"Well they're still interested. Look at this."

She tossed another pile of newspapers at Lia's feet. With a sense of foreboding, Lia stooped down and picked up some of them.

'Biker's Girl Found!' screamed the headline on the top paper, alongside yet another photo of Lia nude. She scanned the story. It told of how 'Biker sources' had informed the paper that Lia was back in the keeping of the owner of the Black Cat, and that she was shortly to star in a film of her own escapades. The other papers had similar copy, with speculation about the film itself and what would be shown, some of it clearly informed speculation. Lia read through a few more, then placed them back on the floor, her face red.

"You see? You're even more of a celebrity now," said Helda. "There's a lot of people looking forward to seeing you. Look at this."

She passed Lia a roll of paper. Lia took it and unfurled it. It was a poster, and she stared at it, her mouth open.

At the centre stood a picture of Lia, hanging naked from chains, whilst a fierce looking Biker laid a whip across her behind. All around were smaller pictures, depicting scenes from the film. In one she was rising from the lake, and in another she was standing on the highway, one hand thumbing a lift whilst the other was between her legs. Across the top, in large red letters were the words 'Biker's Girl', and below, in smaller type, 'A new dimension in erotica'. Lia's colour deepened as she took it in. She rolled it up and passed it back to the smiling Helda.

"I hope you're good at public appearances," she said. "The film opens tomorrow, and you're the guest of honour. A personal appearance, no less. You'll enjoy that, won't you?"

Lia said nothing.

"Meanwhile," she went on. "We'd better put a few fresh stripes across that pretty little behind of yours. We don't want to disappoint your public. After all, they'll be expecting it. Now bend over that chair."

And she pulled her riding crop from her belt.

Chapter 29

Lia peered anxiously from the heavily tinted window of the car as it swept through the streets of the city, a pair of Bikers in front and behind as escorts. This was the first time she had returned to the city since her escape from the watchman all that time ago, and it was strange to see all the old sights once more. Nothing much seemed to have changed. The streets were still strewn with litter, the shop fronts fitted with heavy metal shutters, gangs of youths gathered on every corner.

The car turned down a road that was very familiar to Lia. At the end was the shabby frontage of the hostel in which she had lived before making her escape and falling into the hands of the Bikers. She gazed out at it. She felt no nostalgia, towards it. Her life at the hostel had not been a happy one. Still, she wondered what the inhabitants would make of her now. When she had lived there she had been a shy and demure girl, who kept herself to herself. What would they think of the naked beauty who sat in the car, her wrists and elbows pinned behind her, her lovely breasts thrust forward as if inviting caresses? Yet she was still Lia, and the shyness had not gone. It was simply that she had discovered a desire within herself that she did not understand, but which drove her to accept, to relish even, the cruel treatment that the Bikers meted out to her.

They swept by the hostel, and made another turn. Lia recognised the area as one protected by the Bikers. This was an area she would not have entered in her days at the hostel. Despite the fact that the crime in Biker controlled districts was much less than in others, no young girl would ever have ventured there without an escort. Stories abounded of such women being picked up by passing Bikers. At best they could expect to be released after a night of depravity. At worst, they could be carried off and not seen again. And now, here she was, right in the middle of the area, staring out at the men and women in leathers who patrolled the streets.

They rounded another bend, and a huge building loomed ahead. It might once have been a sports stadium. Certainly it seemed far too large to be a cinema, though that was the legend in six foot high letters across the wall. But it wasn't that sign that caught Lia's eye.

Above the entrance to the building was a huge figure, at least forty leather. Her legs beneath were encased in black fishnet stockings, and the suspenders that held them up were revealed with every step she took. Her shiny boots were of knee length, with a thin, high heel. On top she feet high. It was a photograph. A vast cutout figure that dominated the front of the building.

It was of Lia.

She was seated on the saddle of a motorcycle, her feet stretched forward, the toes pointed. Her body was leaning backwards, her hands stretched behind her and cuffed to the back of the seat. She was totally naked.

Lia stared at the image in fascination. She had never seen anything like it. It was extraordinarily erotic. She recalled the day it had been taken. Afterwards the photographer had been so turned on that he had fucked her twice across the padded seat of the bike. She had never dreamed the shots would be displayed so publicly though. She glanced across at Helda, who sat beside her in the car. The woman smiled.

"Do you like it?" she asked. "It's certainly caused a stir. That cinema will take three thousand people and we expect to sell every ticket tonight. . Look, they're queuing already."

Sure enough, outside the cinema were hundreds of people, all queuing patiently in a line that ran alongside the building and round the corner out of sight. A set of crash barriers had been erected, along which patrolled a number of Bikers. The people gazed idly at the car as it passed them. Lia wondered what their reaction would be if they could have seen who was inside.

They passed the cinema and sped on through the city streets, finally pulling up outside a huge reinforced gate. As Lia watched, the gate swung slowly open, and the car purred through.

They came to a halt outside a large town house. It was completely surrounded by the high fence, with small lookout towers overlooking front and rear. A man opened Lia's door and she stepped out. He took her by the arm and led her inside. Helda did not follow.

It was two hours later before she saw Helda again. In that time she was bathed, her hair was brushed and her face made up. Then her hands were shackled as before and she was taken out into the courtyard once more.

There, parked in the drive, was the most magnificent motorcycle she had ever seen. It was covered in gleaming chrome, the paintwork airbrushed with scenes of Bikers riding along open roads in golden sunlight. The tyres were wide and fat, the exhaust pipes spotless and shining, sweeping up the machine on either side. It was almost a work of art.

Footsteps sounded from the house, and Lia turned to see Helda walking towards her. She wore the tiniest of miniskirts, made of fine black wore a short leather jacket, tailored perfectly to her shoulders, but only reaching to just below her breasts, so that her midriff was bare. The jacket was joined at the front by a shiny chain, which left it open about an inch. Beneath it she wore nothing. On her head was a cap, again of leather, almost military in appearance, and her eyes were shrouded by mirrored sunglasses. Lia had never seen her look so sexy.

She strode toward Lia, the ever present whip dangling from her belt.

"All ready for your big night?" she asked.

Lia did not reply.

Helda took hold of Lia by the chin, turning her head round to face her.

"Now listen carefully," she said. "I want no funny business tonight. You're to do exactly as you're told. Do you understand?"

"Yes Mistress."

"And don't even think of trying to get away. My people are everywhere. All right?"

"Yes Mistress."

"All right. Get on the bike."

Lia straddled the magnificent machine, the leather feeling smooth and soft against her backside There was a click as her cuffs were fastened to the seat behind her. Once Helda was satisfied that Lia was in position, she too climbed aboard, apparently careless of the fact that her skirt rode right up in the process, baring the creamy white of the top of her thighs and revealing the tight leather thong that covered her sex.

Lia's heart beat fast as she saw the gate begin to swing open. She looked down at herself. Her nipples were hard, and she knew that this was in anticipation of the ride through the city that was to come. Even for Lia, this would be an outrageous act. At least in the country, the people were few and far between. The city teemed with people. And she was about to be driven through them totally nude. Her stomach gave a little lurch as the machine's engine growled into life.

The ride took them through the busiest part of the city. Everywhere people turned their heads and pointed as they passed. They did not ride fast, so that passers-by were treated to a long look at the sexy woman Biker, carrying her naked captive along. Behind them rode two more Bikers, there to prevent trouble. But their presence was unnecessary. The people kept well clear of the machine, awed by the presence of Helda.

At last the bike swung round a bend, and the cinema came into view. The image of Lia was brightly lit now, and as they came closer Lia could see that the queue had grown, so that it now snaked round and back to the front of the building. As they came closer, Helda revved the engine, and all eyes were turned their way. Lia could see fingers pointing at her, and across the street cars were drawing up as their occupants craned their necks to get a view of her. She had never been naked in such a public place before, and her stomach churned at the thought of her outrageous situation.

Helda drew the machine to a halt and cut the ignition. Immediately Lia was able to hear the hubbub of the crowd as it surged toward the barriers.

Helda climbed from the machine, pausing to adjust her skirt before turning to Lia.

"See that poster?" she said, unnecessarily.

Lia nodded.

"Pose like that."

Lia glanced nervously about her. It had been one thing posing in so lewd a manner before a photographer. To do so here, in the middle of a busy city street was quite another. She turned her eyes pleadingly on Helda, hoping to see a spark of mercy, but there was none.

"Pose!" the Biker ordered.

Her face glowing red, Lia slid her backside down the saddle, at the same time opening her legs a little wider. A wolf whistle sounded from the crowd, then another. Lia knew that every eye was upon her, and that what she was doing was totally brazen.

And at that moment, as Helda had known it would, the perverseness of Lia's nature came to the fore. In her mind, Lia could picture how she must look, naked and apparently shameless before all these normally clad people, showing off her body with abandon. The thought sent a sudden thrill right through her, and instead of showing the modesty she knew she should, she found herself raising her backside slightly, aware that this made her open sex still more visible. She did not understand her lack of shame, but she knew that the eyes of the crowd excited her greatly. She wished she could caress her sex.

Suddenly there was a bright flash. Then another, and Lia blinked as a crowd of photographers pushed forward. So Helda had invited the press! Of course she should have realised that would happen. After all the pre-publicity she had arranged, it was obvious they would be here. And there would be no question that the authorities would intervene, despite the indecency of her situation, lying bound and naked across a motorcycle in the middle of a busy street. This was Biker territory, and what Helda wanted she got.

"Look over here love. Pout your lips. That's it."

"Raise your backside a bit higher."

"Over this way. Can you push your tits forward a bit more? Great!"

"Lick your lips. Look as though you really want it."

Lia responded almost automatically to their demands, displaying her young body to them as best she could, despite her bonds, spreading her legs as wide as she was able to ensure they could see the wetness within her. The cameras were exciting her greatly, as they always did. Why was it that she felt the need to display herself in this way?

"Jeez. Someone's been whipping her arse. Untie her Helda so we can have a good look."

Lia's face reddened as she heard the request, aware of the sight that the stripes across her backside must make, and of the way in which they emphasised her submissiveness.

Helda move forward and undid the lock that secured her to the seat.

"Kneel up on it," she ordered.

It wasn't easy with her arms pinned, but Lia managed to manoeuvre herself up until she was kneeling on the machine, the flash bulbs still popping all round her.

"Press your tits down on the seat and raise your backside," ordered Helda.

Lia obeyed with an eagerness that was obvious to those watching, raising her bottom as high as she was able, displaying the cruel red stripes to photographers and crowd alike, a thrill pulsing through her sex as she realised what a sight she must make.

The photo session went on for a further ten minutes. Lia was made to take up every pose imaginable as the photographers took their shots, her sex pulsing with excitement at being so publicly nude. Somehow, the thought of the crowd gathered in the road, and of the cinema queue that was filing past her just a few feet away made her position overwhelmingly arousing. The men and women's stares as they slowly made their way into the building were like physical caresses to the passionate young girl.

More than anything else she wanted to frig herself, and would have done so, even here in the street, but for her bonds. When they made her straddle the front wheel of the machine she was able to rub her sex against the roughness of the tyre, small cries escaping from her lips as her hips pumped back and forth. But Helda spotted what she was doing at once and dragged her off. The watchers laughed at this, pointing at the streak of wetness that had been left behind on the rubber.

At last the photographers were satisfied, and Lia was ordered to stand beside the motorcycle. There then followed a news conference, still out in the street. The reporters shouting their questions to Helda, whilst Lia stood by her side.

"Why is she naked?"

"She prefers it that way. She has no clothes."

"None at all?"

"She has no need of them. She exists only to give pleasure with her body."

Lia pondered that answer. It was true, of course, though not something she had admitted to herself before. And in a way she felt proud of it. Who else could thrill so many people at the same time? If her function was to give pleasure, then it was a function she carried out very well. She looked at the faces of the reporters and saw that they hungered for her. She wondered how many men would masturbate over her photo in the following day's paper, and her sex convulsed once more.

"Was she forced into any of the scenes in the film?"

"Every orgasm depicted is genuine. She is an extremely sensual young person."

"And the punishments?"

"The beatings too give her pleasure. There is physical evidence of arousal after she has been whipped."

"Why is she shaved?"

"To keep her sex visible. To remind you of her desire to be fucked."

"Can't she speak for herself?"

"She speaks in the film, don't you my dear?"

"Yes Mistress."

The questions went on, and Helda continued to answer them, somehow never admitting Lia's status as a captive, or her desire to be with the one she loved.

At last Helda called a halt. The doors of the cinema were closed now, and the Bikers on the door were turning the unlucky ones away. Taking Lia by the arm, Helda led her inside.

She took Lia down a dark corridor that led beneath the auditorium, and into a small, bare room. Here she released the cuffs, and Lia was allowed to stretch her cramped limbs. Helda patted the girl's hair and checked her all over.

"Right," she said. "Time to go to your premiere."

She led Lia up a narrow staircase. As they climbed higher the noise of the crowd reached her ears, faint at first, but growing louder with every step. Lia realised that they were headed for the auditorium itself, and her heart began to beat fast.

The stairs ended in a door, and as Lia stepped through it the roar of the crowd washed over her. She was actually stepping out onto a stage in front of the cinema screen, and before her were a sea of faces, all cheering and whistling. Helda took her to centre stage. She held up a hand, and the deafening roar began to die down, until at last the auditorium was silent.

"As you can see," she began. "The star of tonight's show is with us."

A cheer went up once more.

"Both she and I are as anxious to watch the film as you are, so I'll be brief. As you will no doubt have noticed, the best seats in the house are in the middle there." She indicated a platform, set about halfway back down the auditorium. It was dead in the centre, the seats directly behind it removed since it would have been impossible to see the screen from them. On each side of the platform was a divan, with one end raised, similar to those used by the New Age priestesses.

"I shall be using one of the couches," Helda went on. "And our star will be on the other. I expect there's plenty of you here who would like to join her."

A roar of approval went up from the crowd.

"Well someone's going to be lucky."

At this, the crowd went silent, and Lia turned to stare at the Biker.

"Each one of you has a number on the seat in front of you," went on Helda to the hushed crowd. "We're going to draw a number, and the winner gets to join our star during the film."

Lia gasped. It was like her first night at the Black Cat all over again. She was being raffled. She glanced up at the divan, and felt an odd feeling in her stomach, that rapidly turned into a warm wetness in her sex. Somewhere out in the crowd was a man, or a woman, who would join her to watch the film. She watched as a Biker came onto the stage beside them with a bag in his hand. He held it out to Helda, who dipped inside and pulled out a number.

"Two three seven nine," she called.

For a moment there was silence. Then someone shouted out from the rear of the auditorium. Heads craned round as a figure rose from a seat in the balcony, hands held aloft. Lia squinted up. It was a man. Quite a young one as far as she could see. Before she could tell any more, though, he had turned and was making his way down toward the stage.

Helda led Lia forward, down a short flight of steps and up the centre of the auditorium. As she walked up beside the seats, hands reached out for her, groping for her breasts. She did her best to ignore them, holding her head high as she made her way to the platform.

She preceded Helda up to the raised area. The Biker indicated the divan, and Lia perched herself on the edge of it, nervously. She looked out at the faces below, waiting for her companion to join her. As she watched, a figure appeared, making its way through the crowd, and she felt a sudden perverse thrill as she contemplated what was happening, her body tingling with anticipation after the weeks of deprivation Helda had imposed on her. She looked across at Helda. The woman was smiling at her, aware of Lia's excitement.

Lia dropped her eyes, embarrassed by her own wantonness.

The man had reached the platform and was climbing up. Lia saw him close up for the first time. He was older than she had thought, probably in his mid forties, his hair slightly greying. He wore dark slacks and a casual jacket. He stood before her now, eyeing her coolly.

Helda had risen to her feet as he approached, and she took him by the hand.

"What's your name?" she asked.

"Jerry." His voice was deep, and full of authority.

"Well Jerry, meet Lia. She's your date for the film."

Lia took his hand, her face glowing red. It all seemed so oddly formal, shaking hands with this man as if they were meeting at a cocktail party, whereas she was naked in front of hundreds of people, and about to give her body to him.

The man seated himself beside her, and there was a break whilst the press moved in and more photographs were taken. He wrapped an arm about her for the shots, his grip firm. Her body tingled as he pressed himself against her, reaching up under her arm as the bulbs flashed and toying idly with her nipple.

The lights dimmed, and the film began. The screen was huge, and Lia watched enthralled as her image emerged from the lake. Jerry sat, his arm still round her, his fingers rubbing up and down over her flesh.

When the men began to whip her, Jerry took her hand and guided it to his crotch. She rubbed his pants, feeling the hardness underneath, and found her own arousal growing by the second.

As the whipping continued, his fingers slid down to her behind, feeling for the marks of Helda's whip. Then her leant across and whispered in her ear.

"Suck me."

The excited girl dropped to her knees at once, her fingers at his belt, pulling it undone. She slid down his fly, and freed his cock from his pants. She fingered its thick shaft, marvelling at its rigidity. Then she lowered her head and began to suck on its swollen end, tasting his arousal as she did so. Out of the corner of her eye she could see Helda watching her, and she knew that many of the audience would be doing the same. From the screen came the cries of her first orgasm. There were many more to come.

"Kneel on the couch, with your tits over the end."

Lia had been sucking him for about five minutes when he gave the command. He spoke quite loudly, so that the people around them could hear. A mass of eyes turned in her direction as she released his glistening cock from her mouth and scrambled to obey him.

She knelt on the leather surface of the divan, then leaned forward over the raised end, letting her breasts dangle invitingly. She spread her legs as wide as she was able, presenting herself to him unambiguously. She glanced up at the screen, where she could be seen struggling through the diner with a tray of drinks as dozens of hands reached out for her body.

When he touched her sex she gave a cry of pleasure. It seemed forever since she had been touched there, and the desire within her was intense. She shoved her backside back at him, revealing the moist interior, and grunted with pleasure as he accepted the invitation, sliding his fingers into her.

She had neither expected nor intended to come so quickly, but the watching eyes and the sight of herself being touched up by the officer on the screen, combined with her recent deprivation, were too much for her. Suddenly her body was wracked by an orgasm, hoarse cries coming from her lips as her sex closed about his hands, her hips pumping back and forth.

Seconds later he was inside her, his cock buried deep within her vagina. He began to fuck her at once. On the screen her alter ego was also being filled with a thick manhood, this one belonging to the officer. In the film version he took her in the diner itself, in front of all the truckers, spread across a table on her back, her legs wide open.

Lia's cries were almost drowning those on the soundtrack now as Jerry fucked her hard. All about her eyes were turned in her direction, watching her breasts bounce back and forth as he rammed his body against hers. Lia knew she was putting on a shameful exhibition, but she didn't care now. All she cared about was the cock inside her, and her own intense pleasure as it plundered her, the thrusts growing faster and faster. She braced herself to accept his spunk.

He came in her with a shout, his hot sperm filling her, making her moan with pleasure, all decorum forgotten as her own orgasm overcame her. His hips went on pumping, shaking her whole body with their ferociousness as spurt after spurt of semen shot from him into her sex. The orgasm seemed never ending to her, but as last she sensed that he was spent, his motions becoming slower and slower until he collapsed on top

178

of her, pinning her to the couch.

The ripple of applause from the crowd rose in volume until a deafening roar filled the ears of the wanton, shameless girl as she lay, her eyes closed, her hips still slowly gyrating.

Chapter 30

For the next three weeks, Lia spent every evening at the cinema, appearing at two performances a night. Each night she would have a different partner. She lost count of the number of times she achieved orgasm on that most public couch. The auditorium was packed out for every showing, as news of the film, and of Lia's performances, spread.

Her lovers ranged from eighteen to nearly seventy, all with differing desires. On one night she was joined by a girl with orange hair and pierced nose and ears who brought Lia off more times than she could remember with the aid of a massive vibrator. On another, the man insisted on taking her in the backside, whilst on a third her companion just watched as Lia masturbated herself

Every two or three days Helda would have her beaten in order to keep the marks on her backside fresh. Sometimes she would do it herself, sometimes she would get another Biker to do it. Occasionally Lia was given the cane and ordered to choose someone from the queue to administer her punishment. She would be made to walk out of the theatre apparently unescorted, though the Bikers were always close at hand to prevent her escape. Once in the street, she would make her way, naked along the crash barriers as the crowd whistled and shouted, until she finally picked someone out and handed him the cane. He would then administer the beating in the middle of the street under Helda's supervision. Somehow Lia found these public thrashings the most arousing of all, and from the moment the beating ended until she had a cock inside her, her whole body would be tense with desire.

It was in the fourth week that matters took a new turn.

The first performance had just ended. Lia's partner had been a young labourer and he had taken full advantage of the situation, managing to fuck her four times during the performance, making her come again and again on the end of his rampant young cock. She was in the shower room, washing him from her in preparation for the second performance when something flew over the top of the curtain and into the cubicle, landing on the floor with a clatter.

Lia jumped at the sudden noise, swinging round to see what it was that had startled her. There, lying on the floor of the cubicle, was a stone wrapped in a piece of screwed up paper. For a second she just stared at it. Then she saw that there was writing on the paper. Hurriedly she snatched it up before the water could wash the words away.

Her heart racing, she unwrapped the stone and studied what was written on the sheet. The ink had run slightly, but the message was clear.

'Go to the Ladies at ten o'clock.'

She turned it over. There was no signature on it, nor any way of telling who had written it. She peered out of the cubicle. Opposite was a window, open, but heavily barred to prevent escape. She crossed the room and looked out. She was on the first floor, and beneath was a courtyard, where the dustbins were kept. The yard was deserted, but it was clear that anyone could have thrown the note from there, had they known where she was. And the sound of the shower would have been audible from below.

She read the note again. Ten o'clock! The second performance began at nine-thirty, so the film would be well under way by then. She wondered at the significance of the message. She was permitted to use the Ladies during the show, provided she was accompanied to the door by a Biker and spent no more than two minutes inside. Escape was impossible anyway, since, like here, the windows were heavily barred. Her mind raced. Of course it might have been a hoax, or some sex-starved punter anxious to fuck her. But in the Ladies?

She glanced at the clock. Nine-fifteen. There was no time to ponder further. She had to be on her way. They would draw the winning number in ten minutes. Hurriedly she dried herself. Then, pausing to flush the note down the toilet, she stepped out to where the burly Biker guard was waiting. Ten minutes later she was in the arms of a middle-aged bank clerk, who was licking her breasts enthusiastically.

The man continued his attentions as the film began. Next to them Helda watched idly. She hardly ever attended the screenings now, but this was a night when Lia had been due for a beating so she had been on hand to supervise. The neat red stripes criss-crossing Lia's backside testified to the fact that the punishment had been efficiently carried out. Tonight, though, her presence made Lia very nervous. Whoever had sent the message clearly didn't want Helda to know about it, and Lia found her heart beating fast as the hands on the clock crept toward ten o'clock.

As the time grew close, Lia found herself on her knees, the man's cock filling her mouth as she sucked hard at it. He was moaning softly and she knew it would not be long before he would want to be inside her. She glanced sideways at the clock. It was one minute to ten. She raised her head, still gently wanking him.

"Please Master."

"What is it?"

"I need to visit the Ladies, Master."

181

"Can't it wait?"

"No Master."

The man turned to Helda and raised an eyebrow. She gave a nod.

Lia rose from the floor of the platform and slowly descended the steps to where her guard was waiting. It was dark in the auditorium and she picked her way carefully between the seats, almost oblivious to the hands that reached out to pinch and squeeze her flesh.

They reached the door to the Ladies, and the guard checked his watch.

"Two minutes," he said. Lia nodded.

She stepped into the toilet. The room was brightly lit, with a row of cubicles running along one wall and sinks and mirrors opposite. At first she thought she was alone, but then she noticed that one of the cubicle doors was closed. She stood, uncertain what to do. Should she knock on the door? But what if it was a trap of some sort?

Her dilemma was solved by the sound of the lock on the cubicle door being undone. As Lia watched, the door swung open and someone stepped out. Lia stared at the woman for a moment, then her jaw dropped in surprise.

It was the Countess.

She was completely naked, standing coolly as Lia's eyes travelled down her body. Her full breasts looked plump and inviting, her waist slim. Then Lia realised with a shock that the woman had shaved her pubis. Her mound was as smooth as Lia's own, her slit completely revealed. The sight of it gave Lia an odd feeling in her belly as she realised that her own sex must be equally seductive.

Lia narrowed her eyes. There was something else different about the Countess. It was her hair. The style and colour were totally different from how she remembered. The woman must be wearing a wig. Lia opened her mouth to ask why, but the Countess put a finger to her lips.

"Hush," she said. "We haven't much time. Come here."

She beckoned Lia across to stand beside her, and indicated the mirror on the wall. Then it struck Lia. The wig, was meant to make the Countess resemble her. So too was her nakedness, and her shaved crotch. Staring at her in this bright light, the similarities were obvious. In the darkness of the auditorium, it was quite possible they would be mistaken for one another, especially since, with her breasts, sex and backside bare, it was unlikely they would be paying much attention to her face.

"Now listen young lady," whispered the Countess. "If this escape is going to work, you've got to do exactly what I say."

"Escape?"

"Certainly. You don't think I'm here like this for the good of my health do you? Although I have to admit it is rather sexy. Feel how wet I am."

She took Lia's hand in hers and guided it to her bare crotch. It was indeed very wet, and felt soft and warm under Lia's touch. She caressed the Countess's love bud gently.

"Mmm," for a moment the woman seemed to forget her mission as Lia's fingers stroked her. Then she brushed the hand away.

"We'll have time for that later," she whispered. "Meanwhile we've got to get you out of here."

"But how?"

"The bars at the end window have been removed. As soon as I've gone, climb through and wait in the courtyard."

"Where are you going?"

"Out there." The Countess indicated the door to the auditorium. "I'm going to play Biker's girl for the evening. And I can tell you the idea makes me horny as hell."

"But what about Helda?" said Lia, anxiously. She'll..."

"Helda won't touch me," said the Countess. "She wouldn't dare. I've got far too many friends in high places. Now pay attention. Once you're outside, just stay put and listen for the bikes. As soon as you hear them approaching, run round the front."

Lia took the Countess's hand. "Are you sure you'll be all right?" she whispered.

"Of course. What were you doing with your partner just before you came in?"

"I - I was sucking his cock."

"A nice thick one, I hope?"

Lia blushed and said nothing.

"I'd better get going," said the Countess. "Now, you just look after yourself." She leaned forward and kissed Lia on the lips. "Good luck," she whispered.

Then she was on her way, her firm backside wriggling just as Lia's did as she set off out of the door.

Lia stood for a second, staring after her, then she turned and headed for the cubicle. She pushed open the door and peered through. Sure enough the bars had gone from the window. She climbed onto the lavatory seat and looked out. The courtyard was deserted. She took a final glance behind her, then levered herself onto the sill, crouched there for a second, then dropped to the ground on the other side.

For a second she remained where she was, staying perfectly still and listening hard. There was nobody about. She straightened and made her way across the courtyard to the corner of the building. She took a quick glance round the corner. The road seemed empty. She leant back against the wall, her ears straining for the sound of a motorcycle. All she could do now was wait.

Back in the auditorium, the Countess had run the gauntlet of the audience and had mounted the platform, where Lia's companion still sat, his erect cock still jutting from his flies. The Countess held her head down as she approached, not looking toward Helda. As soon as she reached him she dropped to her knees and took the man into her mouth, letting the long tresses of the wig fall across her face, obscuring it from view. She began to suck, her head bobbing up and down as the man gave a sigh of satisfaction.

Like Lia, the Countess too was listening hard for the sound of the bikes. So far everything seemed to be going like clockwork.

"On the couch."

At first the Countess barely heard the command, as it had been delivered in a low voice.

"I said on the couch."

Suddenly she realised he was addressing her. Still keeping her head low, she rose to sit beside him.

"On your hands and knees, and get that arse of yours up in the air. I want to see everything."

Despite herself, the Countess felt a thrill of pleasure at the command. When they had made the plan, she had decided that if she was going to go through with it, she might as well enjoy it. She perched on the couch, deliberately facing away from Helda. Then she pressed her breasts down against the surface, raising her behind toward the man. She gave a little gasp of pleasure as his fingers penetrated her.

He frigged her for a minute or two, sliding his fingers in and out, feeling the heat and wetness that was welling up inside her. The Countess was very aroused now, her hips pumping back and forth in anticipation of the fucking she knew was to come.

"Raise your behind higher."

It was when he made this demand that Helda must have glanced across at them. The Countess made quite a sight, her lovely rounded backside raised up for the attention of her lover, her gaping sex stretched wide to receive his swollen cock.

Helda turned back to the film. Then she blinked and stared at the Countess's behind once more. Her eyes widened.

"Wait a minute. You!"

The man turned his head. He was crouched behind the Countess and about to penetrate her.

"Get out of the way," Helda ordered.

The Countess remained where she was, her face buried in the leather of the couch as she felt the man move slightly to one side of her. Behind her she heard Helda rise to her feet, and the click of her heels as she crossed the platform.

For a second there was silence. Then she felt Helda's gloved hand on her behind.

"Where are the stripes?" Helda shouted suddenly. "The bitch was whipped less than two hours ago. Where are the stripes?"

The Countess said nothing, her face still hidden. She could feel the man's cock pressing against her backside once more as he hesitated, staring at Helda.

Helda grabbed the Countess's hair, trying to yank her face round. All she got was the wig. Then the Countess turned to face her. For a moment nothing was said as the two women stared at one another.

"You!" said Helda, incredulously.

The Countess giggled. "Expecting someone else, dearie?"

Helda opened her mouth to reply. Then closed it again. She swung round. "The Ladies," she shouted. "That's where she went."

She set off at a run in the direction of the toilet, shoving people aside in her haste to reach it. The Countess's companion stared after her, his mouth agape.

The Countess reached for his cock. There was nothing else she could do.

"Come on," she said, guiding him toward her aching sex. "You've got me so horny I can't stop now. Fuck me. Fuck me hard."

Outside Lia was unaware that the Countess's plan had been discovered. She stood with her back pressed against the wall, still trying to pick up the sound of the Bikers. Then she heard a shout. Across the courtyard a face had appeared at the window. It was Helda.

"You!" she shouted, pointing at Lia. "Come back."

Lia's heart sank. Discovered. The plan had failed. She was back in Helda's clutches. A feeling of desperation gripped her. Escape had seemed so close. It was all too disappointing.

Then suddenly she knew she had to go on. After all, the Countess had worked so hard on the plan, and she was already halfway towards freedom. She couldn't stop now. She felt a sudden surge of adrenaline fill her veins, and, without stopping to think, she made a dash for it, heading out towards the open road, oblivious to her nakedness.

The road at the front of the theatre was almost deserted, just one or two passers-by staring in amazement at the young girl who suddenly appeared from behind the building. She stopped at the junction for a second, looking right and left. Then she set off up the road, praying that she was going the right way.

Lia ran hard, not daring to look behind her, but aware that she was being pursued. She hoped desperately that they would not have time to go for their motorcycles. The road was hard, and her bare feet made a slapping sound as she rushed along.

Ahead the lights were getting brighter, and she could see there were more people about. Still she ran on, oblivious to the shouts and whistles of the people as she sprinted past them, her breasts bouncing deliciously as she went. Behind her she could hear shouts and she recognised the voice as that of Helda, who must be pursuing her in person. Lia knew that it was only a matter of time before she encountered another Biker, who would head her off.

Then she heard it. The far off roar of a motorcycle. At almost the same time she saw three powerful headlights appear in the distance. The machines were rocketing towards her, and she was afraid they would not see her. She ran on in the centre of the road, waving her arms frantically. She could hear the footsteps behind her now, and she knew Helda was close.

Just as the bikes were nearly upon her there was a screech of brakes, and together the three of them wheelied round so that they were facing the way they had come. Lia felt a gloved hand touch her arm, but she made a final effort, leaping onto the back of the middle machine. At the same instant the Biker dropped the clutch and the machine roared away. Clinging tight to the rider Lia glanced behind her. Helda was standing in the middle of the road, shaking her fist at the departing machines.

Lia didn't need to see the Biker's face. She could tell by the flowing blond locks that her rescuer was Thorkil. She hugged herself to him, burying her face in his jacket as they sped through the streets toward the city gate.

They rode a long distance from the city before they pulled off the road into the woods. They put a good mile between themselves and the road, then drew up in a small clearing. The moment Thorkil dismounted Lia threw herself into his arms and they kissed long and hard.

"Oh Thorkil," she said at last. "It's been so long."

He smiled down at her. "But worth waiting for."

"Yes." she snuggled close to him. "Don't let me go again, will you?"

"I won't."

His hand dropped to her breast, kneading the soft flesh, feeling the nipple harden under his touch. He pushed her backwards, so that she sat on the rear of the bike seat, her legs apart as he slid his fingers down over her mound. Lia shut her eyes, a moan escaping her lips as his mouth closed over hers again. Then she felt a hard cock brush her thighs and she looked up in surprise.

At once she recognised Thorkil's companions. It was Rico and Lara. Rico was standing over her, his fly open, his rampant cock jutting out from his pants, whilst Lara gently wanked him. Lia felt Thorkil's grip tighten on her, forcing her back over the seat of the machine. For a second she struggled, then relaxed as Lara guided Rico's thick weapon into her vagina.

She gazed up into the eyes of her lover. He was watching her closely as Rico fucked her, trying to gauge her reaction. She knew she should be outraged, but she couldn't be. She simply smiled at him.

After all, she was a Biker's Girl.

THE END

If you like one SILVER MOON book you will probably like them all. EXTRACTS this month concentrates on one author: Rex Saviour.

ERICA:PROPERTY OF REX:- (opening Part II)

I awoke lazily that morning, to find myself lying on my back with a hard-on. The delicious sensation of warm lips and timid tongue told me that Erica had come into my bed during the night - as she often did on windy nights or when the owls hooted.

But her face down there between my legs - that was something new!

Perhaps she thought it would put me in a good mood for the day?

Well, maybe so, but it was also extremely frustrating, having to deny myself sex because of her youth.

I wound my fists into her long auburn hair and pulled her slim body up over my naked one. I was rewarded with the sight of the face that turned me on so, masses of lovely long shining auburn hair, bright mischievous blue eyes, apprehensive now as I brought her lips to mine.

My hands were free to play with her uncovered bottom, for her flimsy nightie barely reached it these days, so fast had she grown, and of course I didn't approve of underwear - she squirmed deliciously under my touch and her kisses grew in intensity.

Why?

Then I remembered!

Today, at long last, Erica was legally of age. From today everything would be different. Her total vulnerability tempted me to roll over on her and put my new rights to the test, but just in time I remembered the little ceremony I had planned for later in the morning.

"Out!" I said.

I suffered renewed temptation, seeing her walk to the electric kettle - it was that upright carriage I had taught her and the easy grace that came so naturally.

I watched her make the tea and arrange it on a tray. As she came and bent forward to lay the tray in my lap her breasts were fully revealed, high, pert and firm, the tips exceptionally rosy. I saw the usual blush rise in her cheeks as she waited for me to accept the tray.

When I did so, she proceeded to the next stage of our morning routine - routine it is, for even when she slept in her own bed she would come to make my tea and do her exercises in my room.

This pleasant little interlude in our day is intended to help Erica with her deportment. She wasn't just standing - she was standing at attention, chest out, head up, hands behind the back but held clear of the buttocks. I had taught her never to hide her bottom, because it was the focus of many of her hang-ups and therefore, in the interests of the systematic desenisitisation therapy, I had to warm it up quite often, with the belt which she always wore, or kept by the bedside, for just that purpose.

Every ninety seconds she moved smoothly to a different posture in a preplanned sequence. First she went on tiptoe with her hands behind her neck, elbows strained backwards, then it was legs apart hands straight up in the air, clasped above the head. That pose allowed me to check the smoothness of her shaven sex. Her skin is a beautiful light golden brown, a legacy from the Argentinian father she so little resembled in any other way. She flinched a little but did not dare to move away.

"Erica!"

"Yes, Uncle?" She still called me Uncle. It sounded better than step-father when I took her into pubs and so on.

"I think I'll have breakfast in bed this morning."

"Yes, Uncle."

"Erica!"

She turned at the door.

"Many happy returns!"

"Thank you, Uncle Rex."

"You can't go downstairs like that now, it wouldn't be decent."

"Oh no, no!" There was great relief in her voice. "I'll get dressed, then."

"It isn't worth it, you'd only have to undress again. You haven't finished the exercises."

"Oh - but - "

"Put your shoes and socks on, that's all I meant."

"Oh!" She sat on a chair and put on her white socks and trainers, then walked reluctantly to the door. "Hold your shift down," I suggested, "it's getting a bit short." By this time I had a small staff - besides the butler there was a chef, a gardener, a stable lad and a chauffeur - loyal, discreet, very highly paid. I think she was worried because they would probably all be in the kitchen gossiping at this time of the morning.

When she came back with the breakfast tray she had fetched from the kitchen she was crying. She was still standing there snuffling when I finished my breakfast.

"You can finish the exercises later," I said, opening the newspaper. "You may come back to bed."

She went to the foot of the bed and raised sheet and blanket to creep in. The timid brush of her hair and breasts, the touch of her hands and the feel of her tongue working its timid way up the inside of my thighs was pleasant.

ISBN 1-897809-02-6 £4.99

BALIKPAN 1:ERICA ARRIVES:-

I was in no hurry to release Oi from her erotic bondage - I liked it and she looked so good, so totally helpless, standing there in the lounge of my temporary apartment, strained upwards and slightly back by the pressure of the slim chain that ran from the crossed arms secured up behind her back to that elongated ring in the front, above her over-exposed sex.

I sat down and had her kneel at my feet, which strained her shoulders even further back, really delightful.

I put my dressing-gown on and opened my legs, took her head in my hands, put it beneath the robe. There was no need to guide her lips. They were eager and fearful, very soft. After a while I asked: "How long does Stephen keep you like this?"

She broke off and looked up at me. "Always, Master." Her voice was low and musical. "Always."

"Always? With that chain on? Even in bed?"

"Yes, Master. Therefore I can do little for him in his bed, I cannot use my arms, I can use my mouth, he too likes that, but truly he has screw-girls for his pleasuring -"

"Screw-girls?"

"Like your one. Erica, I think? Some men get quite fond of them. Like you, I think. I don't think your Erica gets beaten as I do, just for the pleasure of her Master. I am a whipping-girl, that is what I was sold as, that is what I have always been and that is what I shall always be. This chain was already upon me the day Master bought me in the market."

"A market? Sounds interesting?"

"It is not velly nice to be sold."

"I suppose not. Tell me about it."

"I was secured like this, except the chain was quite loose so people could feel me ploperly."

Her English was excellent, she just lost her Rs occasionally.

"I had to stand on a block all day. But always if somebody wished to buy me, they were told I was reserved. It was tellible. Then at last Turk came to buy me."

"Turk? A Turkish man?"

"I do not know. He is not of Balikpan. Turk is Master's butler. I think he saw me and reserved me for Master."

"I see. So Stephen has tightened the chain?"

"No, Master, Turk sees to that."

"I see. He must like it tight."

She shuddered. "Sometimes it is more tight than this!"

"Oh?" It really was indecently tight already. "And he didn't unlock you?"

She would rather be sucking me off than talking, but I was interested. "There was some fuss about the key," she said at last. "The butler - Turk - he said it was the wrong one, but Master said never mind. He told Turk to feed me and wash me and groom me - "

"Groom?"

"Do my hair - clip finger and toe nails - wash me -"

I could feel her shuddering. She applied her mouth again, but I pulled her face away from me by her hair and looked into frightened brown eyes, deep dark pools of mystery.

"Go on!"

"And shave me, master, every day, down there."

The feeling of revulsion was even stronger. "Don't you like the butler?"

"N-no Master."

"So - Stephen bought you and never unchained you? You must still be a virgin, then?"

"Oh no!" She was surprised. She hesitated, and then continued: "It was not a matter of much concern at orphan school. It hardly affects the price of a whipping-girl, most men don't even ask when they buy."

"What happened there?"

"Must I tell, Master?"

"You must, yes."

"It was the masters, I suppose."

"The masters raped you?"

"Sometimes, of course - they first -"

She dried up.

"That wasn't the worst?"

"At night - there should be night clothes and sheets but there were not - they laid us on our backs - they tied our wrists and ankles to the bedposts - Turk - the first time I saw Turk - he undid my arms and - and - I slashed his face with a broken bottle -"

"He doesn't like you very much, then?"

She shivered...

ISBN 1-897809-99-9 £9.99 (mail order)

ROBIN:PROPERTY OF OGOUN:- (the opening)

Suppose, suppose - he licked his lips as he studied the young woman, an erection coming upon him - suppose this girl was his plaything, this particular girl, his to do with exactly as he wished?

She looked delicious, so vulnerable sitting alone on the cold pavement, slim but with the promise of lush curves, probably in her early twenties.

Suppose - suppose she had served his evening meal and now stood naked in a corner of his study, at attention except that her hands were clasped upon her head, frightened eyes upon him, expecting him to beckon, trembling and maybe whimpering as she awaited his pleasure, his pleasure and her punishment?

It was deep into a cold snowy night and still no taxi. She didn't notice his interest as he gazed at her from a discrete distance, knew nothing of the fantasies she had unwittingly roused in him: what had attracted him was the way she was squatting on the cold wet pavement near the empty taxi rank, her head sunk in apparent misery upon knees that were drawn up to her chin and held there by the bare brown arms that clasped them.

And the small tatty brown suitcase beside her - surely that suggested a runaway?

If only life were different and fantasy ruled, how easy to take her home and use her to achieve his secret lusts: it seemed to him that a whiff of the exotic cloaked her, the shape of her face perhaps, the unusual slant of the cheek bones and closed eyes, suggesting that almost anything was possible if he were bold enough.

He had just arrived back in London from Thailand via Bahrain and Gatwick, and here he was at Victoria, but the eroticism of the Patpong bars, with those delicious brown girls dancing on platforms, or rather writhing their supple sweat sheened bodies, must still be affecting him.

He was beginning to wish he had let himself go more. Bangkok was a place to indulge one's every sexual whim, and yet he had done very little. Oh, he had gone into the bars, even the massage parlours the taximen took him to without being asked, he had been propositioned often enough, but he had been too frightened - frightened of his own desires, frightened of Aids ...

But with this girl, what could he not dare do with this one? She looked so helpless and cold, he could take her over his knee, pull up that flimsy apology for a skirt, put his fingers in her knickers and pull them slowly down, right off, touch the naked flesh...

He must snap out of his fantasies. Things such as he was prone to imagine just did not happen in real life, at least not to him, he had never actually been rude to a real flesh and blood woman nor expected to get to spank one, not even for money.

Snow flakes were whirling round the girl, the edge of the storm outside, a few settling on the shiny black of her hair. She had no coat, she just wore one of those sleeveless woollen dresses that outline breasts and cling closely to the figure. Long glossy hair fell over half her face but he had already discerned a delicate dusky beauty, and his splendid imagination - the imagination of a photographer - told him that the body inside that dress would be slim but rounded, lissom in motion, graceful in submission, with the eminently spankable bottom that had stirred his imagination.

He wanted to speak to her, to hear her voice, to establish real life communication. He longed to do that, but she was too young, very early twenties. There was no coffee bar open. Besides, he, in his late sixties, was not the sort of benefactor any young woman would welcome. He was bold only in his mind, not in real life, dominant enough in fantasy but soft in reality.

As he retreated from real life action, so his imaginings came into sharper focus, strong and erotic, very real to him, a fantasy as real as life and far more satisfying.

Suppose, just suppose...

...they would be in his study. She would have her back to him of course as she faced into a corner, hands upon her head, elbows braced back, legs wide apart, bottom stuck out as he had commanded, very still and quiet for fear of attracting his attention. Now and then he would glance up from the comfort of his arm chair by the warm fire, and gloat over her nakedness, set off only by a ribbon round her neck, tied in a butterfly bow.

Bells? Yes, little bells dangled from her pierced nipples, and that was why she was so still, knowing he would be angry if the bells tinkled, dreading his anger ...

He would be sipping brandy, smoking a cigar perhaps. Yes, he, a non-smoker in real life, was definitely smoking a cigar. He let the blue smoke trickle through his lips as he lay back and admired those rounded buttocks so invitingly presented. In fact he had a spot light trained upon them. Would there be a quiver of fear to be detected? Or felt? Maybe he would get up and pat them, or snap his fingers to call her to his side so he could run his hands over them yet again. There would be delicious tremors then, coming from deep down, and he would make her turn round and look at him so that he could delight in the fear that would be so plain to see, deep in her eyes.

What colour eyes did she have? He could imagine what he wished, for the waif's head was down, her eyes shut, she just sat there all alone in the cold with her arms clasped round her drawn up legs, the hem of the very short dress slipping unheeded down her thighs, very provocative, though he was sure that was unintentional. He imagined that her eyes were brown, deep brown, which was probably correct, for she had long raven black hair and high cheekbones, and dusky skin, suggesting a touch of the east.

... in his imagination she was holding a broad leather strap in her mouth as she stood in his study, chewing on it to stop herself from whimpering, knowing that it would soon come whistling down to bite into her plump bare bottom, waiting as she had done for the last hour or two for the order to display herself before her usual evening beating. Her usual evening beating? Yes, he liked that. Usual was good. It would be for no particular fault, just to get him in the mood for bed, warm her up for it too...

Oh yes, he thought, as he marched up and down in the cold waiting for a taxi, flapping his arms without much effect, this particular girl would be very spankable, very spankable indeed. He had never actually beaten a woman, but he often chose a passer-by to suffer in the sort of fantasy the cold had just snapped him out of. Sometimes he followed them for quite a while, but he had never come across a more convincing subject than this. The very way she sat there, her small battered case by her side, made her seem vulnerable, like an abused child who had run away and had nowhere to go.

He looked round and continued to swing his arms to warm himself a little. Still no taxi. Not surprising, perhaps, at 3 am on Christmas Eve, a bitter night like this. Her dress looked very thin as well as the skirt of it being so short and she had no coat.

Oh yes, very spankable, very spankable indeed...

ROBIN is part of our '3-in-1 Special' BOUND FOR GOOD
ISBN 1-897809-05-0 £4.99